AMERICA'S AGATHA CHRISTIE

"I keep saying 'urbane, witty, faultless, delight-
ful'; what other adjectives is one to use for
Lathen's precise blends of formal detection and
acute social satire? John Putnam Thatcher,
senior vice-president of the Sloan Guaranty
Trust, is one of the very few important series
detectives to enter the field—a completely civil-
ized and urbane man, whose charm is as remarkable as his acumen."
—Anthony Boucher,
The New York Times Book Review

"Miss Lathen boldly tackles United States/Soviet
trade relations in a charming book of classic
quality. . . . [Her] touch with international relations is perfectly balanced, and her light
asides, such as the performing otters and the
beatnik club, are charming."
—(*The* London) *Times Literary Supplement*

MURDER AGAINST THE GRAIN
was originally published by
The Macmillan Company.

Books by Emma Lathen

Accounting for Murder*
Ashes to Ashes*
Banking on Death
Come to Dust
Death Shall Overcome*
The Longer the Thread*
Murder Against the Grain*
Murder Makes the Wheels Go 'Round
Murder to Go*
Pick Up Sticks*
A Place for Murder*
A Stitch in Time
Sweet and Low

*Published by POCKET BOOKS

Murder Against the Grain

by Emma Lathen

PUBLISHED BY POCKET BOOKS NEW YORK

MURDER AGAINST THE GRAIN

Macmillan edition published 1967

POCKET BOOK edition published May, 1975

L

Standard Book Number: 671-78885-X.
Library of Congress Catalog Card Number: 67-20183.
This POCKET BOOK edition is published by arrangement with The Macmillan Company. Copyright, ©, 1967, by Emma Lathen.

Front cover photograph by Mort Engel.

Printed in the U.S.A.

Contents

Prologue

From New York, New York:

RUSSIAN-AMERICAN TRADE TREATY SIGNED
COLD WAR THAWS OUT
100 Million Tons Grain for USSR
Consulates Opening New York and Frisco

American foreign policy scored a major success today when the Soviet Union accepted the proposals of the American negotiators in Geneva and signed the Russian-American Trade Treaty. The Treaty is the first phase of a step-by-step program designed to dissipate US-Soviet tensions. Prominent features call for major purchases of US grain by the Soviet Union and opening of Soviet consulates in New York and San Francisco later this month.

"The first step was bound to be the most difficult," said the Secretary of State in his press conference immediately after the accord was reached. "The peaceful goals of the American people had to be communicated to the Soviet Union so that they would be willing to lay aside their distrust and suspicion. . . ."

From Moscow, USSR:

US-SOVIET TREATY SIGNED
Grain shipments this winter

Representatives of the United States today accepted Soviet proposals in Geneva and signed the US-Soviet Trade Treaty. Thus the first step has been achieved in the program of the Central Committee to reduce areas of conflict between the capitalist and communist worlds. The treaty calls for major sales of US grain to the Soviet Union and the establishment of American consulates in Leningrad and Odessa.

The Foreign Minister said here that it was a source of great personal satisfaction to him to have succeeded in bringing home to the American people the peace-loving aspirations of the Soviet peoples. He is confident that American belligerence and aggression will melt before the . . .

From Paris, France:

The French Government of course applauds any diminution of world tensions caused by the mutual distrust and ignorance of the non-European great powers. It would, however, warn that any attempt to bypass the European community in the settlement of world problems cannot be acceptable . . .

From Bonn, Federal Republic of Germany:

Germany has the most to gain by the lessening of prospects for a third world war which would necessarily be fought on German soil and with German blood. However, agreement with the Soviet Union on collateral problems, without first reaching accord on the question of German reunification, is a direct violation of the commitments to the Federal Republic of Germany made by the United States.

From East Berlin, German Democratic Republic:

. . . and with German blood. However, agreement with the United States on subsidiary problems, without first reaching accord on either German reunification or the Oder-Neisse territorial demarcation, is a direct violation of the commitments to the Democratic Republic of Germany made by the Soviet Union.

From Peking, China:

And thus the hostile forces encircling the Peoples Republic of China have joined hands to further the course of imperialism in Asia. The Soviet Union, once again abandoning the principles of Marxism-Leninism, has embraced the bastion of capitalism in a transparent maneuver aimed at the enhancement of right-wing deviationism. . . .

From Manchester, England:

A LONG COOL LOOK AT THE TRADE TREATY

But existing undertakings do not spell out how the rapprochement is to be effected. Both powers are acutely conscious of their commitments to their allies and some of those commitments are disturbingly at variance with the immediate goals of the pact. Close agreement between the United States and the Soviet Union on policy in Central Europe will therefore be the yardstick by which any major realignment will have to be assessed by future British governments. . . .

1

Sing a Song of Sixpence, A Pocket Full of Rye

"MISS CORSA DID SAY IT WAS AN EMERGENCY, Mr. Thatcher!"

Miss Turvin delivered this message, cast a frightened but defiant look at the startled conference table, then fled. She had interrupted an Investment Committee meeting and even the newest employee of the Sloan Guaranty Trust knew that never, under any circumstances, should this occur. No messages, no calls, no announcement of visitors waiting in twenty-five important offices. The Investment Committee's solemn deliberations were sacrosanct.

Yet Miss Turvin, a veteran of twenty years' service, had not only shattered tradition, she had compounded the offense by transmitting his secretary's message to John Putnam Thatcher, who was senior vice-president of the Sloan, presiding officer of the Investment Committee, and currently acting executive officer of the bank. It took Miss Turvin several days before she could think of the whole thing without shuddering.

"Hmm," said John Putnam Thatcher thoughtfully, while

a muted buzz sped around the vast conference table. Leaving the Investment Committee at this particular juncture would constitute a departure from protocol. In addition, there were certain perils: Walter Bowman, the perennially exuberant chief of research, was waxing dangerously eloquent about a dubious investment in liquid sandpaper.

On the other hand, if Miss Turvin could be believed, the imperturbable Miss Corsa was running up storm signals.

"Charlie, do you want to take over?" Thatcher decided finally, pushing back his chair. "I'd better look into this."

"Sure," said Charlie Trinkam with his usual cheeriness. "But if we're on fire, be sure to tell the firemen that we're up here, won't you, John?"

The Investment Committee's proceedings resumed before Thatcher had left the tower conference room, but as he strode vigorously toward the waiting elevator, he knew that twenty-five bankers' brains were running over the list of mishaps that could befall a bank. The list was varied and, unfortunately, virtually endless.

When Billings, the elevator operator, debouched him at the sixth floor, a rapid glance told Thatcher that at least no one had run amuck in the Trust Department. (It had happened once, in 1934.) Typewriters were clacking, file drawers were rolling, and trust officers were telephoning with their usual hushed efficiency. Thatcher strode down the corridor to his corner suite with the athletic vigor that belied his years, catching fleeting glimpses of offices as he passed; nothing looked out of order.

In his outer office Miss Corsa sat at her desk, calmly checking the monthly portfolio summary reports. She looked up as Thatcher entered and announced:

"It's Mr. Quentin, Mr. Thatcher. He's waiting."

Without wasting time, Thatcher continued into his office. There, the acid angularity of modern architecture and décor was moderated by the old-fashioned and comfortable furniture that Thatcher had wrested from the original Sloan by brute force. In a big, red leather chair sat Victor Quentin, chief of the Commercial Deposits Division of the Sloan Guaranty Trust. One look told Thatcher that, as usual, Miss Corsa had spoken only the literal truth: this was an emergency. Victor Quentin was flushed and shaking with suppressed emotion.

"John! Thank God! I told Miss Corsa that I had to talk to you . . ."

Deliberately slowing his pace, Thatcher circled his desk and settled himself, maintaining an imposing air of calm. One question was answered: whatever it was, it was big. Victor Quentin was normally quiet-spoken, competent, and —if the truth were told—something of a cold fish. As Thatcher watched, he ran a shaking hand through hair that was carefully brushed to lie flat and smooth.

". . . God knows I didn't want to call you out of the Investment Committee, but I couldn't sit on this any longer . . ."

Thatcher interrupted. "No, that's fine, Victor. It was a pretty dull meeting. What's the trouble?"

". . . you know this new Russian-American Trade Treaty? Well, of course, we've arranged to handle some of the commercial paper from the wheat sales . . ."

Quentin seemed to find it difficult to stop talking. Thatcher raised a hand to silence him. Then, without a hint of impatience, he said:

"Forget the background, Victor. Why don't you just tell me the bad news in a sentence? We'll get to the details later."

Momentarily Victor Quentin looked panicky. Then, after a deep breath, he said:

"Four days ago we were robbed of $985,000."

There was a moment of silence. In the distance Miss Corsa was typing.

"Yes," said Thatcher with measured appraisal that was perfectly genuine. "Yes, that is quite a sentence."

Quentin, to do him credit, tried to smile. He did not succeed. "When this came over me today," he said with a catch in his voice, "I thought I must be going crazy."

Thatcher nodded. The Sloan Guaranty Trust is a big bank, but $985,000 is a lot of money. And four days is a long time. For that matter, the Russian-American Trade Treaty was a very important document. Question after question leaped to his mind. He did not ask any of them. Instead, studiously neutral, he said:

"Well, Victor, you'd better fill me in on some of those details. What happened?"

"God knows!" Quentin replied, sagging back in his chair. But with Thatcher implacably waiting, he made an effort to marshal his resources and explain; the familiar workday terms served to revive him slightly. Thatcher watched the shock recede. Victor Quentin was once again the quiet-spoken, eminently competent head of the Sloan's Commercial Deposits Division.

"It all began with the Russian trade treaty," he said.

"I'm sure it did," said Thatcher tartly, and to himself. The opening of wider channels of trade between the U.S.S.R. and the United States had already involved him in ceremonial festivities including gala performances by the Bolshoi Ballet, dinners addressed by Soviet and American dignitaries, and more bad luncheons than he cared to remember. Still, it seemed excessive that it should also involve a theft of $985,000 from the Sloan.

With growing self-assurance, Victor Quentin continued his recital. One of the first actual transactions to be consummated under the newly liberalized trade agreements was the sale of forty million bushels of U.S. wheat to Russia. This colossal undertaking required the efforts of hundreds of grain brokerage firms, flotillas of ships—and many banks, including the Sloan.

". . . and Russian ships," said Quentin, sounding bitter. "That's why it was possible, John! My God, nobody could pass off forged bills of lading from an American ship on me. But this was the first time I had seen these damned Russian bills . . ."

What had happened was this: a week earlier, the grain brokerage firm of Stringfellow & Son had called the Commercial Deposits Division of the Sloan to report that the first Russian vessel had begun loading. The news had been confirmed by the Port Authority. Three days had passed, culminating in a second call from Stringfellow's office —his secretary reported that Stringfellow expected the final papers any minute. These documents would be speeded to the Sloan, where financing to the tune of $985,000 had already been arranged in a long, tedious series of conferences.

"So I made out the check," Victor Quentin went on, goaded by the recollection. "After all, it was perfectly standard procedure . . ."

"Yes," said John Putnam Thatcher, walking the narrow line between sympathy and authority.

"Well, in about two hours a messenger brought in the package from Stringfellow. Of course, I examined it carefully—checked to see that the bill of lading was okay, and the invoices, and the consul's certificate. Hell, they looked fine!"

He shook his head.

"So, I assumed they were all right. I signed the check. And since Stringfellow had asked me to send it to him at the Registry of Deeds—he's buying some land out in Jersey—I sent it right out since the messenger was going there anyway. And that was that . . . just a simple little $985,000 . . ."

Before he could relapse, Thatcher prompted him. "That was that until . . . ?"

Quentin shuddered. "Until two hours ago—when Stringfellow called me. He said he was sending down the *Odessa Queen* papers, and would I ship that check to him as fast as I could! My God, John, I don't know how I finished that call! The minute Stringfellow was off the line, I rushed out to look at the papers I had accepted—and Goddammit, they still look good! But an hour ago, the messenger brought these—and hell, you can see!"

He almost flung the envelope onto Thatcher's desk as he went on savagely, "Oh, it's a beautiful job, all right. They got the letterheads—from Stringfellow and from the Russian Consulate! That's what made it look so good—but the rest is a forgery! A smooth, high-class forgery!"

Thatcher picked up the envelope and opened it. Inside were two bulky sheafs comprising the familiar, elongated receipts given by the ship's officers on loading of goods, the promises to pay on delivery, and all the documents that constitute the commercial paper of trade which—in some circles, including the Sloan Guaranty Trust—is virtually indistinguishable from cold cash.

"The check has been cashed, I suppose," he said finally.

Quentin nodded somberly. "I've started an investigation, but I think we can take that for granted."

Thatcher agreed. That was the point of the theft, after all. "That means, presumably, that the messenger did deliver the check, it was picked up—what's the matter?"

Quentin slumped forward again. "I didn't use a bank messenger. Baranoff's chauffeur brought in the Stringfellow package. Since I knew he was going up to the Registry of Deeds—well, I made him wait and take up the Stringfellow check . . ."

Thatcher repressed a sigh. Quentin was clearly bent on self-flagellation. It made no difference at all who had carried the check; the point in question was who had cashed it. Abe Baranoff was an important Sloan customer. His many employees were all used, at one time or another, as couriers for checks, contracts, securities, and other financial instruments of their master's far-flung empire of theaters, movies, concert tours, and real estate deals.

"Unless Baranoff's chauffeur has taken to crime," he said somewhat pointedly, "it doesn't make much difference whether he carried the check or the U.S. mails did. The question is, who cashed it? I wonder . . ."

Hopelessly, Victor Quentin watched Thatcher frown in thought.

"I don't suppose that there's any possibility of a mix-up at Stringfellow," Thatcher mused aloud.

Quentin hitched himself forward. "That's why I wanted to talk to you, John. I don't know whether it would be wise to call Stringfellow. It would certainly cause a lot of talk if . . . if . . ."

If, in fact, word leaked out that the Sloan Guaranty Trust had been fleeced of $985,000.

Thatcher closed his eyes. Unbidden came mental pictures of Russian ambassadors shaking presidential hands, of U.S. trade missions talking to Russian trade missions, of speakers dwelling lovingly on the rich potential for peace inherent in growing trade between the great Union of Soviet Socialist Republics and the United States of America. Let Russian vessels steam into American ports to load agricultural bounty for the long trip across the seas to Russia. Let American fleets anchor in Baltic waters, for vodka, gold, and furs to be brought to the Western Hemisphere. Transform the armadas of war into harbingers of peace. Let peaceful trade herald the promise of a new dawn. . . .

"No," said Thatcher wearily. "We certainly don't want to rouse any talk if we can avoid it. But we have to check with Stringfellow." He drummed his fingers for a moment, then came to a decision. "I've got it!"

Without waiting to consult Quentin, who had obviously passed beyond constructive thought, he stabbed the buzzer on his desk.

In a moment, it produced Miss Corsa.

"Miss Corsa," said Thatcher. "We need your help with a little problem."

Composedly Miss Corsa waited, untouched by the tension in the room.

"We want you to call Stringfellow & Son. Get hold of Stringfellow's secretary—do you know her name, Victor?"

Quentin started. "What? Oh, no, no I'm afraid not."

"Well, say that you're closing out a report—or something of that sort. The point is that we want to know if Stringfellow has got our check—yet. And we want to make it seem like a simple, routine question—nothing to get excited about. Do you think you can?"

"Certainly, Mr. Thatcher," said Miss Corsa, in effect reminding him that she was never excited about anything.

She moved to the extension phone and Thatcher marveled, not for the first time, at the psychological power of that instrument. Miss Corsa had been raised by loving but strict parents and carefully trained by the good sisters of Our Lady of Lourdes School for Girls. In consequence, she had a painfully high regard for veracity, as Thatcher knew to his cost. Yet put a telephone in her hand, and she could lie like a trooper—without the slightest sense of guilt. Nothing transmitted by AT&T was a sin in Miss Corsa's catechism.

Silently, he and Quentin watched her find a telephone number. Then, with the artificial courtesy of telephonic discourse, Miss Corsa located Mr. Stringfellow's secretary —a Miss Marcus—and launched into an elaboration of Thatcher's sketchy instructions. Her side of the conversation bristled with references to "closing out the check count" and "drawing up account records." There was a silence; Miss Corsa added something about "a new girl here in the office." Then:

"Yes . . . yes . . . well thank you, Miss Marcus."

She hung up.

"Well?" cried Victor Quentin.

"Miss Marcus says that they just sent the *Odessa Queen* papers over this afternoon. They're expecting our check later today—or the first thing tomorrow."

Again there was a pause as Miss Corsa waited for further instructions.

"That's all, Miss Corsa," said Thatcher. "And thank you."

"Certainly, Mr. Thatcher."

She had barely closed the door behind her when Victor Quentin burst out:

"That means that we've been swindled out of $985,000! By forged paper! Now what do we do?"

For the first time in their interview John Putnam Thatcher let steel show.

"What do we do? We call the police!"

He knew where his duty lay: Washington and Moscow could look to their own interests. Now was the time for him to concentrate on the Sloan Guaranty Trust.

2

Separating the Chaff

"BASICALLY THE SITUATION IS QUITE SIMPLE, Inspector," Thatcher was saying an hour later to the large, smooth-faced man from police headquarters. "It's as if someone had passed a forged check. Unfortunately the details are a little more complicated."

"I knew it," said Inspector Lyons, congratulating himself and sounding rueful at once. "Can you give me the bare outlines?"

Reducing the intricacies of foreign trade to bare outlines is not a task for everyone, but Thatcher was willing to try. "You know, foreign sales are usually made by what we call a letter of credit. Let's say that we're selling something abroad—wheat to Russia, for example. Now the Russians will pay for that wheat only when they get control of it. The seller of the wheat—that's Stringfellow & Son in this instance—wants to get paid as soon as it hands over the wheat."

Quentin nodded encouragingly, but Lyons merely looked wary. "Okay," he said.

Thatcher hoped so.

"That's where the banks come in," he said. "The Russians have a bank account in London. And the London bank has an account here at the Sloan. When the wheat seller—Stringfellow & Son—presents us with the loading documents that prove he has handed over the wheat, we pay him. Then London pays us later. That's the whole transaction in a nutshell."

Lyons was game. "And those loading documents were your forged check?"

Thatcher nodded. "That's exactly it. When you're shipping wheat, the steamship company gives you a bill of lading after the wheat is safely aboard—and that bill of lading is what Stringfellow brings to the Sloan. We pay, and in the normal course of events, we send the bill of lading to London and they pay. Unfortunately . . ."

He let the sentence trail off and kept from looking at Victor Quentin. Unfortunately this bill of lading was a high-class forgery; the Sloan should not have handed over $985,000 for it—and the London bank certainly would not.

Lyons thought for a moment, then spoke with resignation. "I suppose it's more complicated than that in actual practice?"

Technical questions had a beneficial effect on Victor Quentin, Thatcher was happy to observe. Quentin sat up. "Yes indeed," he told Lyons. "For instance, there are insurance certificates and export licenses and tax exemption forms. What Stringfellow & Son ships to us is really a packet of official documents—but the bill of lading is basic. That's what says the wheat is aboard ship."

"And that was forged," said Lyons.

He deflated Quentin.

"It was. And the invoice too," Quentin said.

Lyons groaned. "What's the invoice?"

"The invoice is the paper that Stringfellow & Son prepared—specifying how many bushels of wheat were sold."

Lyons was trying to sort this out in his own mind. "Let's see if I've got this straight. The Sloan is responsible for this wheat really being on board the ship . . ."

Thatcher and Quentin were both horrified.

"Certainly not," said Quentin. "Banks don't get involved in responsibility for the quality or even the existence of goods."

Thatcher saw the bafflement on Lyon's face. "Look, Inspector," he said, "it really is like a check. If you give a check to a car salesman, your bank isn't responsible if the car turns out to be a lemon. You can even write a check to buy the Brooklyn Bridge—and the bank doesn't care."

Lyons smiled. As it happened, his last car had been a lemon. "So, on this letter of credit—all the bank really cares about is whether or not those bills of lading—yeah, and the invoice—were forged or not."

There was a silence during which Thatcher and Quentin looked at each other.

"On letters of credit," said Thatcher with real regret, "things are more complicated."

"Somehow I thought they would be," said Lyons.

"Normally the Sloan would only be responsible for determining that these documents were in order. We're not expected to spot forged signatures or anything like that. We are responsible for noticing that the paper we accept comes from the correct ship. Do you see?"

Lyons thought that he did. He also thought he had spotted something new. "But since these forgeries are all in order—from the right ship and everything—doesn't that mean that the Sloan isn't going to be responsible? You said that Mr. Quentin here isn't expected to be able to verify signatures?"

Thatcher sighed. "The key word is 'normally.' You see, this wheat shipment isn't at all normal. Half the wheat is being shipped in American bottoms, half in Russian. And the Soviet government wants the wheat as quickly as possible, so they're sending over every boat they can lay their hands on."

"Boats from the Black Sea," said Quentin gloomily. "From the White Sea. Even naval vessels. The *Odessa Queen* is a converted troop transport. She's never issued a bill of lading in her life. And there aren't any steamship offices in New York—to check."

Lyons was not unduly impressed by this catalog of woes. "But couldn't you see the foul-up coming? Couldn't you prepare for it?"

Quentin simply shook his head, but Thatcher spoke for him. "We did," he said, "We prepared, and the Russians did too. So the arrangement requires that every bill of lading has to be authenticated by an official certificate from the Russian Consulate here—with signature and seal—"

"And that . . . ?"

"Yes, that was forged too."

Lyons was developing some sense of identity with the Sloan. "That's what's going to sting you, eh?"

"Who knows?" said Thatcher philosophically. "It certainly raises a tricky legal problem for our lawyers. They'll probably be working on it for years. I just want you to see how abnormal this whole transaction has been. And the forger seems to have known every detail of it. Just look—he forged a bill of lading from the *Odessa Queen,* he forged Stringfellow's invoices, in triplicate, he forged consular certificates with Russian seals and signatures, and this draft . . ."

As he went down this melancholy list, he tossed photostats of these documents across the desk to Lyons. The originals had already been dispatched to laboratories and specialists. Lyons looked at them without enthusiasm.

"There's just one more point, Inspector," Thatcher said.

"Yes?"

"You do realize that when Washington hears about this all hell will break loose? This Russian-American Trade Treaty is important—and the whole wheat sale is, too. I'm afraid we've got to be ready for tremendous repercussions if we don't handle this right."

Lyons, a man who knew you can't fight city hall, expelled an exasperated breath. "Senators!" he muttered. "The FBI! The CIA! All of them underfoot, all of them hamstringing us . . ."

Thatcher was pleased with this realistic and ready acceptance of the inevitable. "I've already spoken to Lancer—he's our board chairman—and he's breaking the bad news to Washington. I think we've got to keep quiet about it until the Russians have been officially informed . . ."

"Fine," said Lyons irritably. "And how do we talk to Stringfellow, without letting him know what's happened?"

"We don't," said Thatcher incisively. "It's out of the question. And believe me, you cannot regret it as much as the Sloan does."

Lyons acknowledged this with a smile. "Still, the trail is already four days old," he said. "If anybody knows anything, he's rapidly forgetting it." He thought for a moment. "I'll tell you what. We can still talk to the chauffeur. We won't have to explain anything to him. And if Mr. Quentin here is right about just shoving the check into his hands—well, that leaves him clean!"

These musings were simply the tools of Inspector Lyons' trade, and his brutality was quite unconscious; it sufficed, however, to turn Quentin ashen again.

Thatcher considered this. "That's all right," he decided cautiously. "But all things considered, I think the Sloan should be represented at the interview."

Lyons nodded. "You said the man's name was Denger? I'll give the office a ring. They'll be able to track him down."

The sign above the double overhead doors read "Halloran's Garage." The doors were up, leaving both driveways clear and forming the only entrance. Inside, fluorescent lighting cast a bright, metallic glow over the fleet of glistening, black cars. One car was being raised on a hydraulic lift, while others were being washed and greased. A mechanic extracted himself from underneath a hood and strolled over to them, swinging a greasy rag.

"Do something for you?" he asked in a genial shout over the prevailing din.

"August Denger around?" asked Inspector Lyons.

The mechanic shook his head. "He's out on a job." He looked at them doubtfully, suspicions dawning. "You want a car? You'd better see the office."

Lyons didn't move. "No, we want Denger. When will he be back?"

"No idea."

Lyons reached for his wallet. Flipping it open, he displayed his identity card. "All right. Fun's over. The police."

The mechanic's eyes widened slightly. "I don't know what the trouble is, mister, but now I'm sure you'd better see the office." He lifted his voice over the stillness that had spread like magic at the sound of the word *police*. "Hey, Ed! Get Rita! It's the cops!"

A man at the far end of the cavern was busy talking through a glass window in a stud partition. "Rita says to come into the office," he relayed, turning back to the garage. "Through that door."

As they filed across the littered floor to the whitewashed door labeled simply "Accounts," Thatcher leaned toward Lyons. "Where are we? I thought Denger was Abe Baranoff's chauffeur."

Because Lyons, after a brief discussion over the phone, had bustled them all into a taxicab, and they had rolled up First Avenue to Halloran's Garage in the upper eighties.

"It's more complicated than that. The Hack Bureau says this is where Denger works."

Victor Quentin was distressed. "But I know he works for Baranoff. He's been running Baranoff's errands for years."

Lyons pushed open the door. "We'll know in a minute."

The woman sitting behind the desk was white-haired and vigorous, probably near sixty. She waved them into the hard wooden chairs and then kept her hand stretched out suggestively. "Eddy said you are police."

Lyons handed his wallet over and she whistled soundlessly. "*Inspector* Lyons, eh? I guess we're not talking about a traffic accident. I'm Rita Halloran, by the way."

"No, it's a lot bigger than a traffic accident. And it may not have anything to do with your operation, except incidentally. We'll know more after we've talked to this August Denger."

Mrs. Halloran made a long arm for a clipboard hanging on a nail in the wall. "Gus is out right now," she announced, "but he should be back any minute. I'll tell Eddy to get him the minute he checks in." She pushed at the sliding panel and spoke crisply to Eddy. When she turned back to them her forehead was creased in a frown. "You can't tell me anything more about this?"

"Not yet."

Mrs. Halloran did not push the point. The garage business seemed to encourage acceptance of the unknown. Inspector Lyons settled himself more comfortably before pursuing the conversation.

"By the way, we were a little surprised to end up here. The way I heard it, this Denger was Abe Baranoff's chauffeur."

"Well, that's simple enough," she said. "This isn't just a car-hire business. I do some hiring for an evening or a weekend, naturally, but mostly it's contract work."

"Come again?"

"Most of our customers don't run their own cars. While they're in town they rent a car and driver from me. And the ones who've been on the books a long time always have the same man. That means the driver gets to know their habits and their ports of call, so they have most of the benefits of a private chauffeur. This Baranoff, for instance. You know about him?"

"Just the usual. Brings a lot of foreign companies over. He's produced some movies, and now he's big in real estate."

"That's right. He spends about six months of every year in New York. When he's in town, he has the exclusive use of a Caddie and of Gus Denger. This has been going on now for about six years. I can look up the exact time if you want."

"There's no hurry," said Lyons easily. "I just want to get the picture. So the fact is, Denger really is Baranoff's private chauffeur for about half the year. The rest of the time he's on call for other jobs."

Rita Halloran nodded. "That's right. He doesn't have any other regular customers because Baranoff's schedule is so irregular."

"Most of your business like that?"

"A lot of it is."

"You use just Caddies?"

"No, I use everything they want. Caddies, Continentals, Rolls Royces. Most of them like the idea of a limousine for New York."

Thatcher had taken no part in the conversation, content to listen to the Inspector and Mrs. Halloran. He was always willing to learn about the ways in which money is made and business is serviced. But now he had a question of his own.

"Did you start out this way or did you work up to it?"

"Hell, this isn't the way we started." Mrs. Halloran took a cigarette from a package on the battered desk and seemed surprised to find Quentin presenting her with a light. "Frank began with one car he drove himself. Frank was my husband," she explained. Her tone became reminiscent. "And what a rat race that was! Calls at all hours. Then he got a bank loan after the war and began expanding. Still mostly the hire-car business, but he had four or five cars and a bunch of drivers. I came down to take over the office end, and when Frank died, I simply kept going. I went into the contract business to simplify things, but it's paid off. Getting bigger and bigger by the year."

Thatcher's unspoken question had been answered. He now knew why Halloran's Garage was run by a woman.

The woman meantime was answering a tapping on the sliding panel. Eddy was again at work.

"Gus is back," she told them. "Here he is. Gus, this is Inspector Lyons from police headquarters. Help him out, will you?"

Without further parley, she left the office and the floor to the Inspector.

Denger stood in the doorway through which she had passed and surveyed the assembly truculently. He was a short, squat man with the beginnings of a beer belly. His feet planted well apart, he rocked back on his heels slightly so that he was peering upward. The requirements of Halloran's Garage saw to it that he was clean-shaven, with a fresh haircut.

"I don't know what you think you've got. But I'm clean. My ticket is as good as the day I took it out in 1949."

"I'm not from the Hack Bureau, Denger. I want to ask you about some errands you ran for Abe Baranoff."

A slow and rather unpleasant smile crossed Denger's

face. "So the King's got his feet wet, huh? That'll be a change from sitting on his ass in a Caddie."

"Well, come in and we'll find out," urged Lyons heartily with a brief glance at Thatcher. Denger was not wedded to the Baranoff interests. And that might make things easier.

"What makes you think Baranoff is in trouble with the law?" Lyons asked when they had finally become settled.

"It stands to reason, doesn't it? Everyone knows he started without a cent. Now he's rolling in dough. Nothing's too good for him. It's caviar and champagne and Sardi's. You should see the parties he throws!" Watery gray eyes searched for approval. "Now, nobody makes a pile like that who's legit. Naturally he's been pulling some fancy stuff. And it must be something big."

"Oh?" Lyons encouraged.

Denger expanded with seedy authority.

"Sure. First off, everything about Baranoff is big. And then it's got three of you tracking him down. Two of you big shots from Centre Street." He paused to look at his interrogators knowingly. Apparently John Putnam Thatcher conformed to his idea of the kind of policeman necessary for somebody as tricky as Abe Baranoff. "And then, to put the lid on, the third one is from the Sloan. That means there's a helluva big stink—about something."

He had recognized Victor Quentin. Thatcher felt a small knot of anxiety dissolve. He was not unmindful of the ambivalence of Quentin's position. Denger's recognition of Quentin was confirmation of Quentin's supposed recognition of Denger.

"Now what can I do for you gentlemen?" asked Denger condescendingly.

"I want you to think back to last Thursday," said Lyons. "Give us a blow-by-blow account of your day."

Denger pushed his visor cap to the back of his head and scowled. "Thursday? Let's see. Oh, sure. I got you. That was pretty confused. Bound to be with His Majesty sailing. That's always hell."

"Sailing?" Lyons broke in sharply. "You mean Baranoff?"

"That's right. Mr. Big himself. I took him and that nance secretary and the whole crew down to the pier at ten o'clock in the morning. And it was no joke, let me tell you. That pier was hell on wheels. You wouldn't believe there were so many bums ready to sit in the sun for a week and relax from the heavy partying they do."

Lyons waved aside Denger's notion of travel on the North Atlantic in early March. "Now let me get this straight. At ten o'clock in the morning you went to the pier. Do you know what time the ship sailed? And also what ship?"

"The *Queen Mary*. Nothing but the best for us. We always go an hour before sailing time. I didn't hang around though. Don't know what time they got away. I had plenty of jobs to do for His Nibs."

"How long did that take?"

"Christ, he left enough for the whole day! He always does. You'd think I'd get a couple of hours for myself after trailing him around for six months. I don't go on to other work until the day after. But not once. . . . Okay, okay," he said as Lyons made a gesture of impatience. "Let's see. I ran around uptown and midtown on my way back from the pier. Then I brought the car in here to be gassed up while I went to lunch. Naturally by the time I got back that bastard had thought up something else for me to do. Luckily it fitted in with the downtown jobs I was holding for the afternoon."

Thatcher wondered if Denger managed to moderate his sullenness when he was driving Baranoff. Lyons, however, was concentrating on the narrative.

"Now wait a minute. I thought you said he'd sailed."

"Yeah, sure. You don't think somebody like Baranoff calls a chauffeur direct?" Denger replied sarcastically. "He'd gotten hold of his office. Some girl there told me he left some stuff at the pier for me to deliver right away."

Tense stillness settled on the little room. Even Denger had abandoned his self-satisfaction. With clumsy curiosity, he said:

"I suppose that's what this is all about, huh? That's the package I took to Mr. Quentin here."

"Let's take it in more detail," said Lyons slowly, carefully. "The girl told you Baranoff had left something for you at the pier. Did she tell you what it was?"

Was Denger alarmed by this question? Thatcher thought he sounded apprehensive as he answered:

"Are you crazy, mister? I'm just the errand boy in that outfit."

"And what exactly happened at the pier? I mean where did you go?"

"Where I always go. You know that kind of booth they have, where you can leave fruit and flowers and telegrams for the jokers who're sailing?"

Lyons nodded.

"Well, it works the other way too. The jokers can leave stuff for messengers. I asked for the package for Baranoff's chauffeur, and the guy there looked at the mess of stuff in the back and gave me an envelope addressed to the Sloan. I had to fight to get it too. There was a real mob of deliveries."

"I see." Lyons was getting grimmer and grimmer. "Now tell me what happened at the Sloan."

"I don't know why you pick on me." Denger was certainly uneasy now. "Mr. Quentin here can tell you as well as I can. I gave him the envelope. He said to wait while he checked it. So I waited, didn't I?"

Lyons gave Quentin no opportunity to reply.

"You gave it personally to Mr. Quentin?" he snapped.

Denger was openly puzzled.

"Sure. It was marked 'Personal Delivery.' A lot of Baranoff's stuff is that way. It means I don't settle for secretaries or assistants. I hand it to the big cheese himself. Say, what is this?"

"And then?" Lyons pushed.

"Like I said, he checked the stuff. Then he was just telling me everything was okay and I could go, when he saw this other envelope I was carrying addressed to the Registry of Deeds. So I let him smooth-talk me into doing the Sloan's errands. He went away for a couple of minutes and brought back an envelope addressed to somebody called Luke Stringfellow at the Registry. I took it to the Registry." Denger nervously ran a meaty hand over his chin, then hurried on, "When I got through the doorway there, a guy came up to me. Asked if I had the envelope for Luke Stringfellow. I said sure and handed it to him. And that was that. I left the rest of Baranoff's stuff with the clerk and beat it."

Quentin was white as this recital came to an end. His mouth opened, but the look from Thatcher forced him back into silence.

Thatcher knew exactly what he wanted to say. It is not every day that someone walks up to a messenger and gets $985,000 without even showing identification. Not that it would have made any difference. The man undoubtedly had ample identification—all forged.

The Inspector was the first to recover.

"Describe the man."

Again Denger ran a finger along his jaw. "God, I didn't really look at him much. It was in that dark entrance way. He had on a topcoat and a dark hat and a scarf of some sort."

"You must have noticed something about him," Lyons pressed.

In his surly fashion, Denger was trying to be responsive.

"Well, there was nothing strange about him, if that's what you mean. Nothing out of the ordinary. He was about medium build I guess. Maybe a little taller than me. He was wearing some kind of glasses—horn rims—and yes, yes, he had dark hair showing around the hat. And that's about it."

His listeners sat silent and disappointed. Denger was relaxing when Inspector Lyons took a new tack.

"All right. Now this girl who called you. What about her? Did you recognize her voice?"

"Nope. I didn't take the call. The message was just waiting when I got back."

"Dear God, couldn't you have told me that before?" Lyons ground his teeth in exasperation.

"You didn't ask me." Denger grinned again in good humor. He enjoyed scoring off mankind in general. But Lyons had abandoned him and was at the door.

"Mrs. Halloran!"

"Yes?" Rita Halloran raised her eyebrows as she appeared from around the corner. She cast a sharp glance at Denger, Thatcher noted.

"Is there any way we can find out who took a call from Baranoff's office during Denger's lunch hour on Thursday?"

"I don't—oh, wait. Was that the call telling him to go down to the pier? If so, I took it myself. I was eating a sandwich at the desk when it came through."

"And could you recognize the voice?"

Mrs. Halloran stared at the Inspector as if he had suddenly gone mad. "Not a chance in a million. You don't know how many calls like that we get from girls in offices."

"Game, set, and match," said Thatcher when they were out in the street again. "An unknown voice on the phone for the pick-up. An ordinary man with no distinguishing characteristics for the drop-off. A complete dead end."

"We'll see about that," Inspector Lyons promised grimly,

But three hours later, Thatcher was doing some grim promising himself.

He had just emerged from an extended session with George Lancer in which he had been privileged to learn the views of the State Department and the United States government in the matter of honoring Luke Stringfellow's second draft.

"And it will interest you to know, Miss Corsa," he said savagely on returning to his own office, "that any delay on the part of the Sloan will be viewed as tantamount to declaring a third world war."

Miss Corsa was far too experienced to be flushed into discussion by this ruse.

"Mr. Quentin has phoned five times. He says it's urgent," she said.

"All right. You can put him through. Not that I have any doubts about what he wants."

Victor Quentin wanted to report that Luke Stringfellow had called repeatedly for his check. Obedient to instructions, Quentin had merely replied that he was still checking the documentation. "But I can't go on saying that forever."

"You don't have to," Thatcher replied shortly. "Lancer has made his decision. Do you have the check there? He can have it tomorrow."

The day, for John Thatcher, reached its climax of unsatisfactoriness when he sat foursquare at his desk and appended his signature to the buff slip just below the words "Nine Hundred Eighty-Five Thousand Dollars and No Cents."

3

A Jug of Wine,
A Loaf of Bread . . .

THE SLOAN GUARANTY TRUST was as mindful of its public responsibility as the next great bank, but there is a limit to high-mindedness, and $985,000, it turned out, defined it pretty neatly. From the directors' room and other important offices came a strong feeling that somebody should do something. Thatcher mildly pointed out that any such action would have to be circumscribed in view of the Sloan's agreement to observe monumental discretion and tact.

"We have complete faith in you, John," said George Lancer, departing.

For a moment, Thatcher considered alternatives. Then, because he was opposed to aimless forays on principle, he decided to make the best of a bad situation.

"Miss Corsa," he told the intercom. "I want you to make some calls. First, Inspector Lyons. Then I suppose that State Department man. Then . . ."

Miss Corsa remained serene.

The next morning, Thatcher stopped at the Sloan only long enough to collect Victor Quentin, who seemed to have lost ten pounds overnight. Thatcher thought briefly of reminding him that it was not Sloan policy to start heads rolling at every setback, then decided against it. It was all too probable that Victor Quentin would have to go; it would be a false kindness to pretend otherwise.

"We're going to see if we can find out how those *Odessa Queen* papers were faked," he explained briskly. Then, to the waiting taxi driver, he added, "Pier Twenty-two."

Apathetically, Quentin clambered into the taxi and asked: "Do you think we can learn anything at the *Odessa Queen?*"

"Not really," said Thatcher truthfully. "But we can see how the bills of lading should have moved. That might suggest something about how our thieves were able to operate."

Quentin looked skeptical, and the driver, who turned right in front of a Broadway bus, splashed dirty rain water from the gutter onto pedestrians waiting for the light.

Thatcher maintained a bracing tone. "Inspector Lyons has gone down to the Cunard Office to see what he can find out about the package that was left for Denger. He suggested we might tackle the *Odessa Queen* at the same time. He'll join us if he gets through early enough."

"I don't see what he thinks he'll uncover at the Cunard pier," said Quentin, rousing himself. "You know what they're like on a sailing day."

"He's just checking anything he can check. God knows there isn't much. And Denger is worth a second look."

Quentin was surprised. "Denger? But I told you, I almost forced the check on him. And he told a perfectly straightforward story."

"The story was straightforward enough." Thatcher was silent for a moment. Then he continued: "Maybe it's just his manner that put me off. You've seen him under different circumstances. Tell me, is he always that pleased with himself?"

"Well, I've only seen him when he was running errands for Baranoff. But, yes, I suppose you could say he's pretty cocky."

Thatcher shook his head dubiously.

"It wasn't just cockiness," he said, almost to himself. "It was as if he were enjoying a secret joke."

The taxi driver, running a red light at Chambers Street, narrowly missed a delivery truck illegally backing out of an alley.

"Jerk!" he summarized over his shoulder to his passengers.

As a rule, Thatcher did not encourage taxi drivers, having long since discovered that what passed for philosophy among simpler minds palled rapidly. But Quentin was sunk in a dejection profound enough to be contagious; moreover, now that he came to think of it, he had a technical question, and here was an expert of sorts.

"Wouldn't it be easier work if you were with one of the private chauffeuring outfits, instead of driving a cab?" he asked.

The lecture lasted until Franklin Street. Private garages, Thatcher and Quentin learned, were slave drivers, exploiting their hapless employees with impossible schedules and endless nagging about standards of service.

". . . and you get a minute, for Crissake! You gotta polish the goddamn car! Who wants to polish a car? You get a bash on the fender, and they dock your pay. . . ."

The biggest liveries in Manhattan were Waley Car Hire, Custom Chauffeurs, and Halloran's Garage.

"About Halloran's Garage," Thatcher began delicately.

"Boy, there's one tough dame!" said the cabby with unstinted admiration. "Got a tongue that would blister paint. And around that garage, does she know what she's doing!"

Thatcher agreed. Running a garage at an enormous profit was not as simple as Rita Halloran had tried to make it sound.

"A lot of garages handpick the chauffeurs," continued

the cabby. "But Halloran's is the only one I know that handpicks the customers too. Well, with her money she can afford to."

He braked to an abrupt halt in a truck-throttled street. "Can't get no closer!"

Thatcher would be willing to bet that Mrs. Halloran's drivers could. He did not say as much, but paid the driver and slipped out into the middle of the street after Quentin. The docks were gray and dirty under a leaden sky. There was the usual din of machinery and wares being manhandled along rough bricks, of shouts and cries, of engines churning. Beyond the echoing warehouses, out of sight, tugs shrieked impatiently over the rumble of the traffic.

"Yes, here we are," said Thatcher, threading his way to the curb.

The smell of the port assailed them like a blow: salt water, rotting garbage, damp and decaying wood, bilge. Overhead, gulls wheeled and screamed insults at one another.

At Pier Twenty-two, a small contingent of police stood about, curiously immobile in the midst of moving men and freight. Thatcher presented credentials and asked if this were routine.

"Nope," said the guard, checking a list. "You're okay. No, we got the boys out at all the Russki ships. You can't ever tell what some nuts will do. Just yesterday, we had twenty-five Hungarians down here. You go right on up."

"You know, I never thought of that," Quentin said as they trudged upstairs. "The theft could be political, couldn't it, John? Some White Russians, or something like that?"

"From what I've seen of White Russians," Thatcher remarked, "they'd find it difficult to break into a piggy bank, let alone forge papers well enough to take you for $985,000, Victor."

"Or some Albanians," Quentin continued.

Who was Thatcher to dash hopes? He did not reply.

In the great echoing cavern, there were longshoremen, customs officers, and other officials, but no sign of Lyons. At the berth, they could see the *Odessa Queen*. Thatcher was no seaman, but the *Odessa Queen,* sitting low in the scummy water, looked both squat and utilitarian to him. At the foot of her gangplank was a representative, not of the New York City Police Department, but of the United States Navy.

"Now what?" Thatcher murmured in exasperation as they moved forward.

The man, with the keen innocent face of the military and the usual dazzling show of ribbons, stepped forth, ascertained their identity, then introduced himself: "Commander Richardson." A pause, then: "United States Navy." This last, Thatcher inferred, was in case they should confuse him with a member of the Coast Guard.

Quentin and Thatcher let their hands get shaken strongly and projected cautious curiosity. Commander Richardson cleared his throat, stepped aside as a burly stevedore rolled toward them with an enormous, canvas-covered load.

"Bureau of Naval Intelligence," he explained cryptically. "New York Branch."

"Move it, mister!" shouted somebody behind him.

This revolted the leader of men in Richardson, but wisely deciding that he would cut no ice with a member of the longshoremen's union, he stepped aside. "A little naval discipline would do them a lot of good," he said tightly. "Well, I'm here because we heard, from unimpeachable sources, that you're boarding the *Odessa Queen*."

It sounded as if they were going to do it with daggers between their teeth.

Thatcher was beginning to feel the dank chill. "You mean the police informed you?"

Commander Richardson again took a quick look around. Thatcher expected a reply concerning enemy ears; instead the Commander hissed, "Washington wants a representative of the U.S. Navy present."

Thatcher repressed a sigh. In view of his other troubles, he did not feel inclined to take on the U.S. Navy. Accordingly, he indicated that Commander Richardson was most welcome to join them, looked around in vain for Inspector Lyons, then decided, as they had agreed, to carry on without him.

"Let's go aboard," he said in smart tones of command.

"Yes sir!" said Richardson, going over the top.

They were welcomed aboard the *Odessa Queen* with a tremendous flurry of salutes. Then the Russian officer said, "If you will please come . . . ?"

He led the way; Quentin, Thatcher, and Commander Richardson—who was looking keen—followed. Six sailors fell in behind.

After walking the length of a short deck, they turned

and proceeded down narrow stairs. The *Odessa Queen* had an odd musty smell; somewhere distant machinery was producing vibrations. The officer turned a corner and finally went down a long passageway to the single cabin door.

"Captain's quarters," Richardson explained in an aside.

The door opened; they were ushered into an unexpectedly cozy cabin, dark with heavy oak furniture and betasseled red velvet draperies. There was a large table supporting decanters and glasses; a gallery of family portraits covered a shelf beneath an oval mirror.

A huge, red-faced man in a rumpled uniform rose as they entered.

"Captain Kurnatovsky!" he bellowed, seizing Thatcher's hand, pumping it and powerfully drawing him in before passing on to Quentin. "Captain Kurnatovsky!" he repeated, reaching Commander Richardson. With a happy shout, he pounded him soundly on the back. The door closed behind them and Russian sailors, Thatcher had no doubt, took up stations outside.

The Captain's quarters on the *Odessa Queen* were not large, yet as Commander Richardson pulled himself together and attempted introductions, Captain Kurnatovsky grinned broadly and stepped aside to reveal three companions. Two of them advanced to cover his flanks and joined in the bedlam of greetings. One was a harassed man, very correct, bearing a briefcase; the second was a dark, vivacious young woman. To the rear hovered a slightly younger man, his broad shoulders stooped and his face paled by anxiety, with "assistant" written all over his deferential posture. The young woman, anything but pallid, was built along lines that made Thatcher regret Charlie Trinkam's absence. Charlie was the Sloan's most serious student of Woman; here was a notable example.

It was she who started the ball rolling.

"Unfortunately Captain Kurnatovsky does not speak English, and I will have to interpret. I will do my best to be helpful." A quickly suppressed twinkle suggested that her best, in all arenas, was very helpful indeed. Sternly she returned to business and indicated the briefcase bearer. "And Mr. Liputin is from the Embassy in Washington."

Liputin gave a formal bow.

"I speak English," he announced. "Not too fast, please."

This augured ill for a fruitful exchange of information,

but Thatcher merely nodded and waited for the final introduction.

"Mr. Voronin is an assistant commercial officer with our consulate in New York."

"How do you do," murmured Voronin tonelessly.

"Excellent," Thatcher said. "Tell me, Richardson, do you speak Russian?"

"Certainly," the Commander answered, implying this was standard equipment at the Bureau of Naval Intelligence.

Thatcher's worst fears were realized. All the seconds could communicate freely. Only the principals were to be prevented from doing business.

But business, it developed, was not to be the first order of the day. There was an explosion from Kurnatovsky, who waved his huge arms and thrashed his way to the bottles.

"The Captain says we begin with a toast," said the interpreter approvingly.

Ominous glasses of colorless liquid appeared, thrust into their hands by the Captain, who was bellowing something high-spirited.

"To full peace and understanding between our countries," said the interpreter.

Manfully, Thatcher quaffed; the interpreter might be young and attractive but he suspected her accuracy. From what he could see, Captain Kurnatovsky was likely to use less lofty formulations as a prelude to a drink. And the Captain was tossing off vodka with a down-to-earth competence that was in sharp contrast to Commander Richardson's prudent sipping. Under the circumstances, Thatcher felt a patriotic pang; if the United States Navy insisted on meddling in the Sloan's affairs, they could have had the decency to produce a real sea dog, someone to yo-ho-ho for a bottle of rum with the best of them.

Liputin, who also managed his vodka with praiseworthy dispatch, opened the subject.

"From Washington I have come upon learning of this crime. The *Odessa Queen* has nothing to do with it. Captain Kurnatovsky knows nothing of it."

"Oh, certainly," said Thatcher.

Captain Kurnatovsky again bellowed something, produced a bottle and replenished Richardson's drink. Victor Quentin, staring at him with awe, nervelessly held out his glass.

"You comprehend," said Liputin earnestly, "that Captain

Kurnatovsky is a simple sailor. He knows not of details. He loads the *Odessa Queen* with wheat, and that is all. . . ."

The interpreter, translating for the Captain's benefit, had reached this point when the simple sailor burst into a torrent of impassioned speech that brought tears to his own eyes and apprehension to those of Commander Richardson.

"The Soviet people are friends of the American people," ran the suspiciously concise translation.

"Hear, hear!" said Victor Quentin (who afterward explained that somebody had to say something, and what could you say?).

"More vodka!"

Much clinking.

Thatcher had no particular desire to break up a promising party, but the Sloan Guaranty Trust had lost $985,000.

"We appreciate that Captain Kurnatovsky and the *Odessa Queen* have nothing to do with this theft. . . ."

This produced relief from Liputin.

"That is what the Ambassador told me," he said.

The Captain, when the gist of Thatcher's truncated remarks was relayed, shouted vast approval. There was a thin line of perspiration on Victor Quentin's forehead. Determinedly Thatcher avoided more vodka.

". . . but we are simply trying to trace details about the bill of lading."

There was a pause for translation. The Captain looked at Liputin, produced a pipe, busied himself lighting it. Then, through a haze of foul black fumes, he spoke.

"He asks," the interpreter said gravely, "what is a bill of lading?"

The Captain rumbled further. Compressing her lips, the young woman turned large, dark eyes on Richardson. "He asks if you, a fellow naval officer, know what is this bill of lading?"

"Bill of lading?" Richardson repeated blankly. He fulfilled at least one sea dog qualification. His eyes, now firmly locked onto the interpreter, had abandoned the rest of the gathering.

"Mr. Liputin, I merely wish to find out a little more about how the *Odessa Queen* issues its bills of lading— since a forged bill was used to rob us."

Liputin nodded intelligently.

"Perhaps you can tell me how . . ."

Liputin drew a deep breath. "The Ambassador tells me that we regret this crime but we have no knowledge of the criminals. Perhaps fascists who wish to destroy Soviet-American trade have done this. We will make no public statements, and we are very much approving that there is no publicity maligning the Soviet people or the *Odessa Queen.*"

In desperation, Thatcher turned to the third member of the triumvirate. Voronin was slightly withdrawn from the group, sitting well back and missing approximately two out of three rounds of vodka. Thatcher's simple question, repeated for the third time, produced a reaction beyond his wildest anticipation. Voronin, who had shown himself completely at home in the English language during the introductions (with traces of a BBC accent, in fact), now retreated hastily behind the language barrier. He addressed himself exclusively to the interpreter in Russian.

"Mr. Voronin," she intoned, "is present only as an observer. He has no authority to discuss these matters."

Liputin seemed to take savage exception to this remark. He rounded hotly on Voronin. Within seconds the interpreter had been sucked into the dissension, and all three were tossing around Slavic polysyllables with frantic abandon. Thatcher resisted the temptation to think that he had thrown the Soviet representatives into a panic. A lifetime of international negotiations had taught him that almost any exchange in a foreign language can sound alarmingly dramatic to the uninitiated.

At length the disagreement resolved itself, and the interpreter again turned to him:

"The details that you desire are obtainable at the offices of the consulate. Mr. Voronin suggests that you make an appointment to speak with Sergei Pavlich Durnovo there. He regrets that he himself must leave us now. He extends to you his best wishes in your inquiry."

Voronin's hasty departure, whether on his own initiative or at Liputin's behest, made it clear that he was not laying himself open to further questions. Thatcher watched him go with a sigh. There went the only man likely to provide them with any information. Accepting the inevitable, he turned to his remaining hosts and said:

"Perhaps I should have expected this. I think the best thing we can do is follow Mr. Voronin's advice. Quentin . . . Quentin!"

Withdrawal from the *Odessa Queen* proved a lengthy process. When Captain Kurnatovsky learned their intention he launched into a lament punctuated by several rounds of vodka and urgent invitations for Thatcher, Quentin, and Commander Richardson to come again, to consider the *Odessa Queen* as their own, to visit Kurnatovsky in Kiev any time. Liputin looked impassive. Surprisingly it was Victor Quentin who replied in kind with warm offers of hospitality at the Sloan.

As he left them at the gangplank an hour later, Mr. Liputin repeated the Ambassador's strongest representations that dastardly as this crime was, it had nothing to do with the Russians.

Unless it was an anti-Russian plot.

"Whew!" said Victor Quentin, wobbling slightly as they left the ship. "I'm not used to drinking so early in the morning."

Neither was Commander Richardson. But, queried as to the recent Russian bickering, he waxed informative.

"That was just one of their bureaucratic squabbles. Liputin wanted Voronin to get permission to answer questions, but Voronin insisted on bringing Durnovo into the picture. Said Durnovo was his boss, and those were Durnovo's specific instructions. Anything else I can do for you?"

Receiving a negative reply, the Commander accompanied them to the street with dignity, then smartly saluted and went his way.

"What good he did, I don't know," Thatcher said sourly, though in fairness he would have had to admit that Richardson had been no more obstructive than any other of the agencies present. He succeeded in flagging a taxi and extracting Amtorg's address from Quentin.

"Well, that's two hours wasted," Thatcher summed up.

Quentin leaned his forehead against a cool metal crossbar and surreptitiously lowered his window. But even with the world spinning around him, he was still functioning.

"Why are we going to Amtorg?" he asked.

"To see this Durnovo," said Thatcher patiently. "The man who can answer a few questions, and won't let anyone else."

"You're not going to make an appointment?"

"Not unless I have to. After all, Voronin left an hour before us. That's given him plenty of time to brief Durnovo, which is certainly what he's been doing."

Quentin started to shake his head, but thought better of it. "Anyway, the consulate isn't with Amtorg anymore."

"I thought they were sharing offices."

"They got too big. They've taken a brownstone of their own on Seventy-third Street."

Thatcher relayed the new instructions.

This driver was melancholy rather than choleric.

"Why not?" he asked sadly as he sped uptown. "Why not sell wheat to them Russians? They're human, aren't they? That's what I say. Anyway, it can't do no harm to anybody."

He was wrong.

How wrong they were soon to learn. As they swung east on Park Avenue, they encountered a crowd that was excessive even for New York lunchtime standards. A group of pickets waving placards was being herded across the street by mounted police, cars were screaming up to the curb to join the cluster of patrol cars and motorcycles.

"Can't get nearer," the cabby announced with gloomy pride as people nearby began to break into a run.

Thatcher paid him, roused the somnolent Quentin and began to struggle through the press. Even so, it took several minutes before he could make any headway and confirm a growing suspicion. The center of the disturbance was the anonymous brownstone which was his goal. But the density of the crowd made any further observation impossible. He paused for thought.

"I suppose it's not worth it," he grumbled, reluctant to give up at this point. "Whatever they have on their hands up there isn't going to leave them any time for our fishing expeditions. The only thing to do—"

His meditations were brought to a halt by a new arrival.

"Thatcher! Quentin!"

Detective Inspector Lyons was alighting from a squad car that had forced its way to the curb.

As Thatcher turned, he caught the word "murder" being passed around the crowd.

Lyons hurried to his side. "I'm glad you're here. You'd better come and take a look."

"We were just leaving," protested Thatcher, naturally recoiling from the detective's suggestion. "This isn't any of our business."

"It is, if the radio in that squad car was right," Lyons rejoined grimly.

Without further discussion they prepared to follow him. Quentin was moving like an automaton. Lyons' ID card brought them to the foot of the steps.

The door remained closed. But several men stood looking down at a body spread-eagled, face down, in a pool of blood.

"Shot," said somebody nearby. "Dead before he hit the ground."

Uniformed attendants with stretchers were moving through the crowd. Lyons knelt down with one of them and helped turn the body over, grimacing with distaste as his hand touched the sodden jacket.

The visored cap fell clear as the face came into view.

"Oh, my God!" said Victor Quentin in a sick voice.

Lyons nodded in macabre satisfaction.

"The radio wasn't wrong," he said harshly. "It's Gus Denger all right!"

4

. . . with a Grain of Salt

IT WAS TOO MUCH to hope that a violent murder on the steps of the Russian Consulate in the midst of New York City's lunch hour should not start political hares in the minds of television announcers reviewing the event. Particularly as the police release confined itself to identifying the victim and specifying the locale. The pundits of radio and television, with these bare bones, were swift to spy political significance. The presence of New York City police outside the consulate at the time of the shooting was underlined, the small band of Ukrainian Nationalist pickets became a fiery uncontrollable mob bent on assault, and the name August Denger by some miracle of pronunciation was invested with heavy Slavic overtones.

After several early afternoon broadcasts in this tenor, the powerful minds at the State Department and in the Russian Embassy concluded that disclosure of the million-dollar theft would be, on the whole, less prejudicial to the

Big Thaw than the continued excitement of Ukrainian passions.

"Because you can't tell how this thing will go," said Wright Dixon. "We have a lot of Ukrainians in this country."

Piotr Rostov lifted weary eyes. "There are quite a few in my country too," he pointed out. This was not irony but simply the transmission of information.

Dixon considered one of those complicated statements maintaining that New York has more Irish than Dublin, more Italians than Milan, more Jews than Tel Aviv, and more Ukrainians than wherever it was, but rejected the idea. There were more urgent problems at hand.

"Let's check this press release once more."

Accordingly the evening newspapers carried the entire story of the Sloan robbery, with full details on August Denger's role as pick-up and drop-off man. The murder was firmly attributed to Denger's criminal accomplices. Without actually misstating any of the few known facts, the release finally issued from Washington laid the whole affair at the door of gangland rivalry.

And what Washington doesn't know about stretching facts is scarcely worth knowing. So ingenious were the drafters of this document that it provoked a whistle of admiration from Charlie Trinkam.

"You have to hand it to them. Those boys haven't missed a trick, John."

"And not a single outright falsification," commented Thatcher.

Everett Gabler, the Sloan's oldest and most conservative trust officer, was rigid with indignation at this coupling of the Sloan to the Cosa Nostra. "It's outrageous. Surely we have some recourse."

"You can't let your feelings run away with you, Everett," Trinkam replied. "Look at the job they've done. They've even managed to bury the fact that he was shot twice with a pistol. It's somewhere in the middle of the biographical statistics. The general idea is that he was given the once-over with a tommy gun from a speeding car."

Thatcher leaned forward, his interest roused. "Biographical details? Where are they?"

"I've clipped them for you, Mr. Thatcher." Miss Corsa, not one to be diverted easily, was still trying to return to the dictation interrupted by the descent of Trinkam and Gabler.

But Gabler also had a one-track mind. "It may well be defamatory. We should consult our attorneys. Or release a statement ourselves. After all, this was a respectable theft."

Thatcher had long ago stopped trying to live up to Everett Gabler's high, if idiosyncratic, notions of propriety.

"There was nothing crude about it, I agree. And highly efficient. The most money for the least effort," he concurred.

"At least a word to the *Times*," said Gabler militantly.

"I'm afraid it would have to be a word to the State Department."

Charlie Trinkam grinned. "Well, you're going to have a chance. They're due here at four-thirty."

"That's all we need," Thatcher muttered absently as he perused the brief biography. "Denger seems to have led the life you'd expect. High school, Korea, milkman, United Parcel truck, then Halloaran's Garage. Nothing there to tell anybody anything."

"Wait until tomorrow. They'll have him the righthand man to Capone."

Certainly by that evening, television had neatly reversed its position. The entire criminal sequence of theft and homicide was now admittedly home-brewed.

The general insistence on a "Made in USA" tag for the crimes was reflected on a more elevated plane by *Pravda*, which wanted to have its cake and eat it too. The crime was undoubtedly the result of America's well-known and flourishing criminal element—oh, undoubtedly—but its purpose was to embarrass the Soviet government. Displaying the egocentricity to which that venerable organ occasionally falls prey, the editorial firmly refused to believe that a million dollars could be sufficient motivation for the crimes.

We are not deceived, nor are our readers. War-mongering elements in the United States, alarmed at the successful overtures of the peace-loving Soviet peoples, have turned to their natural allies, thugs and hooligans, to introduce division and factionalism in Trade Treaty. As a new dawn for a great concord of amity between these nations sheds its first golden light, militarist and materialist have joined hands to prolong the black night of dissension. They shall not prevail. The American people will not be confused by this transparent attempt to attribute an exclusively economic motive to these outrages. They will demand the implementation of the great Soviet-American enemies . . .

"They don't know much about Americans," Thatcher muttered to himself over his breakfast coffee.

The article then went on to castigate the Ukrainian mobsters in front of the consulate and, perhaps fortunately, strayed into the quagmire of the Russian national problem.

The New York papers, however they may have bent to the wishes of the State Department in their own treatment of the story, had stuck to their guns and republished the *Pravda* article on their front pages—where it made very strange reading in the midst of articles with references to the Brink's robbery and a gangland slaying in a hotel barber shop.

It was a copy of the *Times* which was spread out on Luke Stringfellow's desk when John Thatcher and Everett Gabler descended on the offices of Stringfellow & Son shortly after the opening of business.

Everett Gabler's protests at personal involvement had been overborne by Thatcher.

"If it's good enough for the Sloan, it's good enough for us."

Calls to Gabler's sense of service rarely failed. He had yielded, but he was still inclined to find fault and he was now inspecting Luke Stringfellow's milieu with a critical eye. The receptionist had passed them on to the inner office with a minimum of formality. Stringfellow himself was in shirt-sleeves, reading pertinent snatches of the paper to his secretary. She was sitting on the corner of the desk immersed in a tabloid. Both held cartons of vending machine coffee.

It was not the way Gabler liked clients of the Sloan to face the world.

Stringfellow hoisted his burly weight from his chair, looking doubtful. "You're Thatcher from the Sloan? Your office called and said you were on the way over. Of course, I expected someone as soon as I saw the paper. I can see you've got your problems, but so have I. What about my check? You can't blame us if . . ."

His voice trailed off as Thatcher, without attempting to

stem the garrulous flow, simply reached into his pocket and produced the familiar buff slip. Laying it on the desk, he said:

"There. I think you'll find everything in order."

Stringfellow picked up the check and examined it admiringly. "Now how about that? I thought you were going to give me a hard time. But this is all right. I'll say one thing for the Sloan. They don't try and stick anyone else for their mistakes. I appreciate this, Thatcher, I really do. There's a big deal hanging fire, waiting for this. And I know a lot of banks would have had me running around in circles before they finally came through."

At his driest, Thatcher said: "You'll appreciate, Mr. Stringfellow, that it would be best if you paid this into your account or dealt with it personally at the bank. It will be a long time before anybody at the Sloan is casual about anything connected with these wheat shipments."

"Once burned, twice shy, eh!" Stringfellow exploded into laughter and turned to his secretary. "Say, Tessie, give Kay a call and ask her to bring in more coffee."

By the time the coffee arrived, their host's elation had subsided enough for Thatcher to return to business. "You understand that, while we have honored the letter of credit a second time, we are extremely anxious to get to the bottom of this affair."

"My God! I believe it! Almost a million dollars! It'd be a cold day in hell before I forgot anything like that."

"Exactly so."

"But say, why isn't Vic Quentin in on this? He was the one I really expected to see."

"Quentin is busy with the police. It seems safe to say that he'll stay that way for some time," Thatcher replied.

In spite of his physical bulk—he was a big man, in both height and weight—and in spite of the crew cut rigidly disciplining his coarse red hair, Stringfellow seemed very youthful as he alternated spontaneous outbursts of fleeting emotion with carefully conventional expressions of sympathy.

"Poor Vic! It's a damn shame! About the robbery of course. But it's even worse that it happened to Vic. Why, Tessie and I were just saying that he must know more about shipping documents than anyone else in the business."

"Yes, he's upset about it all," Thatcher said tersely.

Stringfellow detected no constraint in Thatcher's voice.

He shook his head in commiseration. "I remember when I took over this business from my dad about fifteen years ago. Every week practically, Vic would have me on the phone to straighten me out on some angle I'd overlooked."

Everett Gabler put down untasted coffee and introduced rigor to the exchange:

"You see, our immediate problem, Mr. Stringfellow, is to determine how much inside information was required to forge the documents," he said precisely.

"Yes, you'd have to have some, I can see that." Stringfellow paused to absorb the implications. "I guess this murder made me forget that. The papers are talking about a bunch of hoods. I suppose Denger was just a messenger, and he had to be shut up."

"Nobody seems to know. You've never heard of him before?" Thatcher asked.

"No. Who was he? Just some guy who worked for a garage, wasn't he?"

Thatcher decided the time had come for a calculated indiscretion. To a man the papers had been silent on the connection between August Denger and Abe Baranoff. It was impossible to say whether this was due to lack of knowledge, to soft-pedaling of the Russian connection, or to fancy footwork on the part of Baranoff's public relations men. But the more Stringfellow knew, the more likely he was to be of assistance.

"The garage was his formal employer. Actually he worked as private chauffeur to Abe Baranoff."

Stringfellow pursed his lips. "So that's the way the wind blows. Baranoff is the one who's always bringing over those Russian troupes, isn't he?"

"That's right."

"So he must have a lot of official Russian connections? Boy, this thing gets bigger and bigger."

"And murkier and murkier," agreed Thatcher. "But what we are particularly interested in is the Stringfellow invoice that accompanied the forged bill of lading. Perhaps you'd like to look at a photostat."

He produced it. Tessie was the first to comment.

"It's one of ours, all right, Luke. It's even a good imitation of your signature. I think it would fool me."

"The police experts say that it was traced. I suppose it wouldn't be difficult to get access to one of your signatures?" Thatcher asked.

"Don't see why. Aside from all the commercial paper

I sign, almost anyone could write me a letter asking for some sort of a quote and get an answer with a signature. Say, the invoice is supposed to be in triplicate, isn't it?"

Thatcher nodded. "Yes, there were three copies all right. The others were just carbon copies. I didn't bother to bring them. But it suggests that someone had no difficulty laying hands on a supply of blank invoices from your firm."

Luke Stringfellow was quick to resent the suggestion of office laxity. "Now, wait a minute. We run a pretty tight shop here. I'm not saying a mastermind couldn't figure out a way to pinch some forms. But I don't see how he did it, off the top of my head."

"May I make a suggestion?" It was Everett Gabler's second contribution to the conversation.

"Yeah?"

"I noticed as we passed through your reception room that the young lady at the desk was typing something. She had a box of forms by her side. If she does typing for the office, I presume that she occasionally does invoice work."

Stringfellow shuffled uneasily. "Hell, I never thought about that. We don't have enough reception work to keep Kay busy. So she pitches in and helps out with odd jobs of typing."

"Including invoices?" Gabler was at his severest.

Stringfellow looked helplessly at his secretary. "Tessie assigns the office work."

"There's no sense in dodging it. Sure, she does invoices. Almost every day." Tessie was not apologizing for anything in her office management.

Before Gabler could comment, Thatcher intervened. It would be just as well if Everett were prevented from developing his impersonation of an MKVD interrogator. There was no point in putting Stringfellow's back up, particularly as Gabler's rigidity sprang not from suspicion but from personal affront at the entire situation.

"Then I think we can regard that as settled. The young lady would naturally be absent from her desk occasionally. Any steady visitor to your office could abstract some empty forms—if he were willing to wait a few weeks. But more than access to forms was required. You realize that the documents presented to the bank conformed exactly to the requirements of the letter of credit. And those requirements were rather unusual."

"I'll say they were." Stringfellow's hearty bonhomie had been replaced by a tough, workmanlike attention to detail. "Those consular certificates were a real joker. It took us almost a whole day to get one out of the commercial attaché. What was his name, Tessie?—Oh yes, Durnovo. The one with that suit—well, he didn't look like a communist to me. He insisted on going down to the docks too. Still, I see what you mean. Somebody had to know all about the deal."

"That was what I had in mind."

"It's not going to help you much, you know. This wheat deal was a big thing. Even after we got rid of the boys from Washington, the place was a madhouse. We had a whole bunch of giant conferences. Hell, we couldn't even use an office. We had to go to the Statler."

Thatcher had expected something like this. But it still could be helpful in narrowing things down. "And who attended these conferences?"

"Every wheat broker in the city, for a start," said Stringfellow firmly. "Then we had the big freight forwarders, the banks—Vic Quentin was there, by the way —the Atlantic steamship lines. And that's not mentioning a few odd men, like the grain elevators in Jersey, the elevators in Chicago, the railroad people."

"And all these people were in on all parts of the conference? I mean, were people concerned only with transshipment from Chicago to New York present at sessions concerning payment by the Russians and ocean shipment?"

A frown of concentration was accompanying Stringfellow's attempts to recollect the meetings. "Now there you've got me. Some Chicago people dropped out early, I remember. And—yeah, now wait a minute—some of this is coming back. That's right. We had to have a Russian interpreter when we hammered out this business about consular certificates. Vic Quentin will remember. The banks were there, and somebody from the consulate and a whole pack of Russian ships' officers. The man from the *Odessa Queen* was one of them. Not that it did much good when he doesn't speak English. Their interpreter is damn good, but it does slow things down."

The frown had been transferred to Thatcher. "I hadn't realized that the ships' captains were actually in on the conferences. I thought all that was being handled by the consulate."

"No, captains, too. Understand, only some of them were there. The ones who got over here early."

Thatcher's gloom was deepening. "We'll have to talk with the Captain of the *Odessa Queen* again. That will mean another round with the State Department, the Russian Navy, the Russian Embassy, and probably a conference in Geneva."

"No, it won't. I thought you realized. It's been forty-eight hours since I sent you the bill of lading."

"Realized what?"

Stringfellow spread his hands. "The *Odessa Queen* sailed yesterday."

5

Flailing About

THERE WAS A MOMENT of silence before Everett Gabler announced the obvious conclusion.

"Then, we have established one fact. The personnel of the *Odessa Queen* was informed about the details of the letter of credit. Now they are beyond the reach of questioning." He eyed the gathering sternly. "It seems incredible that they should have been allowed to decamp in this fahion."

Gabler's intractable sobriety sparked a demon of perversity in Thatcher.

"Not so incredible, when we recall that the entire purpose of the trade treaty was to have this wheat shipped as soon as possible, Everett. And remember, the State Department has made it perfectly clear they do not intend to let our troubles stand in their way."

"Now wait a minute," protested Stringfellow. "I don't want you two to get me wrong. The Captain was at some of our meetings. But how much he found out, I couldn't swear to. There's one thing we didn't discuss, I know for a fact, and that's the business of triple invoices. That's so commonplace no one would raise the point."

"Because everybody already knows it," Gabler argued.

"I don't want to disillusion you, Everett, but it will be a long time before I credit the slightest commercial knowledge to anyone in a naval uniform," Thatcher objected, mindful of his experience at the docks.

Stringfellow was undeflected by this exchange. "And there's another thing. No Russian has been hanging around my office with his hands free to snitch things from the reception room."

"Maybe we should reverse our tactics," suggested Thatcher. "I've been trying to find out the widest circle of people who might have known the details of your arrangements. What about the narrowest circle? Those who absolutely had to know? Besides the brokers and the banks, of course."

"Let's see." Stringfellow passed a hand over his stubble of red hair. "The big freight forwarders. You know, one of our problems was trying to synchronize the deliveries to Russian ships and American ships. The forwarders broke us down into subgroups based on our elevator holdings. One elevator, one subgroup. That's how they decided to handle it, and it's worked pretty well so far."

"And your subgroup?"

"Just Willard & Climpson and Stringfellow & Son. We two are the biggest single purchasers in the whole wheat deal."

"And I suppose each subgroup met for discussions?"

"With our bankers. Sure."

Thatcher's meditations on this point were interrupted by the buzz of the telephone. Stringfellow's face sharpened into joviality as he identified his caller.

"Hello . . . That you, Len? . . . How's the boy? . . . Yes, I was just going to call you. The check's come through. We can go ahead with the deal. . . . No, I'm expecting Yates. What about this afternoon? . . . What? . . . Just a second."

He laid the receiver on the desk while he turned to consult his secretary. "You know that surveyor's report, Tessie? Len wants to know if the right of way is blocked in. What the hell is he talking about?"

"It's the Farquarson right of way. I went over it with him."

Stringfellow turned back to the phone. "Len . . . say, I've got some people here. Tessie's coming on. She knows all about it. Okay? . . . Yeah, that's right. See you this afternoon."

Thatcher was pleased to see the conversation cut short. Time was running out. But he was also interested to have received corroboration of the Stringfellow real estate purchase. He watched Tessie root out a folder from the filing cabinet before moving the phone to a side table and starting to speak about the surveyor's report with brusque competence. She was the kind of secretary he had come to associate with the Stringfellows of this world. Men who were specialist traders, buying and selling in large sums out of small, untidy offices; simple men who did one thing and did it quite well but needed a steady no-nonsense woman to run the office, manage the paper work, and listen to their domestic troubles.

Tessie must have been in her late thirties, Stringfellow about forty-five. Thatcher was willing to wager that Tessie had worked for him fifteen years, had called his wife by her first name for the past ten years, and would be as willing to arrange a Nevada divorce as a gala party to celebrate his twentieth wedding anniversary. With Luke Stringfellow she was friends, but it was to Stringfellow & Son that she was committed.

During this lull Stringfellow had gone to have a word with his receptionist. He now returned with a visitor, a dark-haired young man busy unbuttoning his topcoat.

"This is Dave Yates. John Thatcher, Everett Gabler from the Sloan. It's a good thing you dropped by, Dave. We're just trying to figure out who might have had the savvy to pull this forgery. You've read about it, haven't you?"

"First thing this morning," Yates nodded. "That's why I called in. Wanted to know if it was going to make any difference in how we handle things."

Stringfellow turned to the bankers. "Dave is a partner at Willard & Climpson. The brokers in our subgroup, you remember. He may be able to dredge up something I've forgotten."

Thatcher acknowledged the introduction and said:

"Before we go into that, let me answer Mr. Yates's question. There won't be any basic changes. But there will be a meeting of all the banks and brokers to tighten up procedures somewhat."

"I guess nobody can complain about that." Yates smiled diffidently. "This is my first big deal as a partner and I thought procedures were already complicated enough. But apparently not."

Stringfellow grinned at the younger man. "Don't let it

throw you, Dave. You can spend your life in the grain business and not have this sort of thing happen again."

"You seem pretty chipper, Luke. I suppose this means that the bank hasn't made any . . . er . . . difficulties?"

Stringfellow's grin broadened. As Tessie took issue with the phone in the background, he produced the check and waved it aloft. "Right on the button."

"That's a relief," his colleague exhaled.

"Believe me, Dave, it isn't always this easy," said Stringfellow with a return to grimness. "But what the Sloan particularly wants to know is who knew all the shipping details besides the obvious people at the meetings."

Yates pulled at his lower lip reflectively. "That's hard to say. I'll tell you one thing, though. By the end of last week the chief longshoreman did. You remember, Luke, that day I came in to tell you that the *Odessa Queen* was loading and you called Quentin on it? Well, by that time Riccardi knew all the details. In fact," said the young man with a burst of frankness, "Riccardi was the only person at all helpful I could find on the docks."

On the basis of his limited experience, Thatcher could well believe the statement. But all he said was:

"You sound dubious, Mr. Yates. Don't you think this Riccardi is up to something as complex as these forgeries?"

"Oh, I expect he could manage it. No, it's the time I was thinking of. Most of the details sort of percolated down to him, bit by bit. I doubt if he had much information before last week. And these forgeries took a lot of time, didn't they?"

Everybody agreed they did. What's more, Luke Stringfellow was prepared to swear that the chief longshoreman had never been to the offices of Stringfellow & Son.

And that seemed to be that. Neither of the brokers had any further suggestions.

"After all," said Stringfellow, "you don't pass the time of day at the clubhouse bar describing letters of credit down to the last dotted 'i'.' "

"That certainly wasn't much help," Gabler complained as he and Thatcher reviewed their findings in the taxicab. They were on their way uptown from Hanover Square to their next call—the Soviet Consulate.

Thatcher shook himself free of the reverie into which he had fallen. "No, it wasn't much help. It all comes down to the same thing. You can, by a vivid stretch of the imagination, picture freight forwarders and Russian naval captains and longshoremen pulling this fraud. But the natural suspects are the wheat brokers themselves and the banks with which they dealt—nothing alters that."

"If anything can be regarded as natural in a business conducted with such astonishing carelessness."

"Oh, come now. I daresay it might be possible to abstract a few blank letterheads from the Sloan."

Gabler's disapproving silence made it clear that it might be possible from John Thatcher's office, but certainly not from Everett Gabler's. In this, he did Miss Corsa an injustice.

Thatcher allowed a few moments for his companion's irritation to dissipate before returning to his chief concern.

"I hope you realize the reason I'm belaboring this point, Everett. It is because the New York City Police have two people in mind. Victor Quentin and Luke Stringfellow."

Gabler was in the habit of finding fault with everything. His colleagues were accustomed to his criticisms; very few of them had ever heard a word of commendation. But like most conservatives, once his back was to the wall, he was prepared to concede that his associates of long standing were, on the whole, not quite so unsatisfactory as the rest of the world. Now, he lost no time in making his position clear.

"Victor Quentin? That's out of the question! I've worked with him for twenty years. He may have been negligent. But dishonest? Never!"

"Then turn your mind to how we can persuade the police of that. And, as a starter, you might consider this point." Thatcher knew that he now had Gabler well and truly hooked. "We are agreed that the banks and brokers are suspect. But if a man were planning such a crime, wouldn't he avoid involving his own firm? Just so that he wouldn't immediately appear on Inspector Lyons' short list?"

"He would if he could. But the reason these men are suspect is because they have detailed inside information."

"That's why I was interested in this curious subgroup feature. As nearly as I can tell, Yates knows as much about Stringfellow's cargo as Stringfellow does. We're going to have to go into this in more detail with Quentin."

Gabler was eager to expand the list of suspects, but it was beyond his power not to raise objections.

"What about that call from Stringfellow to Quentin, the morning before that chauffeur turned up? That can't have been an accident. If it hadn't been made, Quentin probably would have checked back with Stringfellow."

"Didn't you hear what Yates said? He was with Stringfellow during the call. Or at least, one of them. And they seem to live in each other's offices. You heard Stringfellow say just now he was going over to Willard & Climpson."

"There may be something we don't know," Gabler said cautiously. "For instance, whether they had equal access to Russian forms."

"We can ask this attaché we're going to see," replied Thatcher as the cab drew up at their destination.

Aside from two policemen the sidewalk was bare. No demonstrators had put in an appearance this morning. Either they were afraid of being involved in a murder investigation, or they were put off by the possibility of another round of gunfire. Somebody might be taking potshots at anyone in front of the consulate. After all, this was New York. You couldn't tell what some people would do for kicks.

The receptionist was expecting them. Within moments they were being ushered into an office.

"Good morning, gentlemen. I am Sergei Pavlich Durnovo, commercial attaché seconded to the consulate. I believe you have already met my assistant, Feodor Voronin."

Durnovo was a tall, slim man with a suavity of manner that suggested the experienced and successful diplomat. He did not affect the rumpled, homespun look of lower-echelon Soviet officials. Sleek silver-gray hair was set off to advantage by the charcoal of his suit and the carefully matched greens of tie and handkerchief. Italian silk tailoring flowed smoothly as he punctiliously seated his guests.

After the introductions were completed, he began solemnly to convey a message from the consul. The rolling sentences unfolded into a statement which met even Gabler's high standards of formality. There were no shirt-sleeves or cardboard cups here. Thatcher, armed with his morning's reading of the newspapers, was not surprised to find Durnovo passing from sorrow at the robbery (and shock at the murder) to a review of the Ukrainian problem.

"They are misguided. Yes. They are foolish. Yes," he said in slow march time. "But they are not murderers."

Apparently the Ukrainians, however apostate, were assured of a true loving socialist welcome if they would return to the fold.

"It is the passion of conviction with them. You must not judge them harshly. We understand them."

Thatcher yielded the point. Gravely he assured the company that he would not judge the Ukrainian Nationalists prematurely. He had come because he knew he could rely on the cooperative spirit of the consulate. He had no wish to involve the Soviet government in his travail; only a matter of detail required clarification.

"I am sure that you have heard the general outline of the forgery. We have already established that a blank letterhead was stolen from the wheat broker involved. I wonder if we could do the same for the consular certificate used."

He produced the certificate for inspection. Durnovo examined it slowly while Voronin bent over his shoulder.

"There is no question that the Consul's signature is a forgery. I have here a genuine specimen."

Thatcher had realized that they would insist on an acknowledgment of this point, whether or not he had already conceded it.

"Yes," he agreed politely. "The signature is a forgery. The seal too."

"As you say, the seal also."

"But the letterhead?"

Minutes passed. Everyone knew that the letterhead was genuine. The attaché had surely received very precise instructions on this point. But damaging admissions are not lightly made by great powers.

Slowly Durnovo rested elbows on the desk and steepled his long tapering fingers into a graceful arch. Light was reflected from the beautifully polished and shaped nails.

"On the basis of my inspection, the letterhead would appear to be genuine." He glanced down at the paper in his hands and frowned.

Everett Gabler was nodding approvingly. Suggestion and agreement were proceeding with the slow solemnity he relished. It occured to Thatcher that Everett would make a fine Soviet foreign affairs officer.

"We understand that a number of the people taking part in these wheat sales have conferred with you here at the consulate. In your opinion, would it have been possible for them to abstract one or two of these letterheads?"

Another pause. Like Luke Stringfellow, Durnovo did not appreciate reflections on his office management. Suddenly Voronin whispered several sentences in Russian to his superior, whose face brightened.

"My assistant has reminded me of something I had forgotten. A Soviet delegation, including several of our captains and both of us, attended a conference at one of your hotels. The purpose of that meeting was to review Soviet requirements for documentation. As an illustration, we took a box of letterheads to the meeting. That would have been sometime last month, would it not, Feodor Ilyich?"

"Yes. I can give you the precise date." A pocket diary was flourished, and Feodor Voronin announced that the date had been February 2. Almost six weeks ago.

"And the letterheads could have been taken at that time?"

At a sign of assent from the attaché, Voronin expanded. "Very easily, I am afraid. Several copies were handed round—oh, five or six, I would say. But that is not all. It was a large meeting and during one of our pauses, the papers were left spread out on the table so that those in the back could examine them. At the end of the meeting, I collected the papers on the table. I think it would be impossible at this date to be more specific about who returned which paper."

Thatcher nodded. "Then it seems probable that the letterheads were taken there, rather than here."

"Yes," agreed Voronin. "Most of the brokers who have come here to the consulate have conferred with me in my office, and I assure you that they have not been left unattended at any time."

Thatcher accepted the statement without reservation. In fact, it was almost a pleasure to have one avenue closed. This seemed to be the only office connected with the entire far-flung transaction which had made any attempt to restrict the freedom of its visitors.

He turned away from the serious assistant, repressing the thought that civil servants look the same all over the world. Voronin could have been any forty-year-old employee of the Bureau of Weights and Measures.

"There is one further point. I don't suppose it will help

us much, but there are a few lines of Russian typed at the top." Thatcher tapped the heading. "Are there any blunders in the language? Does it suggest that someone who knew no Russian used a dictionary carelessly?"

Durnovo was interested. He leaned forward almost eagerly. But in a moment he was shaking his head. "There is no room for pitfall here. You understand, these are not sentences. Only unconnected phrases. The name of the ship. The number of tons of wheat. The classification of the wheat. For what it is worth, the itemizations are all correct."

"Then I am afraid there is nothing further for us to do than thank you for your courtesy and for your time."

But Durnovo had fallen prey to abstraction. He roused himself and replied that the Soviet Consulate was willing to do everything in its power to identify and punish the miscreants. They were not unmindful of the loss suffered by the Sloan, or the signal contribution to world understanding inherent in the Sloan's immediate decision to honor its commitments.

"Indeed it is a lesson to men of good will everywhere."

And a damned expensive lesson, thought Thatcher, as Durnovo unwound toward his conclusion. For a diplomat, the fellow had seemed reasonably short-winded until now. Leave-takings probably brought out the lurking ambassador in all foreign service officers. Or was he talking for time? If so, nothing seemed to happen to make it worthwhile.

At the conclusion of the amenities, Thatcher reached for the forged consular certificate. Durnovo abruptly abandoned his public platform manner.

"I wonder if you would permit us, Mr. Thatcher, to photostat that document? Although I am afraid we have not been of much assistance this morning, it is possible that further examination might reveal something I have overlooked. Indeed, I am asking Feodor Ilyich to make further inquiries among our staff. And such a photostat would be helpful to him."

This seemed to be Voronin's first intimation of his new assignment, but he pulled himself together and looked decorously eager. Thatcher raised no objection. The photostating was accomplished in record time, and the Sloan party was bowing itself out when Durnovo's secretary delivered a message.

Inspector Lyons had called and suggested that Mr. Thatcher might wish to join him at Halloran's Garage when he completed his business at the consulate. There were new developments.

6

Keep Off the Grass!

INSPECTOR LYONS was waiting for them in Rita Halloran's office. He was looking pleased, in marked contrast to Thatcher's companion. Their trek northward had been enlivened by a return of Everett Gabler's fractiousness.

"I don't see what we can expect to accomplish by dashing around to garages, John. And to be honest with you, I hate to think of what Charlie may be up to—while you and I are out of touch."

One of the many burdens of Everett Gabler's life was the nominal superiority in rank enjoyed by Charlie Trinkam at the Sloan. During Thatcher's absences, Trinkam was acting head of the department and, according to Gabler, in strong need of a restraining influence.

The no-frills exterior of Halloran's Garage and its utilitarian premises did not allay Gabler's alarms. Thatcher had not expected them to; the blast of a hyradulic jack, the echoing clatter of tools, the begrimed mechanics staring incuriously were calculated neither to exorcise the specter of raffish Charlie Trinkam plunging the Trust Department—if not the entire bank—into chaos, nor to encourage the conviction that they were on a foray worthy of the Sloan. Field work would never be Everett's cup of tea.

"This is one of the largest car rental agencies in Manhattan, Everett," Thatcher offered in propitiation, as he forged his way to the rear of the building.

Gabler continued to register fastidious disapproval. Big money without the proper accessories left him untouched. The only two institutions ever known to have elicited his wholehearted approbation were the old Union Pacific (back in the days when a railroad was a railroad, by God!) and Du Pont. It was not to be expected that Halloran's Garage could compete in this company.

The introductions caused a further compression of his lips. Inspectors of the New York City Police Department rang no bells for Everett. In a better world, the Sloan would simply have been granted full police powers.

"We're waiting for Eddy," explained Inspector Lyons. "It seems that he's got something to tell us. Although he may be getting cold feet about it."

"Eddy is a fool," Rita Halloran said in a perfectly level voice.

Whether this remark pertained to Eddy's story or to his cold feet was not clear. Nor did the lady's tone encourage a search for clarification. Thatcher certainly felt no temptation to pursue the subject, and Gabler looked as if he had just sighted his first native in Basutoland and didn't like it.

But Lyons was made of sterner stuff.

"Not enough of a fool to skip, I hope," he said easily. "That could make trouble for everyone."

Rita Halloran looked at him unenthusiastically. "Don't worry, Inspector. He's just sneaked out for a pick-me-up. The boys will find him."

"Good! We all know how much this means to Halloran's Garage."

Mrs. Halloran's lips tightened.

"Don't waste your time painting me a picture, Lyons. I'm willing to play ball with you. Hell, I've got to! You can ruin me, and we both know it. But don't push it!"

"Nobody's done any pushing"—there was an artful pause —yet."

"You don't have to. I've gotten enough bad publicity from Denger's murder and the Sloan robbery. Any more, and I can kiss good-bye to the good will of Halloran's Garage."

Lyons settled back more comfortably. "That would be a shame," he said.

Mrs. Halloran's eyes narrowed.

"It's not going to happen," she announced flatly. "I've spent too many years building this up to watch it go down the drain."

The Inspector was prevented from supplying further provocation by a head suddenly appearing in the hatchway.

"Eddy's here. He's right outside."

"Well, come on," called Mrs. Halloran peremptorily. "Come in, and let's get this over. I've got to get seven Caddies out for the Home Show crowd this afternoon."

Thatcher's recollection of Eddy was immediately refreshed. Small, ferret-faced and grimy, he hesitated in the doorway, avoiding Rita Halloran's eye. He ducked a shoulder in greeting to the rest of the assemblage before taking up his position, leaning against a battered filing cabinet.

Lyons nodded quietly. "Oh, I know you're busy. But then, we're all busy, what with the murder of one of your drivers and the big robbery he helped pull."

"That's a lot of—"

Realizing abruptly that she was playing the detective's game, Rita Halloran stopped in midstream and drew a deep breath. Her voice steadied and fell back into its normal register. "Now, just tell your story, Eddy."

Eddy, once again the focus of attention, ran a dirty hand down his shirt.

"I just thought it might mean something. After I read about that big haul and after they got Gus. Hell, I don't want to make trouble for the garage, or anything like that. I just thought . . ."

Without turning to look at him, Mrs. Halloran interrupted: "The garage is clean, and you know it. We all know it."

"Sure," Lyons agreed amiably.

For the first time Eddy and Rita looked directly at each other. It was an exchange of two troubled glances. They were both unnerved by the Inspector's reassurance. Eddy, in fact, started to edge backward.

"The story, Eddy," she reminded him remorselessly.

"Like I said, I thought it might mean something. So I told Rita and—"

"And I said we better call you, Lyons," Mrs. Halloran finished smoothly.

This simple statement deprived Eddy of what wits he had. He goggled speechlessly at his employer.

"That's fine. Now suppose we hear this story."

Eddy produced a crumpled pack of cigarettes from a shirt pocket and struck a match. He drew a deep lungful of smoke before speaking.

Stripped of false starts, of broken sentences, of panicked silences, Eddy's story was short and simple. The day that

Gus Denger was shot on the steps of the Russian Consulate, he and Eddy had slipped off for a mid-morning beer. (Here Eddy cast a frightened look at the sphinx-like Mrs. Halloran. If, as Thatcher suspected, beer during working hours was forbidden, there was more to Eddy than met the eye. Flouting one of Mrs. Halloran's rules was not something to be undertaken lightly.)

". . . and Gus, he says to me, he's got a good thing going. No . . . hell, no! He didn't have anything to do with the robbery—God, I'd swear to that on my last dollar. No, he's got something else—a little easy money coming his way. So I ask him if it's the horses, and he says no, it's a lot surer than that. So he makes this phone call, see?"

They all saw.

"Well, I been thinking about it, and I see the name in the papers . . . and we don't do no work for them, so why is Gus calling him? Hell, Rita, I thought it was the right thing to do . . ."

Thatcher had had a trying day, and he had no intention of straying again into the tangled relationship that seemed to obsess Eddy and Mrs. Halloran.

"Well, get on with it! Who did he call?"

Almost suddenly, Eddy ground out the cigarette under his heel.

"Stringfellow. This guy, Luke Stringfellow."

Thatcher saw Mrs. Halloran's lips move soundlessly. He wished he knew what she was saying.

Inspector Lyons had listened, without interruption or comment, to the broken narrative. Now he proceeded to take it apart, straighten it out, examine it from all angles and put it back together. He took Eddy backward and forward through his story, again and again, until the mechanic's eyes glazed, and he lost all awareness of his surroundings, even of Rita Halloran's measured appraisal. But though the words varied (Denger was first too "honest" to be in on the Sloan robbery, then too "chicken," and finally too "small-time"), and the details changed (the one beer had become two by the end of fifteen minutes), though Eddy produced some surprisingly ingenious speculations of his own, though he hemmed and hawed about what "a little easy money" might be in round numbers, the two basic facts remained unaltered. Denger had said that he was onto a good thing, and this had prompted him to place a call to Luke Stringfellow.

The question raised by these facts also remained constant. Was it this call to Stringfellow which had caused the shooting of Gus Denger some three hours later?

Finally Lyons was satisfied. "Okay. I guess that's all."

But Eddy, wound up like a top, couldn't leave it alone. "I just thought . . ."

"You thought!" remarked Rita Halloran with good-natured contempt. "From now on, you leave the thinking to me."

Somehow, peace had been tacitly established in the midst of that labored recital. Perhaps Rita had feared some disclosure which had not come. Certainly Eddy no longer feared mysterious reprisals. He sighed with immense relief.

"Sure, sure thing, Rita," he agreed eagerly.

Lyons, while missing nothing of the byplay, was not to be distracted from the central problem. "It's interesting," he summed up. "Denger knew something. He was keeping it under the rug, thinking he could parlay it into a roll, somehow." He looked mildy at Mrs. Halloran to see how she took the suggestion.

She was not as ready to leap to Denger's defense as Eddy had been. She was too busy defending her own interests. She paused for thought, before pronouncing judgment.

"Denger was no big-time crook. You heard his story yourself. Did it sound as if he thought he had a piece of a million dollars? Besides, my boys are bonded, and they get checked up and down the line. I'm not saying they don't like pickings. That's only natural. They see a lot of loose expense-account money floating around this business. The smart ones settle for tips on the market. With the rest, it's five bucks, maybe ten bucks, for keeping their mouths shut about something. Hell, what do you expect? You don't get plaster saints lining up for a job pushing hacks."

Shortly thereafter, Lyons, Thatcher, and Everett Gabler were adjourned in a small nearby cafeteria.

"What was going on back there?" asked Thatcher. "Between Eddy and Mrs. Halloran, I mean."

Lyons was amused.

"The old lady was sore because Eddy blabbed. The less she has to do with the papers or the police, the better, as far as she's concerned. But Eddy was big with his story and told someone. My bet is that he told his beer klatsch about it this morning. Anyway we got an anonymous call at Centre Street advising us to ask Eddy what Gus Denger told him the day he was shot. Then about an hour later, Rita Halloran called me."

"Hmm," Thatcher mused. "You might almost think she had something to hide."

"You might," Lyons agreed carefully. "A surprising number of people do. And if so, Eddy's in it with her. Eddy is her nephew, by the way. Or her husband's. He's got a stake in the garage, too."

"Of course, Eddy could be lying," Thatcher observed. "He's clearly not one of the world's truth tellers."

Lyons nodded. "Yes, but we've got confirmation of his story. The telephone at Tumulty's is at the bar, and old man Tumulty thinks he heard Gus making this call . . ."

Waspishly Gabler said, "Luke Stringfellow was most emphatic about not knowing this man Denger." He lofted a dripping tea bag and glared at it. "I suppose we are sure that it wasn't Luke Stringfellow himself who picked up that check."

"We aren't sure of anything, Everett," Thatcher said, exchanging a glance with Inspector Lyons. "But I certainly got the impression that Denger was telling us the truth about that when we talked to him. He said that he handed over that check to an essentially anonymous man— middle color, middle height, middle weight." He recalled Stringfellow's burly build, shock of red hair, and weather-beaten face. "And whatever else you can say about him, Luke Stringfellow is not anonymous looking."

"No, he certainly is not," said Gabler, making it sound like an accusation.

Lyons thoughtfully stirred his coffee and thoughtfully rose to Thatcher's bait. "You can bet that we'll be double checking on Luke Stringfellow. But I agree with you, Mr. Thatcher. I thought Denger was telling us the truth . . ."

"Then why was he calling Luke Stringfellow just before he was killed?" Gabler asked unanswerably.

They thought in silence while a busboy collected crockery and managed to remove Gabler's teacup before he was quite finished.

"There is something going on at that garage I don't understand," Thatcher said suddenly. "I didn't like Denger's smugness when we questioned him. And now we know he was hiding something. I don't understand what Mrs. Halloran is up to or what she's so furious about. And why is Eddy acting as guilty as if he had just murdered five people in a row? Somehow, it all seems to center right there."

But even as he spoke Thatcher wondered if he was being fair. Halloran's Garage was, after all, in serious peril; the carriage trade does not hire limousines associated with robbery, with murder, or with the police. Fast deals do not flourish under official scrutiny.

On the other hand, a blue-ribbon livery would certainly provide an excellent opportunity for extralegal activities ranging from the transport of call girls to the dispatching of checks, Sloan checks, out of the country—fast.

No doubt Inspector Lyons would be investigating this as well.

"A very competent woman," said Thatcher as they prepared to leave.

"But not a lady," said Everett Gabler. "John, I do think it's high time that we got back down to the Sloan."

7

Not by Bread Alone

THE SLOAN to which they returned was scarcely the Sloan of Everett Gabler's fond recollections.

While they had been pettily preoccupied with the recovery of their money, more powerful intelligences were grappling with the international implications of the sordid tangle in which the Sloan had become enmeshed. The governments and agencies pursuing these investigations had varying goals; but they were united on one issue. The Sloan was not, by a puerile insistence on its commercial rights, to imperil the unexpected accord which had suddenly emerged between East and West.

George Lancer, after extended consultation with his own legal department and with almost every law firm on Wall Street, could see one small ray of hope. The Sloan might be able to pass off some of its loss onto the foreign bank representing the Soviet Union. If so, the foreign bank might insist on penalizing its client.

"My God!" remonstrated the long distance line from

Washington. "Do you want to play into the hands of the Chinese?"

Lancer, who occasionally wrote articles on international events for *Foreign Affairs*, hastily denied the charge. Hadn't he been one of the first to recommend exploitation of the Sino-Soviet rift? He was advised darkly to stay in the realm of theory and leave the implementation to the professionals.

Victor Quentin, finally managing to devote a few hours to his professional duties, succeeded in tracing the first check for $985,000 when it came in for payment. Three telephone calls gave him further information. The check, he reported, had been paid into a Puerto Rican bank account and the funds immediately withdrawn to buy Mexican bearer bonds. Should he go further?

"No, no!" shrieked a voice from Washington. Any attempt to interfere with the liquidity or anonymity of Mexican bearer bonds would be regarded as provocation by the Organization of American States, and could constitute a death blow to the Alliance for Progress. Tactful inquiries on a government-to-government basis would naturally be made, but private intervention would only endanger the already delicate balance of interests in the Western Hemisphere. "Do you want to play right into the hands of Castro?"

Victor Quentin, as befitted his lower station, did not have George Lancer's pretensions to a statesmanlike view of the Sloan's international operations. He didn't care whose hands he played into if he got his money back and the police off his neck. But long and lively experience with Mexican bearer bonds led him to acquiesce in the Washington policy. For all practical purposes, the thieves and murderers now had $985,000—in cash.

At this point, an even humbler exmployee made an interesting discovery. The Sloan did not have the massive insurance portfolio affected by most industries. Banks do not expect to bear risks; they expect to fob them off onto their unfortunate customers. The only area in which they protect themselves heavily is that of the peculant employee. But young MacDonald thought it worthwhile to take a look. And amidst the lavish piles of certificates from bonding companies, richly crackling with their 100 per cent rag content, there reposed a rather unusual policy with Lloyd's of London—a testimonial to that firm's readiness to insure against bizarre risks. Hours passed as heavy legal case books were consulted. Yes, MacDonald thought, he rather thought, that just possibly there might be a chance. Inflamed at the prospect of solving a problem which had baffled mightier minds, he wrote a memo. Within hours his phone was jangling.

"Do you know what you're doing?" a voice sternly inquired. "Do you know that there's a by-election coming up in England?" The election, it developed, was going to turn largely on the question of the future of NATO, thereby giving the electorate of Little Puddingford a respite from the cares of Rhodesia. And NATO meant only one thing to Washington. "Do you want to play right into the hands of DeGaulle?"

Well no, now that the subject had been raised, young MacDonald did not want to play into the hands of De-Gaulle. It had never occurred to him that they were on playing terms.

It has been given to few American institutions to become the involuntary ally of China, Cuba, and France within the space of a few days. The Sloan, ever willing to break new ground, might have sustained the role with fortitude. But Washington was not content to stymie all the bank's moves toward recovery; it insisted on reporting to the Sloan the results of its own efforts. Accordingly, almost every major officer of the Sloan was closeted with an emissary from some government agency.

And bank business ground to a halt as effectively as if Exchange Place had suffered a direct hit.

"Yes," said the man from the CIA to the directors' meeting especially invoked for his benefit, "I think we can assure you that this was not a plot on behalf of the Soviet government."

"But—" said someone at the table.

The CIA man raised a calming hand to quell the riotous relief evidenced by old Bridewell's polishing his glasses. "Of course, it's not final yet. We still have to receive verification from some of our sources. I don't want you to think we're being precipitate. But so far, we haven't raised a flicker of suspicion."

"These sources?" asked a doubting Thomas. "Do they know anything?"

"Some of them are assessed as being alpha reliable," was the dignified reproof. "I can't go further than that. It would not be in the national interest."

"That's all right with me," said the first director. "The whole point of this trade treaty was that the Soviet Union had lots of gold and no wheat. Doesn't make sense for them to endanger the delivery of wheat, in order to steal some money. Right?"

"You're trying to look at this as a simple commercial transaction."

"Well, it is a commercial transaction."

The CIA man smiled bitterly.

The FBI man didn't get the full board. He got Charlie Trinkam.

"Communism," he explained kindly, "isn't the simple thing a lot of Americans think it is. It's a worldwide conspiracy, and there are dissensions and failures of discipline there, just like every place else. We never thought your robbery was Russian inspired. We've had our eyes elsewhere."

Charlie Trinkam tried, without conspicuous success, to summon an appearance of decent interest. "Oh, where's that?"

"The New Left! You're surprised, huh? Sure, a lot of their money comes from the C.P., but to them Russia is just another great power. And they're against all great powers. They'd welcome the chance to throw a monkey wrench into the works."

"So that's what you've been doing, is it?"

The FBI man looked around cautiously before admitting: "Some of our best men have been at work in Berkeley for a long time now."

"And what do they say?"

"Not a peep about robbing the Sloan." He sighed heavily, then tightened his jaw. "There it is. You can't blink at facts."

The Internal Revenue was pleased to report that their investigation had failed to reveal any link between the Syndicate and the bank's loss.

Everett Gabler was sufficiently startled at the source of this information to break his seething silence.

"And would *you* know?"

The thin man across the desk permitted himself a restrained chuckle.

"We know more about their income than they do."

The Office of Foreign Commerce announced this was not a plot by other wheat-exporting nations, the Bank Examiners asked the Sloan to set an early date for a conference, the United States Navy offered to post guards at the Sloan for the duration of the wheat shipments, and every bank in New York wanted a careful rundown on exactly how the swindle had been worked.

And last but not least, Capitol Hill in the form of an old friend of Lancer's called to pass a veiled warning. The report on the theft now circulating in Washington had roused congressional interest. Lancer would be well-advised to leave a week free in his schedule to testify before the inevitable House investigation.

"What report?" Lancer growled resentfully. "For God's sake, how could anybody write a report at this stage? What did they do? List the conspiracies that aren't involved?"

"Well, there wasn't an awful lot of material," said his friend, "but they managed to spread it over thirty pages."

George Lancer went out for a drink.

John Putnam Thatcher had avoided the tidal wave by abandoning the premises. He was keeping his feet dry by fraternizing with yet another of the Sloan's dubious allies. Only Miss Corsa knew that he could be reached at Centre Street, in the office of Detective Inspector Philip Lyons.

Lyons had naturally lost no time in confronting Luke Stringfellow with the information extracted from Eddy at Halloran's Garage.

"Not that it got me anywhere," Lyons grumbled. "Stringfellow sticks to his story that he never heard of August Denger."

"You mean he denies the call was made?"

"No. That, at least, would tell us Stringfellow was lying. We've got definite confirmation of the call from Tumulty's Bar. It's less helpful than that. Stringfellow was out of the office, and says he never heard of Denger. The call was taken by that girl of his, Tessie Marcus. She told Denger that Stringfellow wasn't in and went through the usual routine about leaving a message. Then, as nearly as she can remember, he just told her to say that Gus Denger called."

Thatcher looked at the Inspector appraisingly.

"And do you think she's telling the truth?"

Lyons nodded. "Yes, I do. She's loyal to Stringfellow,

but she's no fanatic on the subject. I doubt if she'd try to cover for him."

"Yet she didn't volunteer the information."

"She says she wanted to talk to Stringfellow first, which is reasonable enough under the circumstances. And she didn't get a chance, until after the murder was announced. Stringfellow didn't come back to the office until late in the day. Their story is that they were coming around to see me if I didn't get to them in the next day or two. Myself, I think they were a little more elastic than that. She decided she'd answer any questions, but she wouldn't take the initiative."

The Inspector's easy, measured judgments underlined the fact that he had spent a lifetime with cases of fraud and embezzlement, and knew a great deal about how innocent bystanders reacted when their testimony about friends and associates became critical.

But to Thatcher's alert ear, the judgments were a little too easy. By rights, the detective should now have been baying at full throat after Luke Stringfellow.

"There's something else, isn't there?" he asked. "Something that points away from Stringfellow?"

Lyons smiled his acknowledgment. "Yes, there is. I wanted to see how it sounded to you. Denger's last hours that morning seem pretty important. We've been over and over this with everybody at that garage. Calling Stringfellow wasn't Denger's only activity. He also called Baranoff's office and asked when Baranoff was due back in the States. Then he asked one of his shopmates if he knew what a certain brownstone on Seventy-third Street was. The guy can't remember the number now, but it was in the same block as the Russian Consulate. And they don't have any kind of sign outside. Then, if it means anything at all, Denger received a couple of calls at the garage. No one seems to know from whom. Does all this begin to add up to you? One point sticks out."

Thatcher frowned as he considered the information. Stringfellow . . . Baranoff . . . the Russian Consulate . . . of course! He leaned forward.

"But all this happened before there was any news release on the Sloan robbery! And we didn't tell him anything, when we questioned him. So he must have found out someplace else that the consulate was mixed up in this. And he was calling everybody involved. And Eddy said Denger was onto a good thing, didn't he?"

"We're thinking along the same lines." The Inspector was pleased. "He was trying to sell something. Our visit probably tipped him off to the value of his information. He may not have known how big a swindle it was, but once the Sloan and the police were on the scene, he knew it was big enough to be worth some money to him. Or, money than he'd already gotten. So he started to call everybody in the picture."

Thatcher interrupted firmly. "Not everybody," he corrected. "He didn't call Victor Quentin."

"No, he didn't call Quentin." Lyons paused as if reaching a decision. "Look, Thatcher, there's no point beating around the bush. We both know that the two men in the driver's seat on this deal were Stringfellow and Quentin. It's only right that those are the two I'm looking at first."

"Of course it is," Thatcher agreed quickly. "The Sloan has every reason to be grateful for the thoroughness of your investigation. I suppose you've already gone into the question of alibis for Denger's murder. Quentin was with me, you recall, on the *Odessa Queen.*"

"Oh, he's clear on the murder," Lyons conceded promptly. "So if the robbery was a one-man job, he should be okay on that too. Only thing is, there's no reason to say it was a one-man job."

Nor was there any reason to say it was not, Thatcher reflected. He decided to abandon the question of Victor Quentin's guilt and move a little farther from home.

"And Stringfellow?" he asked.

"Stringfellow of course was out of his office. That's why he didn't get Denger's call. All day, he was hopping from place to place. He ate lunch alone in a cafeteria uptown. There's at least an hour when he isn't covered. And I can tell you one thing. It's going to be the same for everybody we question. You know what lunch hour is like in New York. Unless there's a business meeting set up, people wander around."

Yes, Thatcher thought, that was probably why the murder took place then. Quite apart from the fact that Denger was unlikely to be able to go to the consulate except during his lunch hour.

Or did that assume the murder had to take place at the consulate?

He shook his head irritatedly at this circular reasoning and returned his attention to Lyons.

"I did get one piece of interesting information when I

was checking into Stringfellow's movements," Lyons continued. "On the day the letter of credit was cashed, Stringfellow left his office for the day after telling his girl to call Quentin. He went over to Jersey to look at some property. So Quentin couldn't have checked back with him when Denger showed up, even if he'd wanted to."

Thatcher absorbed this item in silence.

"It works both ways," he finally pointed out. "If Stringfellow was guilty, he wouldn't want to be available. If he was innocent, then it was a great benefit to the guilty party to have him out of the way. Unless you can narrow down the number of people who knew he was going to New Jersey, it doesn't seem to be much help."

On this discouraging note, both men lapsed into their own thoughts. As he stared out the grimy window, Thatcher was reminded of David Yates's perpetual presence in the Stringfellow office. He had been there during the Quentin call. He probably knew about the trip to New Jersey. But it was idle to speculate with so little data. There might have been other people in the office. Anybody could have called and ascertained Stringfellow's absence. Someone could even have instigated the trip. The trouble was that there weren't enough facts.

"Do you know anything about Stringfellow?" he asked, pursuing this train. "His general background, I mean."

"Quite a bit." Lyons reached for a folder. "We've checked into Stringfellow and Quentin and Denger, so far. That is, we've checked their current position. We're not getting an awful lot of attention from Washington—as far as national records go." The Inspector's voice shaded into irony. "Not that it makes much difference with the first two. They've been doing the same thing for a long time. Quentin's been at the Sloan for over twenty years. He's lived in Scarsdale for over thirty years. Got a big house with the mortgage all paid up. He keeps talking about getting a smaller place now that his kids have grown up and married, but doesn't do anything about it. Let's see, they belong to the club and go there occasionally on Saturday night. Quentin golfs and has picked up quite bit of business at the club. By and large, they live quietly and don't seem to have any trouble, either between themselves or with the kids. The only known debt is on one of the two cars they run. They seem to live well within their income."

Thatcher contented himself with a silent nod. He did not point out that, with a man in Quentin's position, the

Sloan had its own system for being alerted to blatant overspending.

"Stringfellow's a little flashier. He inherited the business from his father and has been running it for fifteen years. He and his wife left the city twelve years ago. They've traded up on houses three times. Now, he's got a big place in Huntington and keeps a boat at the yacht club. They like to step out some. Two kids in high school, one in grade school. They've got mortgages on the house and boat, and are still financing two of their three cars. What's this?" Lyon's peered in perplexity at the paper. "Oh, it must be one of those little foreign sports jobs. Probably the kid's car. Anyway he's getting a lot of mileage out of his income, but nothing beyond reason. My information about his income is from Quentin."

"Who knows what he's talking about, I'm sure. Well, all that sounds predictable enough. What about Denger?"

"Also predictable. Lived in a rooming house, passed his evenings in a tavern mostly. I managed to get hold of his brother. Seems he had a marriage that went sour a long time ago, no kids. According to the brother, most things did go sour for Denger, he was that kind. Liked to play the horses, liked the idea of easy money in general. But he had no big criminal ideas. Brother thinks he wouldn't have burned his fingers on this deal if he'd known how big it was. Just an ordinary small-time bum, maybe a little more surly than most."

Thatcher decided to enter an objection. "I realize that you have to look into people's financial position, but it isn't really relevant, is it?"

"How so?"

"Because this was a theft of almost a million dollars." Thatcher paused to emphasize his reasoning. "And nobody really *needs* a million dollars. You might discover some irregularity in the Stringfellow or Quentin background. They might have betting losses, they might be blackmailed, Stringfellow's business might be in trouble. But not to the tune of a million dollars. Neither of them could have gotten unsecured credit for that amount, in the first place."

Lyons nodded encouragingly, as if Thatcher were following some path he had already explored. "Blackmail?" he suggested. "A bank officer would be very vulnerable to that pressure."

"What kind?" Thatcher insisted. "If someone were

blackmailing Quentin on personal grounds—someone who didn't know anything at all about the wheat deal—he'd ask for forty or fifty thousand dollars. Quentin could raise that on his property. No blackmailer could expect him to raise a million dollars. If you're talking about a black-mailer who didn't want money from Quentin but wanted to use him as an accomplice in this theft, then you're talk-ing about somebody who knew all about the wheat deal. That takes us right back to where we started—to another insider."

Lyons followed Thatcher's reasoning, step by step. Then, almost sheepishly, he said:

"There's another angle. It's what I always call the new life approach, people who want to get away from every-thing and start all over again. Sometimes that's set off by financial trouble. That's why I'm trying to get an idea about domestic backgrounds. If Stringfellow, for instance, was fed up with his wife and kids already, then his busi-ness was suddenly in the hole for fifty thousand—*that* might be enough to trigger him into trying for a new life in Brazil."

Thatcher was intrigued. "I hadn't thought about that," he confessed. "But it makes some sense. Now that I come to think of it, almost all the major coups that have been outright thefts—I don't mean the financial juggler spin-ning to keep himself alive—have been on your new life principle. Very few people, after all, are in a position to have a million dollars flow into an old life without raising a good many questions."

"I'm glad you agree." Lyons grinned broadly. "When it comes down to money, there's nobody I'd rather listen to than a banker."

8

Sowing the Wind

WITH THE SLOAN still smarting from a $985,000 theft and with unknown sharpshooters littering bodies over the steps of the Russian Consulate, the entire situation could fairly be described, in Everett Gabler's terms, as a revolting muddle. It was only to be expected that the passing days should produce fresh convulsions. What surprised John Putnam Thatcher was their nature; the last thing he expected to see introduced into an already roiling scene was a troupe of one hundred and twenty-two highly trained otters.

These otters were no ordinary otters, if various respectful but guarded press reports could be believed. Not for them the mere balancing of rubber balls on shapely noses, the disjointed tooting of childlike tunes.

No, these were Russian otters, fresh from a triumphal tour of Europe, quivering with eagerness to show American audiences that the genus *lutra* had nothing to learn from the Lippizaners. These otters could sing *The Volga Boatman,* dance a rousing mazurka, and assemble a three-stage rocket. Their leader, a strange other-worldly zealot named Plomsky, had devoted thirty years of his life to creating Plomsky's Otter Ensemble and was known in some circles as the Stanislavsky of aquatic mammals. He was also a Hero (Second Class) of the Soviet Union.

"Such otters," Abe Baranoff told the press on the chilly deck of the newly docked *Cristoforo Colombo,* "such otters America has been waiting for. They are artistry in motion, beauty of form, a not-to-be-believed grace . . ."

"For fish?" suggested somebody from the *Times* (who had already learned that Plomsky's Otter Ensemble had boarded the *Cristoforo Colombo* only after the Cunard Line had politely, but firmly, declined to place a first-class cabin at the company's disposal).

"Fish?" replied Baranoff, drawing a silk scarf against the icy wind whistling up the Hudson. "Fish for artists like this? Would we give fish to Callas? To Rubinstein? To Horowitz?" He brandished a malacca walking stick. "Tell them, maestro."

He inclined his majestic head as Plomsky commenced a detailed description of the sugar pellets used to coax prodigies of effort from his protégés.

"Soaked in champagne," added Baranoff grandly. He cared more for the spirit than the technique of the performing arts.

Pained, Plomsky protested.

"But no! Not champagne. Sometimes when they are tired, a little vodka, yes! But champagne . . . no." He resumed his lecture. "You understand, of course, that not every otter has it in him to become a Plomsky virtuoso. First, we must find unusually intelligent otters . . ."

With a lordly gesture that, in effect, dismissed Plomsky and the gifted otter, Baranoff gathered the journalists around him like a cape and began a proconsular stroll through the departing crush of passengers and porters, toward his cabin.

"In America, Plomsky's otters will swim in champagne!" he declared.

In a word, Abe Baranoff was back, and already busily working to insure full houses in Boston, Rochester, Dallas, and anywhere else Plomsky's Otter Ensemble was booked. A practiced impresario, he brought to bear the tools that had worked so successfully with the Anatolian Puppet Theater, Grimya Pelaguin, the noted Peruvian counter-bass, the Upsala Boys Choir, and the many other cultural and artistic events introduced to an eager American public for well over forty years under the banner: "Abe Baranoff Presents . . ."

Besides being time-tested, his method was simple. First, he provided a tantalizing glimpse of his stars (to a photographer from *Life,* if possible). Then he gave vivid, and sometimes accurate, descriptions of mad opening nights in Madrid, Rome, and London. Then last, but by no means least, he would lead the whole group to his cabin, where today he seriously incommoded secretaries, assistants, and the functionaries of the *Cristoforo Colombo* by insisting that champagne and brandy he produced for his good friends, the ladies and gentlemen of the press. Since Abe Baranoff tipped, as one steward put it, like a Grand Duke at Monaco in 1908, he got what he wanted.

"Ah, little did I think when I was a small boy in Omsk that one day I—Abe Baranoff—would have the privilege of introducing this great ensemble of Russian artists to America," he confided, settling himself next to the *Daily News.* Baranoff was a great believer in the personal touch and did not intend to let Plomsky and the otters upstage him. "A childhood dream come true."

The *Daily News* was sipping Piper-Heidsieck with other goals in mind.

"Abe, did you cut your European trip short because this chauffeur of yours was involved in the Sloan robbery?"

Abe Baranoff was wounded. Magnificent eyes under overhanging brows became infinitely sad.

"What does Baranoff have to do with bankers?" he said.

"Bankers, always bankers. Ah, if my mother—who starved to buy me a violin—if she should know. But, at least God has let me play my small part, although I could never be a great artist. I have helped bring the finest talents of our times to America. And today, I am bringing Plomsky's Otter Ensemble—that is why I am back! I know nothing of robberies . . . yes, what is it?"

This last was directed to the slim, pallid aide-de-camp hovering nearby with a sheaf of cables. Silently the underling handed Baranoff the papers. The impresario sighed deeply, then produced glasses from a pocket, affixed them, and with lightning rapidity riffled through the sheaf, meanwhile dictating replies.

". . . no answer to this . . . send this to Weinstein and tell him to get an estimate . . . tell Myra to make me an appointment. . . . My God! Who does this swine think he's dealing with? I said ten per cent, and I'm not going one penny higher . . ."

After making a few notes, the young man retrieved the papers and disappeared.

"Business, always business. It pursues me," said Baranoff, removing his glasses and holding out his hand for more champagne. "Ah, if Mother could see this, her heart would break. Now, what was I saying?"

"You were saying," said the *Daily News* with a straight face, "that your interest is centered on otters—not on the chauffeur of yours who got shot."

"Ah!" Was this a tribute to the champagne, or to something else? "Ah, such otters! My friend, when you see them your heart will quiver . . ."

He rose and moved off, to give *Time* a revealing glimpse into the heart of a great artist *manqué*.

After he had completed his circuit and his confidences, Abe Baranoff donned a billowing coat, lofted his walking stick, and prepared to debark from the *Cristoforo Colombo*, still touting the brio of Plomsky's otters.

(His entourage managed the usual leave-taking amenities: "Always nice to have Mr. Baranoff with us," the cabin steward said obsequiously.

The pale young man, who was charged with distributing largesse, smiled humorlessly. "Isn't it?")

But ashore, things proved to be different. The press sweeping down on the Baranoff party here had not been hand-picked by Baranoff's very wily press agent. And of course, they had not spent the preceding twenty minutes drinking champagne.

"Hey, Abe, what about this driver . . . ?"

"Baranoff, got anything to say about the robbery?"

"Pete, get a picture of them here . . ."

The press agent, alerted by a minatory look from Baranoff, forged his way to the head of the group.

"Gentlemen please, we're here to introduce a great company of performers . . ."

The gentlemen merely continued to howl.

"The world is too much with us," murmured Baranoff tragically in *The New Yorker*'s ear.

Little did he know. More important forces were conspiring to distress Abe Baranoff. They were lying in ambush at the Customs Office. Within twenty minutes his accent had deepened, and shifted from vaguely French to wildly Mittel-Europa. In thirty minutes, Abe Baranoff was, to put it baldly, screaming:

"Quarantine! What nonsense is this! I have a letter of clearance from the American Ambassador! I have certificates of vaccination . . ."

A meaty-faced official gazed at Baranoff's long hair with mild dislike and repeated something about regulations.

"Regulations! What regulations? I'll call my Senator! I'll call the White House! George, you dummy! Why are you standing there! Get me Weinstein! Get Mulloy! What do I pay these lawyers for when they're not here when I need them? Regulations! We'll see . . ."

The ensuing uproar did not alarm Baranoff's retinue, all too accustomed to angry cries for lawyers. The customs officials, who had dealt with the furor when Baranoff brought seventy-two Lapland reindeer to America (for a Christmas spectacular), stared into space.

"They can't do this to me!" Baranoff howled, speeding George to a telephone for legal reinforcements. The press, except for those who knew Baranoff well enough to review his performance without seeing it, scribbled furiously.

"Assassins! Cossacks! Bureaucrats! The curse of my life! All I want to do is bring beauty and art into our country . . . and this!" With a gesture worthy of a nineteenth-century Hamlet, he placed a manicured hand on his heart. "And for this, I am persecuted."

The customs officials not only had the imperturbability

of civil servants; they had coped earlier with a middle-aged Idaho lady trying to smuggle four Florentine leather purses in her corset. They watched Baranoff impassively.

"These otters," he told them vibrantly, "have performed before all the crowned heads of Europe."

Grigori Plomsky gave an anguished yelp.

"Now what?" Baranoff demanded, goaded beyond endurance by human folly.

"Crowned heads?" Plomsky said. "Baranoff, are you trying to kill me?"

Baranoff was nettled. "Kill you? Listen Plomsky, leave these details to me. Let Abe Baranoff take care of you as he has taken care of the Astrakhan Folk Ballet . . ."

But the dread specter of royalism had touched Plomsky on the raw. Moreoever he was not a mindless ballet master. To some, otters might be non-ideological, but not to Grigori Plomsky, artist and intellectual. He stood up.

"I want to see my consul," he announced. "This confusion . . ."

"Viper!" shouted Baranoff.

"Viper, perhaps," said Plomsky with dignity. "Revisionist, no. I want my consul!"

Baranoff hurled himself into a torrent of invective. Remaining aloof, Plomsky folded his arms, stared over Baranoff's head, and maintained a cold silence.

"Stabbed in the back," said Baranoff brokenly. "Always stabbed in the back!"

But despite being stabbed in the back, Baranoff was constitutionally incapable of emulating the silence of Plomsky and the customs officials; he must talk. Accordingly the press finally managed to divert the Niagara of his eloquence from otters to matters of greater interest to the newspaper reading public of New York, including John Putnam Thatcher.

"Denger? What should I know of Denger? No, I gave him no orders to pick up papers . . ."

"What was he like, Abe?" somebody yelled.

"What was he like?" Baranoff repeated, his imagination fired. At his elbow, the press agent spoke urgently. "Be careful? Why should I be careful? No, I, Abe Baranoff knew this man. I understand such men as he. . . ."

He lowered his head in ponderous thought.

"Denger was . . . not ordinary."

A groan went up from the assembly, and the customs men began inspecting their watches.

"Ah, you do not understand," Baranoff declaimed. "One had to look beneath the surface. He was not an artist, no. There was no music in his soul. And that an artist is born with or he is . . . he is nothing."

The press stirred restively. They had all been exposed to the Baranoff theory of soul music. Ever sensitive, the showman realized he was losing his audience. Hastily he shifted gears.

"But still, he had something. He had the thoughts, but he could not put them into practice. It is the tragedy of so many." Here the great figure drooped in a pantomime of suffering. "And so he was frustrated. By the knowledge that he was a failure. By the sight of others who were not."

It was clear to everybody who was the biggest success in Denger's immediate circle.

"Could he plot a big crime?" somebody shouted.

"He could plot; he could not plot well. I understand them, the failures." The arms swept out in a dangerous gesture designed to embrace the failures of the world.

"Listen, Abe, lay off this!" his press agent pleaded, anticipating Weinstein. But Abe Baranoff was caught up by his own performance. When someone asked what he and Denger had talked about, he had his lines ready.

"What do they all talk to me about? Their hopes, their fears, their hidden dreams. Ah, the pathos of it! The dreams of little men!"

"Why was he shot?"

"Who knows? Something in his own miserable life. But nothing to do with me . . ."—and here an idea visibly came to Baranoff—"and nothing to do with the great Russian nation. A people with a profound and reverent esteem for the arts . . ."

In the corner, Plomsky's head went up slightly.

"Abe, did you know Luke Stringfellow?"

Cut off in midstream in his observations about the culture-loving nature of the Slav, Baranoff was momentarily off balance. With a quick look at his press agent, he said:

"Luke Stringfellow? Who is Luke Stringfellow? I have never heard of him . . . Ah, Weinstein, at last! About this quarantine! You must do something!"

Weinstein, who looked depressed, managed to do one thing at least; he put a speedy end to Abe Baranoff's public utterances.

"Hmm," said John Putnam Thatcher, finishing a rather tidied-up version of the scene in that evening's paper. "Of course, the question is whether or not Baranoff knows the difference between fact and fiction."

Everett Gabler, who was in Thatcher's office on quite another matter, was torn between personal dislike for anybody photographed in a fur-trimmed coat and a certain decent respect for substance.

"He does have that string of theaters," he said unwillingly. "And God knows how much real estate, in one holding company or another."

"True," said Thatcher idly, letting his ever active imagination play with the possibility of dispatching Everett to Plomsky's Otter Ensemble. "Still, it's hard to believe that anybody who waxes lyrical about otters is a good judge of men. Think of those unbelievable books. But Baranoff probably was right about Denger . . ."

To his surprise he had touched a chord.

"These otters are quite remarkable from what I hear," said Gabler, gathering up papers preparatory to departure. "I understand that it takes years to train them. Fascinating."

Thatcher watched him leave in some mystification. He had forgotten Everett Gabler's enthusiasm for animals, if not for human beings. He buzzed Miss Corsa.

"Miss Corsa, I think I'd better talk with Abe Baranoff. Will you try to make an appointment for me? I don't know exactly where you can get in touch with him . . ."

Miss Corsa received these instructions with calm.

"They are having a terrible time about those otters," she informed him. "Temporarily they have to keep them on Ellis Island. I'll try there first."

Since Miss Corsa was conspicuously not interested in animals, this could only mean that, not for the first time, she had anticipated him.

"In the meantime . . ." he began slyly.

"I've got the forged documents here for you to look at again," she replied.

He recognized defeat when he saw it.

"Thank you, Miss Corsa."

9

Cover Crop

TRACKING DOWN ABE BARANOFF was not easy, but it was naturally well within Miss Corsa's powers. Her step-by-step campaign promised to last most of the day, however, with some of the minor engagements fought under Thatcher's eye after she started taking dictation during the lulls. Fascinated, he overheard her converse with informants backstage at the Metropolitan Opera (even across the desk he was exposed to the vibrations of a *Heldentenor* limbering up), and the administrative offices of the Bronx Zoo (strange grunts and yips suggesting that their offices were livelier than most), and at the Fulton Fish Market (still stranger grunts and yips).

When the phone next rang, Thatcher expected another report from Miss Corsa's intelligence network, but she turned to him and murmured:

"Mr. Voronin of the Russian Consulate would like to speak with you."

Foreign names did not provoke in Miss Corsa the half-hesitations and false starts of the self-doubter. She simply decided how she was going to pronounce them, then did so firmly and swiftly. She might be wrong, but she was never embarrassed.

Voronin, while wrapping the matter in courtesies, wanted Thatcher to come up to the consulate and was unwilling to say why. Thatcher did his bit for world peace by agreeing to go immediately.

In the taxi, he surrendered himself to speculation. Voronin was the subordinate assigned to further investigation of the forged consular certificate. Obviously he had come up with something. Thatcher was not such an innocent as to think that Voronin had promptly reached for the phone to tell the Sloan all about it. There must have been a session among the reigning powers at the consulate; they had decided on this action.

In other words, what Voronin had discovered was hot

enough to require transmission to the Americans. On the other hand, the consulate did not wish to attach to it the importance that would surround participation by either the Consul himself or Durnovo, the commercial attaché. So the scene had been laid for a casual, underplayed approach.

Just how casual, he had not bargained for.

When Thatcher presented himself at the receptionist's desk, there stood the commercial attaché, Sergei Durnovo. He was staring at an envelope he had picked up from the desk. His surprised recognition of Thatcher was masterful.

"Mr. Thatcher! What an unexpected pleasure! I did not know you were to visit us today."

Thatcher had too often pulled the same trick himself— who has not?—to be taken in. But he was perfectly prepared to play the game.

"Yes, I received a call from Mr. Voronin. I'm on my way to see him now."

An elegant frown flitted over the high, domed brow. The smooth silver hair added the suggestion of statesmanlike concern.

"Ah, yes, he was looking into the question of those forged certificates, wasn't he?"

Without a quiver, Thatcher agreed.

"Allow me to show you the way to his office. It is just down the corridor from mine."

Durnovo indicated the way to the stairwell and fell into step beside Thatcher. The abandoned envelope fluttered back to the desk.

"I believe that Feodor Ilyich did say he had uncovered something that might interest you. We are naturally anxious to inform you promptly of any little fact we unearth, no matter how insignificant. We are so unversed in your tortuous ways of finance that you must excuse us if we trouble you with trifles."

Thatcher confessed he was without sufficient words to express his unbounded sense of obligation. Then he waited to see if there was more to come.

There was.

"Naturally," murmured Durnovo gently, "had we dreamed of these official seals being put to improper use, we would never have exposed them to any casual passerby walking in from the streets. Now, of course, we will take more rigorous precautions. It is, I am afraid, another case of locking the stable after the horse has been stolen."

Durnovo had oiled his way silkily to Thatcher's destination and now, with one last beautiful smile, delivered him into the hands of Voronin's secretary.

While the intercom was being brought to life, Thatcher reviewed the points made by the commercial attaché so casually.

First, whatever Voronin had learned was insignificant to the point of triviality. Second, the seal, which had obviously been found in some Soviet purlieu, had been used for forgery by someone who wandered in off the street. (And who wanders in off an American street? An American!) Three, the Soviet personnel stationed in New York were such lambs in the jungles of American finance that they could barely understand its complexity, let alone bring off brilliant strokes of fraud. (And what an admission *that* was from a commercial attaché who had probably cut his eye teeth on letters of credit!)

That was a lot of information to pack into a charming two-minute chat. Thatcher decided that Sergei Durnovo's professional eminence was indeed well earned.

Meanwhile the intercom had produced not only Voronin, but a visitor he was ushering out.

"You made excellent time in the traffic, Mr. Thatcher," he commented. "I don't know whether you know Miss Marcus."

Thatcher recognized Luke Stringfellow's Tessie, as she greeted him staidly.

"Luke is getting ready to load a second boat," she announced. "Mr. Voronin and I have been going over the papers."

"You can understand our concern, Mr. Thatcher," said the Russian. "There will be no mistakes in the papers this time."

"Well, there weren't any last time. Not in the real papers. God knows we spent enough time working out the details. And much good it did us," Tessie ended grimly.

Thatcher examined Stringfellow's secretary with interest. Her manner might be as brusque as ever, she might be cooperating with Inspector Lyons, but she could not hide the fact that nobody at Stringfellow & Son was relaxing until official suspicion ceased to center on Luke Stringfellow.

"I don't think you'll have any trouble with your second

ship," he promised her. "The Sloan's only interest is in seeing that the remaining deliveries go through as normally as possible."

"That's what we're all hoping," said Tessie as she picked up her plastic portfolio and departed.

Voronin came straight to the point.

"I've discovered an interesting fact, Mr. Thatcher. Perhaps it isn't important enough to justify disturbing you, but we would like you to have all the information that is available to us."

Thatcher expressed appreciation and concluded that Voronin was ignorant of Durnovo's end play.

"It's about the seal. You recall we agreed that it wasn't the consulate seal."

Suddenly Thatcher recalled more than that. He remembered how Durnovo, after examining the seal, had become absent-minded and then suddenly wanted a photostat.

"Yes?"

"Although the seal was not from this consulate, it did have characteristics which were familiar. So I have been checking the seals and stamps in use by Soviet agencies in this city—the Intourist Agency, Amtorg, our office at the U.N."

"What an excellent idea," said Thatcher.

"Of course if the seal had been in use any length of time we would have recognized it. But it turned out to be comparatively new."

"Then you succeeded in locating it?"

Voronin nodded. "Oh, yes. Some months ago we opened a permanent trade show in New York, primarily to display Soviet-produced articles. A small section, however, operates as a store. Purchases can be made only for delivery to individuals in the U.S.S.R."

"I remember. It's somewhere on Fifth Avenue, isn't it?"

"Yes, near Fifty-third Street. I have already spoken with the manager by telephone, and he cannot explain the use of their stamp," Voronin continued. "However, as it is only used to indicate that the processing of an order is completed, there is no elaborate security procedure. I am about to go to the store and inquire further. Perhaps you would care to accompany me?"

When Thatcher said he would be delighted as well as interested, it was no mere civility. If his days and nights were going to revolve around Russian-American trade treaties (and the attitude of both governments to the Sloan's little embarrassment suggested that the wheat deal was the first of many), then he might as well familiarize himself with the Soviet agencies in New York.

On Fifth Avenue they were greeted by a delegation of two—the manager and the vivacious young brunette who had been the one bright spot in Thatcher's visit to the *Odessa Queen.*

"We shall do everything we can to help," the manager assured them. "Everyone on our staff speaks some English, but only those on the floor of the store are fluent. Katerina Ivanovna will be available as an interpreter when you speak with the office staff."

Voronin interrupted. "But will it be necessary to speak with the office? I thought the stamp was used by the clerk taking the order?"

"It is not quite that simple. You understand your operations have become rather more complex than we had anticipated. Let me show you."

The manager led them down an aisle flanked by large pieces of machinery, bristling with cogwheels, levers, and oversized tires. Labels identified these industrial items as: "grinders," "lathes," "drop presses," and other objects rarely seen on Fifth Avenue. As they progressed to the back of the store, however, the atmosphere became more familiar and the goods smaller. Here, under a sign that said "For Sale" were clerks, instead of engineering consultants, and display cases of watches, sewing machines, radios, toys, and bicycles.

The manager halted at a case filled with cameras. Picking up a small 35-millimeter model, he continued:

"Suppose a customer wishes to buy one of these cameras. The order, of course, will be filled from stock in Moscow and delivered in the Soviet Union."

"Very rapidly," interjected the smiling clerk, obviously a born salesman. "On this model, which is extremely popular, we have been making delivery in under a month."

The manager waved away this ill-timed enthusiasm. "Yes, yes. In the procedure we originally set up with the consulate, the customer would have made payment and the clerk would have stamped the order. But two problems have arisen. On our more popular items, the Moscow inventory may be temporarily exhausted. This was particularly troublesome last fall when everyone wanted delivery for Christmas. Then another problem arose." He turned apologetically to Thatcher. "Most of our customers have relatives in the Soviet Union and are sending presents. But occasionally we wonder how much they know about their relatives! We have had addresses that turn out to be in Turkish Armenia, or in Finland. And, as for Poland! Of course, we realize that the last fifty years have been eventful for Poland, but you would think they would know what country their sister is living in. Then, we have Americans who wander in, who seem to think that all of Eastern Europe is part of the Soviet Union. It makes things very difficult."

Thatcher and Voronin nodded their sympathy to these geographic woes.

The manager continued:

"It has, therefore, become necessary to verify the addresses our customers give us. The sales clerk takes care of the obvious ones, like Prague, but all others go to the office. Under our new system, therefore, the order goes back to the office, where it is cleared by the inventory clerk and by the address clerk, before it is stamped with the seal. Only then can the salesman accept the order and take the money."

Voronin's face had been falling steadily during this recital. It was apparent to Thatcher what had happened. Durnovo and Voronin had seen the original procedures calling for stamps in the front of the store. The consulate, when it made its discovery about the provenance of the stamp, had assumed that a stamp could be stolen, or at least used, by any customer who wandered in. But the change in procedure since adopted made this impossible. Access to the stamps now rested with the office staff—all Russians.

So much for Durnovo's tactics!

"I hope I have made it clear," the manager asked anxiously.

"Extremely." Voronin paused, trying to make the best of a bad bargain. "I think the next thing for us to do is locate these stamps in the offices."

The manager led the way. Thatcher was not surprised to find Voronin pulling ahead for a quick Russian conversation with the manager, leaving Thatcher to bring up the rear with Katerina Ivanovna.

"I am afraid our robbery is adding considerably to your duties," Thatcher said to her.

She smiled at him with a shade of mischief. "I know

the robbery is a great misfortune and, of course, I am sincerely sorry. But it has made my work much more interesting. I am seeing so many places that I would otherwise not have seen."

"That is true for me too," he said appreciatively. "I would not have come to this display without the robbery."

"And I would not have visited the docks."

"And I would not have met Captain Kurnatovsky."

Katerina laughed as she recalled the festivities aboard the *Odessa Queen*.

The next hour was spent in following the route of order slips and stamps. Voronin was more morose than ever when they finally reemerged to the display room and came to rest by a pile of paid orders waiting to be pouched and shipped.

"And this is the end," announced the manager. "At this point, our duties are completed."

Voronin sighed. "It has all been most instructive," he said heavily as he picked up an order form and looked at it with distaste.

Thatcher knew that the man from the consulate did not wish to discuss their obvious findings here. Tactfully he disassociated himself from the final exchange and idly leafed through the orders, looking at the addresses. Ekaterinburg, Kazan, Vladivostok, Irkutsk, Smolensk. . . . It all sounded very romantic. Orenburg . . . shades of the Trans-Siberian Railroad.

Suddenly alerted, he looked at the order more closely. No, it wasn't Orenburg that had caught his attention. It was the customer's name.

David Yates.

Could it be? It must be. It would be too big a coincidence to have another David Yates on the scene.

There might, of course, be some perfectly innocent reason for Yates to be sending a record player to K. I. Ogareva in Orenburg. For all Thatcher knew, Yates was married to a Russian and sending presents to his in-laws. Or even simpler, he was making a gesture of appreciation to a business colleague. After all, Yates must have met a good many Russians in the course of negotiating his share of the wheat deal. He might merely be doing errands for Willard & Climpson. But, still, it was interesting, very interesting, to have found a wheat broker in the vicinity of the misused Russian seal.

Thatcher roused himself to thank the store manager for

his courtesy. A round of farewells, during which Katerina dimpled roguishly at the visitors, released Thatcher and Voronin to the sidewalk where they eyed each other cautiously.

"I think we should discuss what we have learned," said Voronin.

Thatcher looked at his watch.

"Then let's do it over lunch," he suggested. To his surprise, Voronin agreed. Thatcher had expected a return to the consulate and a briefing session with superiors to precede any discussion. But he had underrated his man. Feodor Ilyich recognized that briefing sessions were fine, when they could serve to regulate the flow of information. But once the cat was out of the bag, facts had to be faced.

"I know what you are thinking," he said over his salmon after they had been served. "Naturally, you suspect an employee of the trade display. But for my part, I am thoroughly bewildered. I do not see how anyone connected with that store could have obtained detailed information about the wheat sales."

"Yes," Thatcher agreed. "I reached that stumbling block too. The one thing we know is that the forgeries were too accurate to be the work of an outsider."

Voronin showed his relief. He had thought he would have to fight for his point. "Did you hear me ask the manager when they changed their system? He said it was during the beginning of their rush, last October."

It was Thatcher's turn to frown. "About six months ago. Hmm? That's a long time, but it's not impossible. It was before the meetings during which your consulate letterheads were probably taken."

"Exactly. Months before."

"So if it was done then," Thatcher mused aloud, "the store's seal must have been stolen outright. It wasn't a simple question of using it for a moment, because the thief didn't have the letterheads yet. Did you ask the manager if they were missing a stamp?"

"No, I did not." Voronin shook his head. "You understand, I would prefer to have the Consul decide how rigorous an investigation he wants. You saw for yourself that there seemed to be many stamps lying around."

"If it's like most offices, it will turn out that three or four stamps have simply evaporated," said Thatcher, who had a difficult time with his own ballpoint pens.

"I am afraid so. But we shall let you know what we discover. We only wish to protect our personnel against premature judgments." Voronin hesitated a moment, then proceeded: "It is all most awkward. That this should have happened here, of all places."

"A major loss of this kind would be awkward wherever it occurred," said Thatcher, defending New York.

Voronin remained serious. "That is not what I meant. I was thinking of it from the viewpoint of a commercial attaché. In other countries, where the Soviet Union has more normal trade activities, everything is not a crisis. But here, everything is sensitive, every single little transaction."

"Yes, I can see how that would make New York a more difficult appointment than most. Have you been here long?"

"I came here from London two years ago. Several of us under Mr. Durnovo worked on the wheat sales. We started at Amtorg—and moved to the consulate when it opened."

Thatcher was relieved to learn that Voronin had had some experience with the city besides gigantic thefts and homicides in broad daylight. "And you liked London better?" he inquired curiously.

"The work was certainly subject to much less pressure. But it is difficult for me to judge the two cities. My daughter was living with me in London. She is now married, in Moscow. It is better so. It is no life for a young woman, living with a widowed father."

Thatcher agreed wholeheartedly. His own wife had, thank God, lived to see their children's marriages. He would not have liked to be left with Laura on his hands. He said as much.

Voronin laughed. "Daughters, they need mothers first, and then husbands. There is not much place for fathers. Sons, I do not know about."

Thatcher could have contributed a few pithy comments on the requirements of sons, but he abstained. Instead, he expressed the hope that Voronin would remain in New York long enough to see the consulate return to normalcy.

"It is a kind hope, and I thank you for it. But I will be content if we can merely live through these wheat shipments without any further explosions."

It was a modest ambition, but not destined to be realized. As they paused at the desk for Voronin to buy cigarettes, they could see the television set over the bar.

"And now for further developments in the ill-omened

wheat shipments to Russia," the newscaster intoned expressionlessly. "Longshoremen servicing New York's docks, after an emergency meeting this morning, have set a midnight strike deadline. Officials of the Port Authority expressed confusion as to the nature of the strikers' demands. The Mayor, after a personal visit to the scene, has announced that he sees no hope of an early settlement. All loading is expected to come to a halt late this evening, even as a new flotilla is steaming toward New York waters. This promises to be the worst tie-up since . . ."

"No!" said Voronin in agonized disbelief. "Oh, no!"

It was, of course, not the kind of normalcy that John Putnam Thatcher had envisaged.

10

International Harvester

THATCHER MADE HIS WAY back to the Sloan at a more leisurely pace than was usual with him. He was not lost in thought, since this would be tantamount to self-immolation on Exchange Place during business hours, but he was reviewing the morning's work.

The trouble, he thought, was that he was spending too much time with, among others, Russians. Thatcher was not exceptionally xenophobic (although he had had his fill of Swiss bankers). It was simply a matter of efficiency; as yet, despite the interesting revelations at the Trade Display on Fifth Avenue, the correlation between Russians encountered and time lost was too high.

As Miss Corsa informed him when he reached her desk, he was about to change all that within the hour. He was going to waste time with a real red-blooded American.

"Mr. Lancer asked if you could fit a Mr. Hosmer Chuddley in," she reported.

"I suppose I could," said Thatcher without enthusiasm. "Who is Mr. Hosmer Chuddley?"

With uncharacteristic doubt, Miss Corsa double-checked her impeccable notes. "Miss Spence"—Lancer's secretary—"Miss Spence *says* that he's a farmer."

Manufacturers, wholesalers, retailers, engineers, consultants, factors, speculators—a whole spectrum of economic specialists regularly passed before Miss Corsa's uninterested gaze. But rarely, if ever, a farmer.

Thatcher was able to reassure her.

Hosmer Chuddley, he now remembered all too well, was the celebrated Iowa farmer who had entertained a former Premier of the Soviet Union, who had visited the U.S.S.R. as the highly honored guest of the Ministry of Agriculture. He could afford such activities since he was several times a millionaire—but what did he want with the Sloan Guaranty Trust? Or, more to the point, with John Thatcher?

As Thatcher learned five minutes later when Miss Corsa ushered Chuddley in, he wanted accomplices.

"Chernozem!" said Chuddley, after greeting Thatcher in a hearty manner consonant with his calling and his healthy corn-fed frame. "I say, chernozem!"

Thatcher circled his desk and remained silent, a technique he found invaluable at moments like this.

Hosmer Chuddley, red in the face with earnestness, elaborated.

"Chernozem! Finest wheat-producing soil on earth! Just like our own prairies. I've seen them, and I know what I'm talking about."

"I'm sure you do," said Thatcher. He only wished that he did.

Chuddley shifted a considerable, if muscular, bulk. "And I'm all for Russian-American friendship, I guess I've showed that . . ."

"I guess so," Thatcher murmured.

He was beginning to feel for all those Russian delegations of agronomists and technicians who were inevitably doomed to a weekend of real American hospitality ("with all the fixin's") at the Chuddley farm near Parched Stream, Iowa.

". . . but I said, and I'll say again, this wheat deal is a lot of political hogwash! Oh, it's going to give a lot of people jobs, but it's not the way to do things. It's a lot of . . ." Chuddley broke off, searching for a word that was not too rural and finally settled on repetition, ". . . a lot of hogwash."

Thatcher, whose own exposure to the hoopla connected with the wheat deal had not impressed him favorably, pricked up his ears as this noted friend of Soviet-Ameri-

can friendship flayed the cookie pushers and bureaucrats—
on both sides of the Atlantic—who were bungling the
whole thing, because none of them had ever seen a farm.
(Most of them had never seen a window box.) What
would cement Soviet-American relations was a solution to
the pressing food problems. That solution was not going to
be reached with grandstand plays and trade deals.

"Mmm," said Thatcher.

Real farmers were needed—not chairbound politicians.
"Draft the Aggie students, if we have to," Chuddley argued.
Then organize an Agriculture Corps to be dispatched to
instruct Russia on up-to-date agricultural methods. That
was the only answer to recurrent crop shortages. Why
those people were still plowing under fallow cropland. . . .

Resolutely, Thatcher kept his head in a flood of nitrog-
enous fertilizers, hot feeds, and corn-hog ratios.

Finally he said:

"This is all most interesting, Mr. Chuddley, but I'm not
altogether sure where the Sloan enters into it."

Chuddley enlightened him. He was about to organize
a Stop the Wheat Deal Program.

". . . not destructive, but progressive! I've already lined
up a lot of support."

Thatcher remained expressionless.

". . . and since you people already got stung, I thought
you'd be interested. You mark my words, this whole wheat
deal is going to be rotten with robbery and graft."

Chuddley continued in this vein, and Thatcher did not
dispute him, largely because he could see that it would be
a waste of time.

"You won't forget your appointment at the aquarium,
will you, Mr. Thatcher?" said Miss Corsa, interrupting
Thatcher's thoughts and Chuddley's speech.

"No," he said, grateful that his guest hailed from
Parched Stream, Iowa, not nearer home. It is one thing
to propel visitors out of one's office by imaginary appointments; it is another thing to become fanciful.

Thatcher sped Hosmer Chuddley on his way to the New
York offices of the American Farm Bureau Federation
with assurances that the Sloan would give an Agriculture
Corps serious and immediate consideration.

"Oh, by the way, Miss Corsa," he said, pausing to phrase
his reprimand as tactfully as possible. "About the aquarium . . ."

Miss Corsa looked up. "Mr. Baranoff said, would you

mind meeting him there? Then you could go on . He doesn't seem to know exactly what his schedule will be this afternoon. His secretary said something about fish."

Her message, however bizarre, conveyed, Miss Corsa returned to her chores.

For a moment, Thatcher stared. Then, thanking his lucky stars that he had not put himself irremediably in the wrong by groundless protest, he said:

"Fine! And if any important calls come for me—say, concerned with the running of this bank—you might try catching me at the Brooklyn Botanical Gardens."

Miss Corsa made a note of it.

Once before, many years earlier, Thatcher had dealt with Abe Baranoff. He forgot the details, although he dimly recalled that it involved financing a sea-borne shopping center, but he remembered the atmosphere. Therefore, before setting forth for the aquarium, he armed himself with a witness.

Unfortunately Charlie Trinkam, possibly the best fitted of the Trust Department's personnel to deal with flamboyancy, was deep in negotiations with the Teamsters. (And Thatcher made a mental note to review *that*.) This left him no choice.

"I am not sure I understand why we have to meet him at the aquarium," said Everett Gabler, shrugging himself into his overcoat.

"Neither am I," said Thatcher. "Hurry up, Everett. We're late."

They did not have to plunge into the shadowy deeps of the aquarium. Abe Baranoff and entourage were just emerging as the taxi pulled up. When both parties joined, Baranoff shook hands heartily.

"Those otters," he said. "You would not believe the troubles. Now it is fish. Special fish, they must eat. Max, you take this cab and go down to Fulton Street. But . . ." Fatalistically Baranoff shrugged. "I am glad to see you again, Mr. Thatcher. Ah, yes, Mr. Gabler. Here's my car . . ."

Whatever he might confide to the press about the sordidness of money, Abe Baranoff evinced no acute discomfort at the arrival of two distinguished representatives of the Sloan Guaranty Trust. Exuding graciousness, he led them to a waiting limousine, pausing only for instructions to various minions before joining them in the cavernous back seat. The pallid young man climbed in front next to the chauffeur.

"Is this a Halloran's Garage car, Mr. Baranoff?" Thatcher inquired innocently.

"Ah hah!" said Baranoff with a shrewd and amused look. "Mr. Thatcher, could I afford anything but a Halloran car and driver—now?"

It was an answer worthy of a worthy antagonist. Everett Gabler brightened and looked more on his mettle.

Baranoff settled back. "I am sorry to hurry you off this way. Something has just come up. There are so many things to do . . ."

He continued a fervent description of the various difficulties raised by Plomsky's Otter Ensemble.

"They are, thank God, off Ellis Island. With the governor, the mayor, I got them off Ellis Island. But now, they are in isolation in an armory in South Orange, New Jersey. You wonder why South Orange, New Jersey? Well, so do I."

This at least explained the George Washington Bridge over which they were speeding as the car skilfully maneuvered out of the city.

"Now, about this Denger," said Baranoff, producing a gold-tooled case and offering them cigars. "No? They are from Havana. Well, as I told the police, I know nothing about what he did. For me, he ran errands, he picked things up. The police are checking with my lawyer, with my secretaries—but that is what they will find. Denger ran errands for me—but so do many others. It is true, he sometimes took things even to the Sloan Guaranty Trust, but as you know, I am doing business with the Sloan. Apart from that, I know nothing. . . ."

Thatcher took advantage of Baranoff's dramatic pause to disabuse him of the notion that the Sloan was subjecting a valued customer to anything so mundane as police grilling (although at this very moment, three Sloan secretaries were searching the files for anything on which the name Baranoff appeared).

"Whatever you want to ask," Baranoff invited him. "I have nothing to hide."

"I wanted to ask you about the Russians," said Thatcher. "You have been dealing with the Russian government recently, and I know you've had dealings with them in the past. Can you think of any reason why the Russians might be party to this kind of thing?"

It was Thatcher's recent experience that inviting people to comment on the Russians was more revealing than the Rorschach test.

"No," said Baranoff promptly. "No, this would not be the Russian way of doing things. First, what advantage would they get? They need the wheat we are selling—that you can see in the markets in Moscow."

"It was the sailing of the *Odessa Queen* that raised suspicion in some quarters," said Everett Gabler, quite probably in all sincerity. Almost everything raised deep suspicions in him.

Baranoff smiled a melancholy smile.

"Ah, that is easier to understand. The *Queen* was loaded, orders were to sail. Why not? Why stay to become involved with questions, with delays . . . ?"

After deliberating a moment, Thatcher briefly told Baranoff about the day's discoveries concerning the forgery of the Russian consulate seal. Baranoff, he saw with interest, grasped the significance of this immediately.

"Ah," he said, "now that—that will make a difference. My Russian friends, you understand, are suspicious, and awkward. Underneath all the noise, they fear to be thought uncultured. So when crimes happen, even when bodies are found on their steps, why, they say: 'No! It is nothing to do with us!' I have known tenors like this. But . . ."

"But?" Thatcher prompted.

"But they are not simple fools," Baranoff said reflectively. "They have scientific minds. When they see that they really have something to do with the crime, and perhaps with the murder—well, then, they will act!"

"How?" Everett Gabler demanded, sounding breathless. Abe Baranoff, Thatcher saw, was a master showman.

"What the Russians will do, only the devil can tell. An old proverb—I just made it up. Here we are? Good, good. Come, let us go in."

They had pulled up before an abandoned National Guard Armory in a derelict corner of South Orange, New Jersey —a community that Thatcher had previously thought lacked derelict corners. Baranoff descended, took one haughty look at his surroundings, said "Pfa!" and strode in. Amused, Thatcher followed.

Within the ancient edifice, distant barking sounds brought a rabbity look of expectation to Everett Gabler. But as they proceeded into the hall, Thatcher was noting, for future reference, that Abe Baranoff was not only a subtle and devious personality—he had the mechanics of the wheat deal at his fingertips. Of course he might have been born with such details at his fingertips.

"My God! I am surrounded by imbeciles!" Baranoff shouted into the echoing amphitheater.

From crates piled along the wall, from seven occupants of an improvised rink just before them, from Plomsky, secretaries, aides, workmen, discontent echoed back.

"Smelt! Give me smelt!" Plomsky said passionately. "Here, Mitya, we are still practicing. Bad otter!"

Four young men, bearing sheafs of paper, immediately cut Baranoff off from his companions, while an incredibly constructed blonde in incredibly high heels stood nearby, balancing boxes of sugar cubes. At the far end of the hall, beyond the rinks, a small orchestra added to the din by taking advantage of the interruption to reprise a tricky portion of "Lady of Spain."

"The music must be Russian!" Plomsky howled. "And smelt! We were promised smelt . . ."

Up came Baranoff's great head. "Call Weinstein! Get me Weinstein . . ."

"Please, Abe, will you look at this?"

"Smelt . . ."

"Abe . . ."

For thirty minutes, Thatcher and Gabler indulged themselves by watching the whole fearsome spectacle. Plomsky, placated upon learning that Max was bringing smelt, turned to attack the orchestra.

"The time, it is important! Mitya enters on the downbeat!"

"Abe, will you tell this clown . . ."

"Pig!"

"Mitya! Bad otter!"

"Get me Weinstein!"

Punctuating the strains of "Meadowlands," to which the otters marched in serried ranks, were hurried arrivals, each clamoring for Abe Baranoff's undivided attention.

After allowing Everett Gabler the privilege of five minutes with Plomsky, made possible by the performing otters' need for a sugar break at regular intervals, Thatcher decided to take advantage of Baranoff's offer of a limousine.

He made his way through the crowd to take his leave. Baranoff shouted at his aides, shook a fist at somebody across the hall, and accompanied Thatcher a few steps.

"A pleasure, Mr. Thatcher. A real pleasure. "And," he lowered his voice, "if there is anything else . . . well, remember I have many contacts."

"Now what did he mean by that?" Everett Gabler demanded once they were speeding into Manhattan.

Conscious that ears from Halloran's Garage might be listening, Thatcher said only, "I wonder?"

And the Jersey flats sped by to Everett Gabler's measured approval of Mitya's solo.

The limousine deposited them at Exchange Place long after the Sloan's customers, clerical help, and middle-rank executives had departed.

But Walter Bowman, the large, jovial chief of research, predictably was still at his post. Moreover he had the look of a man with a blockbuster as he followed Thatcher into his office.

"It came over the tape," he said. "You mean you haven't heard?"

"You don't keep up with the ticker when you're driving to and from New Jersey," said Thatcher, idly inspecting the notes Miss Corsa had left for him. "What is it, Walter?"

Bowman drew a happy breath; for him, life had few pleasures greater than the breaking of news.

"The Cuban Navy is blockading the port of New York! The Russians have threatened to send gunboats . . ."

Startled, Thatcher let the papers fall. Had Bowman's mind finally given way to the strain of overwork?

Everett Gabler retained his waspish calm. "For heaven's sake, Walter! Cuba doesn't have a navy."

Bowman smiled broadly.

"You ain't heard nothing, yet . . ." he said, as he began a complex tale of small mosquito boats flying the Cuban flag and disrupting harbor traffic with their zigzag maneuvers.

When the lurid catalog was complete, Everett Gabler had the appropriate comment ready:

"That's one in the eye for the longshoremen!"

11

Cereal Story

HOSTILE NAVIES ENCIRCLING New York might be an embarrassment to the United States government, but other people had other problems. In a small frame house in Astoria, the brother and sister-in-law of Gus Denger wrestled with the vexations of interment.

"All I want," said the brother for the twentieth time, "is to do the decent thing."

"Sure you do, Al," replied his wife, "and, believe me, I'd be the last to grudge the expense, if anybody was going to come to see it. But who is there?"

Gloomily Al shook his head. "It doesn't seem possible that Gus lived over forty years without leaving someone who wants to come to his funeral."

Elsie, being no fool, did not remind him what Gus had been like. Instead she discussed tactics.

"How about his rooming house? Did you tell them when it will be?"

"I called yesterday. What could you expect from guys in a place like that? They've all got something else on . . . they say. That means sitting around having a beer and picking their horses."

His wife had gone on to further problems. "What are we going to do about the mass? After Father Fitzsimmons has gone out of his way to help. And you know what he must be thinking."

Al was stirred to pugnacity. "Look, I'm not the only one in this parish with a bum in the family, and Father Fitzsimmons knows it!"

Elsie refused to be drawn into a discussion of Father Fitzsimmons, a subject on which the couple did not agree. "It's going to look awfully funny if no one but us shows up."

"Now, honey, don't worry about it. That Mrs. Halloran at the garage said she wanted to come. I'll just give her a ring and let her know the time."

As he headed for the phone, his wife slumped back in her chair. "Will I ever be glad when this is over," she muttered. "Gus has never been anything but trouble, trouble, trouble. First it was that tramp he picked up, then it was liquor and the bookies. Now he can't even have a respectable funeral."

"Yes," said Rita Halloran. "I've got that. Ten o'clock at Saint James. And I'll bring a few of the boys along. Anyone who isn't out on a job."

She checked the thanks evoked by this offer and cradled the phone. Mrs. Halloran had years of experience with her drivers. Half of them were much-married men living in the midst of rampant fecundity. But the other half were rootless drifters, like Gus Denger. She knew all about the problems associated with their funerals. She had managed one or two herself.

"Denger's funeral," she said in brief explanation to the client across her desk.

"You are going to it?"

"Yes. There won't be many people there, and it'll be a help to the relatives. Particularly if the press shows up."

"The press?"

Abe Baranoff straightened. If he had been the kind of man who waited for opportunity to knock at his door, he'd still be waiting behind that door in Omsk. For a moment he nursed the malacca stick planted between his knees, then reached a decision.

"Reassure these relatives! There is no need for concern. I shall attend!"

The audience for Gus Denger's funeral obsequies had just trebled. For where Baranoff went, so did his entourage. Even now a platoon of them lurked uncomfortably just outside the office, in the midst of hydraulic and air hoses.

Rita Halloran stared at her visitor in open amazement. What was he up to now? Did he know something? Could he possibly have found out anything after only two days back in the country? And what was he doing in her office? The Baranoffs of this world do not come to garages (unless, of course, they have just unearthed the world's finest troupe of Armenian mechanic-acrobats).

He said he wanted to discuss his contract. Baloney! He would call, or send a flunky. But here he sat, shrewd eyes taking in everything, in no hurry to move on. A man with a hundred irons in the fire! Acting as if he had nothing to do but drop in for a casual chat. Rita Halloran's nerves were not as strong as they had been a week ago. She thought to herself, if this fat slob goes on like this, I'll throw back my head and scream!

But Abe Baranoff had exhausted his pleasantries and was now getting down to brass tacks. He sighed heavily.

"This Denger business," he brooded, "it could mean trouble, real trouble."

The press *did* cover the funeral. What's more, the murder, which had almost been lost in the shuffle of Soviet-American relations, reemerged as front page news. Official records had yielded additional details about Gus Denger's early life—an obscure high school in Queens accepted the responsibility for his education, the army admitted that he had advanced to the rank of technical sergeant during his Korean duty. There was a picture of Albert and Elsie Denger looking shellshocked. Their determined bid for respectability had been blasted sky-high. Predictably, the funeral had turned into a Baranoff spectacular.

Luke Stringfellow shoved the paper aside and stared blankly at the wall. He was sick with apprehension. Everything was coming to a head at once. Some invisible net was closing, shrinking around him with each passing day. My God, there must be something he had overlooked, something he had never considered important! How had he ever gotten involved in this? If he could only think, if he could only think, there must be some way out.

Tessie had to speak to him twice. She was slitting open the afternoon mail.

"It's the grain elevator," she persisted. "They want to know what's going to happen with this strike. Jim says—"

"Tell him to drop dead!" snapped Stringfellow.

Tessie examined him in silence. She hadn't expected Luke to go to pieces this way. God knows, trying to run the office as if nothing had happened was hard enough anyway. It was going to be damn near impossible if he started having hysterics.

"All right," she said at length. "I'll tell Jim he knows as much as we do. We'll all have to wait and see."

Stringfellow did not bother to answer. His thoughts were already a mile away. Imperturbably she continued to read the mail, scribbling a note here and there. It would be a waste of time to consult him now. When she finally rose, the movement made Stringfellow give a sudden start. Almost accidentally, their eyes met. He shifted under her level gaze.

"Look, Tessie, I don't feel so hot," he said, running a finger inside his collar as if suddenly choking. "I think I'll call it a day. I can catch the four-ten if I leave now."

Tessie stared at him, more disturbed than she wanted to admit. "Alice is picking you up in five minutes. You're going up to Westchester with her. Remember?"

"Oh, my God! That's all I need! Today of all . . ."

He was still at it when Alice Stringfellow arrived. A tall, voluptuous blonde, normally in good temper with herself and with her world, she narrowed her eyes as her husband made his preparations for departure. He barked a few commands at Tessie, jerkily shoved some papers into a briefcase, reached for his hat, then dropped the hat to re-check his papers. With an exclamation of annoyance he plunged out of the office. Tessie called after him:

"You might sign those letters on my desk, Luke."

"All right, all right!" he exploded as if subjected to some intolerable nagging.

Alice Stringfellow lost no time after his exit. "What's the matter with him? He's as jumpy as a rabbit."

"He says he's not feeling well. He's been edgy all afternoon."

"All afternoon!" snorted Mrs. Stringfellow. "More like all week! What's gotten into him?"

Tessie suppressed a sigh. Being in the middle was the price you paid for being on good terms with both. "There's been a lot of pressure about this Sloan robbery, Alice. Luke's involved, whether he likes it or not."

"It's more than that," said Alice stubbornly. "He's been like a cat on a hot stove since this whole Jersey business." She looked at Tessie out of the corner of her eye. "He's been spending a lot of time out in Jersey, hasn't he?"

"It's a big deal, Alice," Tessie said pacifically, "and Luke isn't used to real estate."

Alice closed her mouth with an exasperated click. She should have known better than to try to get anything out of Tessie. Tessie had raised to a fine art the science of keeping her eyes open and her mouth shut. Normally that was fine. But if things were going to blow up, Alice String-fellow wanted to know. She wasn't the lying-down type, and there was something very funny going on. She could smell the difference in the office.

"Okay, let's go." Her husband had reentered and was

now in a frenzy to be gone. Come on, honey, we'll be late. Tess, don't forget to ring Quentin about the strike."

Tess nodded as she watched the two leave. Usually they were a well-matched couple. The easy-going tolerance which characterized both of them could float their marriage over ordinary little sore patches. Unfortunately, neither of them had any real sympathy on which to fall back when they hit serious trouble.

Tessie shrugged. That was up to them. They were both adults and could look after themselves.

"Yes, I understand, Miss Marcus," said Victor Quentin for the last time before hanging up the phone. Two minutes later the entire conversation might never have taken place. His thoughts were again circling frenziedly, like rats in a maze, around the two papers on his desk. What would happen if he walked upstairs and thumped them down before John Thatcher? Was it too obvious? Maybe nothing would happen. Maybe he was losing his mind. With a shaking hand he started to shift the two documents, first that on the right, then the other. One thing was certain, he wasn't cut out for his sort of business.

Victor Quentin had lost all resemblance to a cool, competent executive. These days he was pallid and indecisive. Desperately he fought for control. There was a chance, just barely a chance, that if this was handled right, it would shift suspicion away from himself. This was the only card he still held. Should he play it now—or later?

Victor Quentin had been in the financial world all his life. He knew that unless someone else were firmly saddled with the Sloan theft, his career as a banker was over. And that had not been in his plans at all.

David Yates was nominally on duty at his office. But he had swiveled his chair around and rested his feet on the windowsill, so that he could gaze sightlessly out the window. Willard & Climpson paid an extravagant rental for that window because it embraced a wide view of the busy harbor.

Now, of course, the longshoremen's strike had left the harbor moribund. The only sign of activity was from the sea gulls, swooping and squawking against the brilliant blue sky. Their outraged complaints rose and fell with melodic monotony. The strike had interfered with their way of life too, interrupting the steady supply of refuse that kept them sleek and shining.

David Yates was not thinking about sea gulls, but about David Yates. He was very pleased at the way things were going. The main thing was to keep it cool. Some people, of course, would say he was playing with fire. Well, there was nothing wrong with fire if you didn't get burned. And the game was worth the candle, there was no doubt about that. In this life you had to decide early if you were going to go around half-dead because you were afraid to do what you wanted to do. Most men after all wanted the same things—Americans, Russians, Laplanders. They hated being tied down by suffocating routine, but most of them were afraid to take chances. Most men—

At this point in his reflections, a spasm of irritation crossed his face. Most men, yes. But women were different. They positively liked being tied down. Remorselessly, his thoughts turned to his fiancée, Dorothy. Dorothy wanted to be tied down, and the sooner the better. What a time for her to turn on the heat for an early wedding! Little did she know! Yates shrugged Dorothy aside and began to dream of distant lands.

Things were better at the Russian Consulate. Nobody was brazenly daydreaming. People were at least pretending to work. Katerina Ivanovna was, in fact, prettily attentive as Feodor Voronin gave her some last-minute instructions before entering the conference room.

Women, as David Yates had just discovered, do think differently from men. Katerina Ivanovna for instance. She had decided that if her activities in New York were not precisely what the Soviet Union had in mind when it assigned her there as an interpreter, then the way to keep everybody off guard was to look as conscientious as possible. This policy had paid handsome dividends. Not only was she establishing an enviable dossier, she was becoming one of the most mobile of consular employees. She went here, there, and everywhere. As a natural consequence of this activity, her location at any given moment was hard to pinpoint. Which was very, very convenient. True, she was walking on eggshells, but that was what gave spice to life. Nothing ventured, nothing gained. It wasn't as if she didn't have her final goal clearly fixed.

Her inner amusement welled up into that expression of

dancing high spirits that her colleagues knew so well. But she said gravely:

"Of course I shall remain on duty this evening, Feodor Ilyich, if it will be of assistance to you."

Feodor Voronin could have used some hidden springs of amusement to get him through that conference. The embassy in Washington, alerted to the latest developments, had descended in full force. Unhappily the consulate staff reviewed its findings for the visitors, produced seals, explained the workings of order clearance at the Fifth Avenue Trade Display. The conclusion was inescapable.

Unbelievable as it was, incredible as it must appear to every right-thinking Soviet comrade, there was certain evidence—yes, they agreed weakly, you could call it irrefutable evidence—that some representative of the Soviet Union in New York had, in some undefined way, conspired to steal from the Soviet Union, to attack the sanctity of Soviet credit, to endanger the shipments of wheat, to take bread out of the mouths of babes, and to imperil the relations between East and West.

In a word, something was rotten in Denmark.

As the awe-inspiring itemization of crimes came to an end, the senior representative from Washington summed up the sentiment of the meeting.

"It is the presumption of it that turns my stomach. A junior official—not even an embassy official—to have the impertinence to meddle in these affairs!"

Somebody said cheerfully there was no proof it was a junior official. After all, there was always the U.N. delegation.

This remark received a chilly reception. Piotr Vassilich had never been noted for his tact.

But all this Voronin had expected. What he had not anticipated was that his superior, Durnovo, should so determinedly try to wash his hands of the whole business.

"No, no," said Durnovo over and over again. "You will have to ask Feodor Ilyich. He handled all the details. I had nothing to do with this."

Subordinates all over the world are acquainted with the maneuvers of their superiors to shift the blame, any blame, onto lesser shoulders. But in a long career as a subordinate, Voronin had never seen a comparable performance. Iron control enabled him to maintain an even voice and a dutifully receptive expression as Durnovo made one resolute attempt after another to hand his assistant's head around the table on a platter. Durnovo was making a tactical mistake. Inevitably others besides Voronin were asking themselves the question: What is Durnovo trying to cover? Why is he so nervous? What is he hiding?

But the only tangible expression of these inquiries came from the Consul himself when he finally interrupted his commercial attaché:

"My good Durnovo! In my report I congratulated both you and myself on our negotiation of the shipment details. Little did I realize that all the credit belonged elsewhere. We must rectify whatever false impression has been created."

After this, it was not altogether surprising that the meeting decided a rigorous investigation was required.

"And not, I think," said the Consul, "by anyone from the New York staff. I would prefer that the embassy send someone from Washington."

The representatives from the embassy agreed with an almost sinister enthusiasm. But they went one step further.

"Not Washington. It shall be someone from Moscow!"

12

Alien Corn

As THESE MEN and women of assorted ages, stations, and nationalities grappled with the problems nearest them, their governments—following Machiavelli's great dictum —were left to cope with strains in the fabric of the general well-being.

The Cuban Navy was a case in point.

After an initial hour of complete pandemonium, the New York Office of the Bureau of Naval Intelligence pulled its socks up and came to a conclusion: despite large homemade signs saying "Viva Fidel," the garbage-hurling vandals were not Cubans. Like Everett Gabler before them, BNI seized on the fact that Cuba does not have a navy. Hurried inquiries were initiated. As the hours wore by, the little boats seemed to bear charmed lives—dashing

out, megaphoning insults at Russian and American ships
—then darting away, to hide as darkness fell. All the
relevant authorities were outraged, but the first hard information came from Halifax, Nova Scotia, not New York.
These gadflies were French-Canadian terrorists.

Precisely why French-Canadian terrorists should be intruding themselves at this juncture, nobody, least of all the
BNI, knew, but the State Department dispatched a stiff
note to Ottawa, then informed the Russian Embassy that
there was no need for Soviet gunboats. Should convoys
become necessary, the United States Navy would provide
them.

Gunboats, said the Russians austerely, existed only in
the fevered imagination of the New York press.

The State Department mopped its collective brow and
phoned the White House. An irascible voice replied that
it didn't want to be bothered with a lot of details when
something really important was at hand—the longshoremen's strike.

"Oh, yes," said the State Department weakly.

The White House snarled, hung up, then got in touch
with the Department of Labor, a Supreme Court justice,
and David Dubinsky. Within three hours, the Mayor of
the City of New York, flanked by a glowering union president and a federal mediator, stood on the steps of Gracie
Mansion to make an announcement. He didn't get a chance
to open his mouth.

"They're twisting our arms," growled Mike Finn. "So
we'll take a seven-day cooling off period! But then we're
going out, sure as hell!"

The Mayor tired to smile.

While these public and private passions seethed, John
Putnam Thatcher sat quietly at his desk, reflecting on the
odd figures attracted to his world by recent events.

For example, Hosmer Chuddley. According to the
News, he was trying from a small headquarters on Ninth
Street to rally public opinion by distributing bumper stick-
ers which read: Farmers Not Flunkies for Food.

Thatcher tossed the paper aside and continued to waste
time. Chuddley was not the only newcomer on the Wall
Street landscape. On his own peregrinations, Thatcher
was beginning to recognize the phalanx of anonymous
young men who trailed in his wake. They waited for
him to emerge from the Sloan; they strolled casually outside the Russian Consulate; they were probably keeping

sharp eyes on Plomsky's otters out in Jersey. Thatcher did not think for a moment that he was their only quarry, but just who was maintaining this surveillance remained unclear. The New York City Police Department, the Federal Bureau of Investigation, and the State Department, upon being taxed, denied responsibility.

More newcomers put an end to his dereliction from duty. The Export-Import Bank wanted the Sloan's assistance in setting up a meeting of the financial institutions involved in the wheat exports. The American Banker's Association wanted Sloan advice on their latest position paper; the ABA was going to come out strong against bank robberies. The New York Federal Reserve Bank, charged with supervising the handling of Russian bullion, developed deep fears about potential gold snatchers infiltrating Wall Street and presented an elaborate security scheme. The State Department told Thatcher that everything was very, very serious.

And his Excellency, Muhammed Ali Fervan, ambassador of Buganda, asked the Sloan Guaranty Trust to underwrite a vast reforestation scheme to the tune of $985,000—which Thatcher could not believe to be pure coincidence. Apparently the Bugandans had been much taken with how little $985,000 meant to the Sloan.

When, at the end of the morning, Miss Corsa announced that the Russian Consulate was on the phone, Thatcher was by no means pleased. He had, he felt, already done more than his duty by the Sloan's high obligations to help maintain public order and international amity. Nevertheless, he wearily reached for the phone, mentally reviewing the Russians he had met.

It was the suave commercial attaché, Sergei Durnovo himself. His phrases rolled as smoothly as ever.

"Mr. Thatcher, if you will not think it positively discourteous, I should like to invite you to dine with us this evening . . ."

Surely this was a departure from the Russian Consulate's punctilious standards, thought Thatcher, moderately taken aback. He was casting about for an excuse that would not unduly emphasize the point, when Durnovo came to the end of his elaborate apologies and continued:

". . . but although it is at short notice, I think that you would be interested to meet Mikhail Maseryan . . ."

"Oh?" said Thatcher. There are times when even trying to be helpful is useless.

"He has just arrived. From Moscow," said Durnovo sounding almost human for a moment.

"Oh yes. I see," said Thatcher, who did. He chalked up another unlikely visitor enticed to New York.

Durnovo drew a deep breath and explained what was already quite clear to Thatcher. When Thatcher and Durnovo's assistant, Voronin, had placed the Fifth Avenue seal squarely in Russian hands, Moscow had started putting two and two together. The other suggestive item was the forged documents from the *Odessa Queen*. And two and two had produced a change in official thinking.

"It was decided at the very highest level," said Durnovo impressively, "that every possibility—however remote—must be explored. You understand?"

Thatcher said that he did.

"Yes," said Durnovo. "Comrade Maseryan has been sent to . . . to look into things. He is a most interesting man. And he has said that he would be honored to meet with you. So, if you do not object . . ."

In other words, another policeman.

Thatcher put an end to Durnovo's suspense by replying that he would be delighted to meet with Maseryan that very night.

"Splendid," said Durnovo with relief. No doubt when ordered to get Thatcher for dinner, he was expected to produce. "He has decided to stay with our Soviet Trade Mission tonight so we will dine there. At seven-thirty. I shall send a car . . ."

Accordingly, at six-thirty, John Putnam Thatcher stepped from the Devonshire Hotel into an exotic limousine driven by a silent, frozen-faced chauffeur. It was too dark to see the expressions of the anonymous young men strolling past the Devonshire, but Thatcher was sure that he had triggered a flurry of some sort of activity. He settled back for the long drive to Huntington, Long Island, and the mansion that had once been the home of Chester Hollenmajor, the famous Sugar King, presently the home of the Russian Trade Mission.

Presumably those members of the consular staff joining him at Huntington were using other transport—transport uncontaminated by the presence of an American banker. He knew that the consular staff, latecomers to New York, had to be satisfied with civilian city apartments instead of North Shore estates.

The party assembled in the lordly living room consisted

mostly of Russians with whom he had already dealt. Standing in the background, like model civil servants, were Durnovo and Voronin, who nodded formally to him. The young interpreter, Katerina Ivanovna, favored him with a charming greeting, then quickly returned to utmost gravity.

"We are delighted you could join our little party this evening," said the Consul, whom Thatcher had encountered some months earlier at a banquet. He introduced a middle-aged, motherly woman as Mrs. Grabnikov, his wife, then continued, "And permit me to present to you our distinguished colleague from Moscow, Mikhail Maseryan. Mr. Maseryan is in our Ministry of Foreign Affairs."

Maseryan proved to be a small bulky man with a luxuriant black mustache, a hooked nose, and shrewd eyes. He greeted Thatcher in serviceable English and said, by way of idle conversation, that this was his first visit to the United States. Thatcher replied suitably, meanwhile noting that this exchange seemed to have mesmerized the company. Durnovo in particular wore a frozen smile. Fortunately, a manservant circulating with drinks broke the trance; Thatcher was happy to see martinis on the tray as well as those ominous clear beakers.

"I have often wanted to visit your country," Maseryan said, after doing justice to his vodka.

"And I have wanted to visit yours," Thatcher replied. He was beginning to be almost unnerved by the painful intensity of the listening silence. Katerina Ivanovna and Voronin were too taut to do more than clutch their glasses.

There was a pause.

Mr. Grabnikov bestirred himself. "Seeing a country that is not one's own is educational," he finally contributed.

"That is very true," said his wife.

Feodor Voronin and Katerina Ivanovna murmured agreement and took tentative sips.

Emboldened, Sergei Durnovo went even further. "It teaches one to value one's own country," he said after clearing his throat.

"That is true."

"Very true."

Maseryan, Thatcher was pleased to note, looked as disheartened as he felt. A second round of drinks and lavish silver cups of caviar did nothing to lighten the atmosphere. Nor could the dinner, once they removed to the medieval vault that was the dining room, he described as a sparkling social moment.

"Tell me, Katerina Ivanovna, what do you do in New York when you are not working?" Maseryan spoke playfully, in the avuncular tone that a very pretty girl frequently elicits.

"I go to concerts," said Katerina Ivanovna quickly, apparently not recognizing either playfulness or avuncularity. Indeed, she sounded like a guilty schoolgirl.

Her colleague, Feodor Voronin, gallantly came to the rescue. "The concerts in New York," he said, "are excellent."

"Yes."

"That is true."

Katerina Ivanovna threw Voronin a grateful look, then concentrated on her bread. Maseryan rolled his eyes slightly and returned to his soup.

For a while, it seemed that the excellent fish might be consumed in total silence. Finally Mr. Grabnikov took the bull by the horns and launched into a long, boring recital of the New York colleges he had recently visited.

". . . then the City College. And the University of Columbia. And, later, out to Queens College. And to the ladies in the economics department of Hunter . . ."

Thatcher himself essayed a brief discussion with Feodor Voronin.

"At least we are spared the longshoremen's strike for a week," he remarked.

"Yes," said Voronin in a low voice. "Yes, that is very fortunate."

Thatcher was not by inclination chatty but he felt an obligation to say something at a dinner table. Accordingly he persevered.

"And I understand that two Russian ships cleared port today."

"Yes, yes, they did."

Thatcher gave up.

Under the circumstances, dinner seemed interminable. Mikhail Maseryan, whose knowing eyes and half smile did not seem intimidating, positively paralyzed his colleagues. Of course, Thatcher thought, as he irritably speared an asparagus stalk, who knew what dark forces Maseryan represented? The knout?

Or was he out of date?

At any rate, he could discern no sensible reason why he should have been introduced into this scene of Dostoevskian gloom. Fortunately, Maseryan appeared to agree. As they left the table, he briskly suggested that he and Mr. Thatcher—if Mr. Thatcher would not object—might take their coffee in the library.

Mr. Thatcher would have taken his coffee in the cellar to be spared more of this.

After they settled in Chester Hollenmajor's library (Gothic arches and matched sets), it developed that Mikhail Maseryan had been as oppressed by the atmosphere as Thatcher.

"I must apologize, Mr. Thatcher. I had thought that a congenial evening with people known to you would be a fitting prelude to our talk. But . . ." He shrugged, spread his thick fingers in an eloquent gesture. "But this . . . wake, is not what I anticipated."

"Of course, the staff of the Russian Consulate is anxious, these days," Thatcher began diplomatically.

Out when Maseryan's fingers again. "No, it is me! These blockheads worry that I shall report things. They are all the same. Moscow sends me to find a connection between any Russian and the robbery of your bank, and the murder as well—and do you know what these people are afraid of? Of buying high-fidelity sets on the installment plan! Of romantic attachments! Of listening to jazz music, or studying modern painting! Bah! They read too much of your propaganda, I tell you!"

Maseryan drew black brows into a fierce frown, then energetically grasped the brandy bottle and splashed two healthy drinks. When he put the bottle down, he glared at the label.

"And I can tell you this, my friend. The head of the Russian Trade Delegation is wondering if perhaps he should not have put the French brandy away, and served Crimean brandy, while I am here. You would not believe the places I have had to drink Crimean brandy! Paris, even!"

Thatcher, although entertained, was not inclined to underrate Maseryan's abilities.

"Of course," he suggested, "somebody might have a guilty conscience."

Maseryan looked at him shrewdly from under those beetling brows. "They all have guilty consciences, Mr. Thatcher. All good Russians enjoy New York, Paris, Rome —and they always feel that it is wrong, that it is a betrayal of their Mother Russia. It is a national characteristic. You Americans are the reverse. You go to London, Paris, or

Rome and enjoy yourselves, then you think that you are the first persons clever enough to have done so."

Thatcher smiled. "I notice that you do not include Moscow in that list."

"No," said Maseryan gravely. "Not yet. But soon. However, I am keeping us from business. It is true that my friends from the consulate all show signs of bourgeois error, but I do not think that all of them are involved in a major crime. We can dismiss that. Let me explain our position . . ."

The Russian position was simply that the discovery of the seal, together with the real competence of the forgeries, suggested the possibility of Russian participation. Technically this meant that the staff of the United Nations Delegation, the Trade Mission, the Intourist staff, and even the embassy in Washington were being considered.

"But of course," Maseryan said, refilling his glass and sketching an offer in Thatcher's direction, "first we concentrate on our friends of the Russian Consulate in New York. On Durnovo, on Voronin, on Ogareva . . . Did I say something to interest you?"

"Who is Ogareva?" Thatcher asked.

Maseryan looked at him. "The little Katerina Ivanova, who goes to concerts when she is not working. Was there something . . . ?"

"No," said Thatcher, not quite truthfully. "I simply had not heard her name before."

"I see," said Maseryan, studying his glass. "At the same time, you understand, my colleagues in Moscow are investigating the crew of the *Odessa Queen* . . ."

"Do you really think that Captain Kurnatovsky is up to high-class forgery?" asked Thatcher, amused.

"Ah, he is more cunning than you think," said Maseryan. "Already, we have uncovered interesting, but strictly forbidden trading in nylon stockings."

"Well I hope that does not mean serious trouble for him," said Thatcher, who recalled Captain Kurnatovsky's uncomplicated approach to life with considerable appreciation.

"Some trouble," said Maseryan, "but not big trouble."

Thatcher was left to ponder this as Maseryan continued to explain that since in this instance the interests of the Sloan Guaranty Trust and the Union of Soviet Socialist Republics marched hand in hand, his government formally requested cooperation. "And," he added, "may I say personally that I would be most grateful . . ."

This eloquence roused the competitor in John Putnam Thatcher. Where Russia led, could the Sloan fail to follow?

"First, I should say that I welcome your presence. Not that I am convinced that a Soviet national is necessarily implicated in this . . . er . . . dastardly crime . . ."

"Let us hope not," said Maseryan formally. "But in that case, it is an American, which is also regrettable."

"Quite so," said Thatcher. "It is too much to hope for somebody from an uncommitted nation. At any rate, I am most happy on behalf of the Sloan Guaranty Trust to offer you what assistance I can," he concluded. If he had not topped Maseryan, he decided, he had at least matched him.

"Thank you," said Mikhail Maseryan, who then dropped the high manner and outlined a long list of requests ranging from an interview with Victor Quentin to a tour of the Registry of Deeds. "And, Mr. Thatcher, we will clear this up, I think. If it is a capitalistic crime, why, you are the expert. If a communist has betrayed his cause, then I am the expert. Between us"—the thick fingers guillotined quickly—"we are more than a match for him."

"Certainly," said John Putnam Thatcher. "Whoever he is."

13

Snap . . . Crackle . . . Pop!

THE NEXT MORNING found Thatcher on his mettle. Mindful of the luxury in which he had been rolled out to Huntington, he firmly directed Miss Corsa to commandeer the Sloan's most impressive automotive transport. He felt, as he so often did these days, that the honor of his country was somehow at stake. At ten o'clock he picked up Maseryan at the Russian Consulate in something long, low, and streamlined. They did not drive to the Sloan; they crested the air waves.

After two hours of solid labor, Thatcher was mentally calling down blessings on Moscow. They had sent him a worker. Maseryan must have stayed up far into the night absorbing his notes of the previous evening. And now he was grimly wading through the material provided by the Sloan's research staff. He was well on the way to qualifying as an expert on letters of credit and the geography of New York City with respect to loading docks, the Cunard piers and the Registry of Deeds.

By God, the Soviet Union was going to learn that when the Sloan decided to cooperate, it cooperated to the hilt!

Thatcher's spirits lifted. A realist if ever there were one, he had abandoned all expectation of help from the federal agencies of the United States within twenty-four hours of the theft. But now, for the first time since the crime, Thatcher entertained the possibility that the Sloan might yet recover its missing funds. He had already lined up Inspector Lyons for dinner. Idly he played with the thought of a triumvirate—Lyons, Maseryan, and Thatcher. Each with his own expertise, his own sources of information, his own access to the leading performers in the drama. Yes, there was a fighting chance.

His visitor having thus become precious to him, Thatcher turned to thoughts of his welfare. Soon it would be lunchtime. Where should he take Maseryan? For a moment Thatcher considered the Seamen's Refuge—a fitting chop house for an upholder of the proletariat. But he had a better idea. If he himself were visiting Moscow as a representative of Wall Street and a notorious exploiter of the downtrodden (witness Miss Corsa), he would like to see his enemies face to face. Maseryan probably felt the same way. Without further ado, Thatcher made a reservation at the Bankers Club, regretting only that J. P. Morgan was not still alive and on the scene.

At twelve-thirty he removed with Maseryan to that Valhalla of capitalist hopes. On the way, mindful of his duties to a tourist, he pointed to some pockmarked striations in the granite wall they were passing.

"Those marks date from the anarchist bombing of Wall Street in 1920," he commented. "There are more across the street."

Determinedly Maseryan crossed the street to examine the evidence. He was not impressed.

"Slovenly work," he decided. "These anarchists. No organization."

Thatcher was amused. "Would Marxists have made a better job of it?"

"Marxism-Leninism has always abhorred isolated acts of terrorism. They serve no useful function in preparing for social revolution," his guest reproved him. He gave a final look at the marks, gazed up at the unscathed buildings looming overhead, and added: "But if Marxists had been involved, they would have been more efficient."

"Almost anybody would have," Thatcher agreed. "I could have done better myself. At least I would have found out when the bankers went to lunch."

"Lunch?"

"Yes. The custom here is that the clerical help goes to lunch from twelve to one, and the executives go at one. The anarchists came at the wrong time and got the wrong people—hundreds of the wrong people."

"But we ourselves are lunching between twelve and one."

"Yes, I thought you might be sick of reading those reports we gave you."

"So, we go at the dangerous time. Maybe I will be bombed by an anarchist."

This put Maseryan in high good humor. He was roaring with laughter as they entered the Bankers Club. A fortunate circumstance, in his host's opinion, as the sounds of merriment brought to the occupants' faces that expression which most of the world associates with bloated capitalists. Thatcher was particularly pleased to see old Bartlett Sims in a corner, looking like a petulant whale.

But a born worker cannot be long deflected from his task. Maseryan looked around, approved the vodka, and then turned to the business at hand.

"It is interesting how little the criminal had to do on the day of the theft," he said. "Regardless of when the seal was stolen, there is no doubt that the consular letterheads were taken many weeks ago. And you say the letterheads from Stringfellow could have been obtained at any time?"

Thatcher nodded. He had already described conditions at the office of Stringfellow & Son.

"Then the paper work was all done a long time in advance. After that, the criminal simply waited for the *Odessa Queen* to near completion of loading. Do you not think that the timing was critical?" Maseryan asked.

"Yes. The papers would hardly have passed Quentin's inspection if there had been discrepancies with an earlier set. I think it was essential that they should be the first set of Russian papers to cross his desk."

"So our criminal simply waits for a suitable day with relation to the *Odessa Queen*," Maseryan continued. "On that day, all he does is deliver the papers to the Cunard pier, call this chauffeur—you know which one I mean, the one who was murdered."

"Denger."

"He calls Denger and goes to the Registry of Deeds. It it not an onerous schedule."

"No," Thatcher frowned, "but there are other things involved. I'm willing to assume our criminal had some luck. But still, there are a lot of coincidences or questions of timing that remain. First, there's Baranoff's departure. Now Baranoff is a public figure, and his comings and goings get a good deal of publicity, but still—"

"Ah, I know what you are about to say. Probably no one in New York knows as much about these Russian trips by Baranoff as the consulate. It is undeniable. Consider that point accepted."

There was much to be said for Soviet realism, Thatcher decided. He continued:

"There's another point—those calls by Stringfellow to the Sloan before the arrival of the forged paper and the fact that he then disappeared for the day. One of them might be a coincidence. But I doubt if both were. I think we have to assume our criminal either knew about the calls or about Stringfellow's trip to Jersey."

"Now I see why you are frowning. That information was probably not known at the Soviet Consulate. But it might very well be known in your own circle of wheat brokers."

"Exactly."

These were heretical sentiments for the Bankers Club, but Thatcher had come to the same conclusion some time ago.

For a moment they sat in silence. Thatcher was the first to speak.

"We need more facts. I thought we'd start at the docks," he said. "The one element in his timing that the criminal couldn't control was the loading of the *Odessa Queen*. We may be able to find out who was unusually interested in that."

At about the time that Thatcher and Maseryan were hailing a cab, Rita Halloran put down the phone, stared angrily around her small office and arose.

"I'm going to be out for the rest of the day, Phil," she said to a passing mechanic. "You cover the office."

Phil nodded and asked if she wanted one of the cars.

"I'll grab a cab," she said, briskly heading toward the street.

On the principle that leads dairy farmers to use oleomargarine instead of butter, Mrs. Halloran rarely used one of her limousines for her own travels. This was sound economics; a limousine that could be earning as much as a hundred dollars a day was no car for a businesswoman.

But today Mrs. Halloran had a special reason to prefer public transport. She had no intention of having everybody at Halloran's Garage know that she was consulting her lawyer.

Joe Kiley's offices were in a shabby building on Lexington Avenue. Joe himself was similarly shabby, with a too-red face, spots on his tie, and a wide range of expressions from piety to ferocity that all looked artificial. Many an opponent had been misled into thinking he was an aging second-rater, but nothing was further from the truth. Kiley had a roll of clients that would have been the envy of some downtown firms.

"You're looking fine, Rita," he said when she had settled down opposite him.

With a gesture that both acknowledged and waved away the compliment, she said, "Joe, I think I've got trouble coming."

Kiley raised his eyebrows. "Well, I know your mother told you to tell the truth to your doctor, your priest, and your lawyer—so let's have it."

She turned to him. "Abe Baranoff came down to see me the other day."

Kiley waited.

Mrs. Halloran fiddled with her purse. "I guess I told you that, didn't I?"

"Yes, you did," he said with elaborate patience. "You said he was worried about Denger. And we both know that Gus was up to something—else he wouldn't be dead and buried. Still, that's the legal end. And apart from that, I don't see that you've been getting too much bad publicity

—all things considered. What's troubling you? Is business falling off?"

Some women might have been offended by this uncompromising appraisal of their genuine interests, but Mrs. Halloran was not one of them. "No, business is all right. Most of the regulars don't care one way or the other. It's the slow season, of course—no, this morning I got *this!*"

She fished a letter from her purse and thrust it at him.

Kiley unfolded it and read. Then he read it again. Then he looked up.

"Well now, this seems like a bona fide offer from a bona fide buyer for Halloran's Garage. At a very good price. And that is a good price, Rita. Now this lawyer I don't happen to know—but the New York Bar's full of Weinsteins, so I'll get the scoop on him." He tossed the letter aside and looked at her again. "I don't see trouble."

She shook her head vigorously.

"I don't like the way things are going, Joe. First, the garage isn't up for sale—never has been. Then, out of the blue, here's someone offering to buy it—at, as you say, a good price! I want to know who—and why!"

Kiley regarded her, then said. "Shame the devil and tell me the whole truth, Rita. What's worrying you—exactly?"

"I'm afraid Baranoff's behind this," she said bluntly. "And I don't like it! Why now?"

Kiley tapped the letter with a nicotine-stained finger.

"If that's all, let's put your mind at rest. I can find out by this afternoon if Baranoff's got a finger in this pie. But listen, Rita. Don't you trouble yourself about why anybody should want to buy Halloran's. Remember, it's a good, going business. And people—*any* people—may be asking themselves why Rita Halloran, who's a wealthy woman, should want to go on working all her life. Maybe she's ready to sell out, to travel, to see the world. After all, Rita, you don't have young ones to leave it to—there's just Eddy, and I know how you feel about Eddy—so why not sell out while you can still enjoy life?"

She looked surprised. "Is that what you think, Joe?"

He indicated exaggerated denial. "I'm not telling you what I think—but what other people may be thinking." He dropped into a sober tone. "Now Rita, take it easy and just put this from your mind. I'll find out who's behind it. And in the meantime . . ."

She leaned forward.

"In the meantime, you give a little thought to the idea of selling," said Joe Kiley. "This wouldn't be a bad time—at all."

Mrs. Halloran left Kiley's office both relieved and troubled in mind. With all its problems, with its ever changing cast of different Gus Dengers, Halloran's Garage and its clamorous phones, its echoing caverns, was home to her.

But, as Kiley said, there were other things in the world. With a sudden spurt of amusement Rita Halloran saw herself down at the docks, ready to board a great liner, to see a new and different world.

"Even Russia!" she told herself. That would be a nice twist.

Currently at the docks were John Thatcher and Maseryan. They had arrived in search of information about the *Odessa Queen*, more particularly anybody who had shown interest in her. From that point of view, the docks were a waste of time.

Otherwise, it was worth the effort of getting there. The seven-day cooling-off period, which represented such a triumph for the city and federal negotiators, had ensured the shipment of substantial quantities of wheat, but it had not quenched the ill-defined fervor which had caused the strike vote in the first place. There were pickets everywhere.

A genuine strike would have created less turmoil. Frenzied efforts were being made to move wheat before the seven days elapsed. As a result, oversize crews labored valiantly while oversize picket lines got in their way. To add to the confusion the United States Navy, alert for the hostile mosquito boats, had posted observers. Between cranes and feed bins and derricks, between sweating stevedores and fiery pickets, moved naval spotters, their work rendered hideously difficult by the armada of pleasure craft afloat in the harbor, hoping to witness a naval incident.

Understandably, the port authorities had no time to waste on Thatcher and Maseryan.

"The *Odessa Queen*? My God, that was back in the good old days! I can't remember that far back. What? . . . Out of my way! . . . That canoe can't land here!"

"Sorry, I'm special dock police drafted in from Philly. Don't know anything about this port."

"Are you the union people? Well, somebody's got to

shift those pickets. There just isn't enough room. No! No! No!"

By dint of perseverance and, more effective still, by making it clear they were not leaving without satisfaction, they did get some information.

In the halcyon days before strikes and garbage-throwing French Canadians, the port authorities had had time to give information to busybodies. And had done so freely. The entire world had been interested in the movement of wheat to Russia—the domestic press, the foreign press, the commercial press, the diplomatic world, the grain world, the banks, the railroads, the exchanges.

Not much wiser, Thatcher and Maseryan finally found themselves back at the entrance hall. Thatcher consulted his guest.

"We aren't meeting Inspector Lyons for two hours. We'll be working with him all night, so I think we could take some time off now. What would you like to see?"

Maseryan reflected. When he spoke, it was with some hesitation.

"You understand, we in Russia are very interested in your problems, your agriculture and space programs and defense efforts, but even more in the problems we do not share. We see the headlines, we see the pictures—oh, those pictures! so compelling, so dramatic!—our curiosity is naturally stirred. And so . . ."

"Yes?" encouraged Thatcher, bracing himself for a tour of Harlem and the inevitable comments.

"And so," continued Maseryan, "I would like very much to see your al-i-en-ated youth," he rolled the words out cautiously. "Do I have that correctly?"

"Yes. That's the current phrase." Thatcher's mind shifted gears hastily. The trouble was that American preoccupations came and went so quickly, there was no way to predict what foreigners would want to see. Alienated youth, however, was better than that Yugoslav fifteen years ago with the wife who read American ladies' magazines: he had wanted to inspect togetherness.

Thatcher stalled for time.

"That may be rather difficult," he said.

The great advantage with Harlem, he reflected, was that it stayed put.

As always in time of travail, his thoughts turned to his secretary. Minutes later he was in a phone booth.

"Miss Corsa, do we have anyone young at the Sloan?"

For once Miss Corsa was shaken. She struggled nobly to meet the challenge.

"Well, there's always Mr. Nicolls," she said doubtfully.

"No, no," he said hastily. "I mean *really* young. Someone who would know about beatnik hangouts. I thought maybe one of the secretaries. . . ?"

Miss Corsa's silence reminded him more plainly than words that beatnik propensities in candidates for secretarial employment at the Sloan did not impress the personnel manager. Not favorably, that is.

But now that a decent, limited objective had been defined, she was willing to try. She rather thought that some member of the staff might know somebody who was young. There was always the possibility of a brother or sister. Would Mr. Thatcher wait while she investigated?

So while Thatcher held the line, irritably fumbled for additional change, finally hung up and waited for the return ring, Miss Corsa gallantly assaulted the barrier between the generations—which quite a startling number of sociologists would have been prepared to tell her was impenetrable.

Within a short space of time Miss Corsa was back on the line dictating addresses and pertinent comments:

"May get rough later in the evening . . . a tourist trap . . . favored by beat writers . . . not for mixed couples . . . possibility of drugs . . . strong on folk songs and Vietnam." She did not reveal her sources.

Armed with this information he returned, only to have Maseryan balk at the cab rank.

"I thought we could take the subway. I hope you do not mind," the Russian inquired anxiously. "After all, we are two strong men."

Thatcher stared. "I don't see how that's going to do us much good."

Maseryan's eyes hooded. "They prowl in packs, I know. But how large?"

"Who?"

"Those subway hooligans."

"Ah!" Thatcher understood now. "Yes, we can take the subway. But its not hooligans we have to worry about. It's the rush hour."

The subway ride, uneventful from the point of view of a commuting New Yorker, filled Maseryan with awe. On the platform he was swept off his feet and bodily impelled into the wrong train, from which Thatcher extracted him (with the help of two burly sailors) in the nick of time. Ensconced in the right train, he was separated from Thatcher and crushed like a sardine without any means of support. At one point, as the express swayed and bucketed around a corner and the entire mob keeled over, a sharp cry told Thatcher that Maseryan had just learned about stiletto heels the hard way.

As they climbed the interminable stairs at West Fourth Street, Maseryan sounded exhilarated. Filth, bad manners, lack of air, and shrieking noise left him unmoved. The Moscow press had prepared him for all that. But the hardiness of the travelers!

"It is amazing! It is truly a communal experience. And how can they say you Americans are soft? Why, I saw little old ladies in there. There was one with an umbrella. You should have seen the way she got a seat! Not nice, no! But efficient, without a doubt."

Getting Maseryan three blocks to a coffeehouse was harder than Thatcher had anticipated. The Russian was fascinated by the paperback bookstores. Approvingly he noted the signs that proclaimed twenty-four hour availability, the hordes of returning commuters, students, artists, residents who poured in and out. But the grunts produced by the display racks in front of each store were more equivocal. By one rack, he remained rooted to the spot as he read the titles:

Some Notes on Swamp: In-ness in our Time
Wrecking Balls: Urban Renewal in America
The Camel and the Chickadee: The Poetry of Urgency
Abortion without Tears: A Medical Study
Seminarian: An Intimate Journal

"But where is the Shakespeare?" Maseryan demanded. "Where is the Hemingway? Where is the infinitely necessary input-output theory?"

Eventually they were deposited at a small round table. Smoke filled the room but did not obscure the art gallery which formed its walls. A group of three people, all in beards and sandals and sweat shirts, stood before the pictures, engaged in furiously contested analysis. A young couple discussed their sex life (unsatisfactory, it appeared) in forthright terms. The illusion of free love was shattered by the proximity of a small baby in a carryall. Girls in what seemed to be shiny black oilcloth sat about in a welter of hair and boots. The high-fidelity record player poured forth with crystal clarity the strains of a guitar and a young voice lamenting unrequited love. Everyone was talking, talking, talking.

Thatcher leaned back satisfied. This he felt sure, was the right place. But Maseryan, looking around narrowly, seemed to be disappointed.

"No drugs," the Russian finally protested.

Miss Corsa was nothing if not thorough. Thatcher reached for his list.

"Well, there's a place further down the street that's rumored to be a source of heroin," he said. "Although I'm afraid they just distribute it there."

Maseryan waved aside heroin. "No, no. I do not mean heroin or cocaine. I mean the drugs your universities have been perfecting. You call them hallucinatory, I believe."

"Oh, those."

"Your young people take them gathered together in order to have a group experience. And I have heard of the powerful effects they induce."

"So have I," said Thatcher austerely.

He went on to explain that the home of the hallucinogenic drug was now in Little Forks, Idaho, the authorities of Massachusetts, Mexico, and Texas having proved successively hostile to the march of science.

Philosophically Maseryan accepted the disappointment.

"Ah, yes, I can see that. The work goes on in your provinces because your metropolis is overwhelmed with other problems. New York must build housing and provide social services and deal with its unemployed."

Maseryan's words were unfortunately audible at the next table. A foxy-faced young man took instant exception and interjected himself into their conversation.

"Ranch houses, white-collar jobs!" he sneered. "That's all you and your kind think of. You can't stand the sight of non-conformity. You have to impose your middle-class attitudes on everybody!"

"Middle-class attitudes! Me!" Maseryan was deeply affronted. "You miserable, pampered offspring of privilege! It is the petty bourgeois like you who stand in the path of social progress."

"Petty bourgeois! Me!" A dull red tide suffused the youth's face as his companions snickered. "You don't know what you're talking about. Why, I was a dropout!"

"Until the draft," goaded an habituée.

Long training in Marxian polemic gave Maseryan the edge over his opponent. Fox-face reeled under charges of "parasitism" and "materialism," but came rattling back when the indictment spread to "philistinism."

"Philistine!" he squeaked. "Why you wouldn't recognize a work of art if it was under your nose."

Maseryan's English failed him. "I can recognize a —— when I see one," he announced ferociously, filling the gap with a few well-chosen Slavic expressions.

The lack of a real common language was probably fortunate, thought Thatcher, enjoying himself. There was no need for him to worry about his guest. Several of the familiar clean-cut young men had entered hard on their heels and were closing in on the disturbance.

Separating the combatants was not difficult. Fox-face's experience had led him to believe that all adult men who wore hats were easy game. The brisk counterattack, particularly with its strong socio-economic frame of reference, jolted him. He was persuaded to change tables even as Maseryan recommended a year or two in a factory as a tonic for his underdeveloped sense of social responsibility.

Thatcher ordered more coffee to indicate they were not abandoning the field. Everybody in the room looked more cheerful. These little excitements do brighten life.

"Me, middle-class? How dare he!" rumbled Maseryan.

"He only means that you're over thirty," Thatcher translated.

"You cannot be serious. Who is to lead youth, if not the experienced?" asked the Russian, displaying that feel for discipline which has made the Red Army what it is.

Thatcher unveiled further horrors. "There's a group of students out in Berkeley who have taken a pledge not to speak to anyone over thirty."

"Incredible."

"Or a blessing for all concerned," said Thatcher drily.

Maseryan reviewed the whole problem of youth. "Of course it is different in our country," he said at length. "Our system does not have the organic deficiencies, the economic and class antagonisms, that form the basis of conflict between generations."

"How interesting!"

"I would not deceive you though. We too have young people who are disturbed, who are unwilling to commit themselves wholeheartedly to the mainstream of Soviet life, who cultivate the culture of the West and reject the individual's responsibilities to contribute to the welfare of the community along prescribed lines." His voice grew steadily less confident as he proceeded. "But with us, this must be attributed to inadequacies in education, in the party's ideological indoctrination."

"Curious," said Thatcher blandly, "how such divergent causes result in virtually identical symptoms."

Maseryan brooded darkly for a moment. Then: "But what do they want? It is clear enough what they are against. But what are they for? That is what I ask myself."

"God knows, I'm no authority," Thatcher replied. "But as I understand it, these people are stronger on the attack than on a purposive program."

"Nihilists! That's all they are! Believing in nothing."

"Well, they always say they're for love and communication."

"Bah!" The word was an explosion. "That is childish. Presumably even Nihilists copulated."

"Presumably," Thatcher agreed gravely.

But he was thinking that it would be hard, after this, to return his guest's thoughts to their engagement with Inspector Lyons and all that it portended.

If he had been wiser, he would have pursued the problem of love and communication in a divided world.

14

Kernel of Truth

ALTHOUGH COMRADE MASERYAN, between bouts with contemporary youth and dinner engagements with New York City detectives, was scarcely ever inflicting his presence on his much-tried compatriots, his spirit nonetheless cast a decided pall over the consulate on Seventy-third Street.

"A trying day," admitted Sergei Durnovo, consulting a wrist watch. He turned to his companion graciously.

"Those papers can wait for tomorrow, Feodor Ilyich. There is no need for you to work tonight."

His assistant looked up. "Thank you, Sergei Pavlich, but I might just as well finish them. I have nothing to do this evening."

"Well, in that case . . ." Durnovo shrugged. Then, instead of departing, he produced a cigarette, sat down, and prepared to while away the idle moments in social exchange. He was still at it, twenty minutes later, when Katerina Ivanovna and a young man from the records department looked in.

"You will not be needing us?" she asked.

Voronin shook his head.

"No, no, Katerina Ivanovna," said Sergei Durnovo. "Work is over for today. Enjoy yourself."

But Katerina Ivanovna did not wave farewell and depart with her companion. Instead, after a hesitant glance at Durnovo, the two of them entered Voronin's small office and joined the party.

"Because I am quite free to help you if you need me," she said, shaking out her hair after removing a rakish little beret.

"No, no, I assure you . . ."

In a few minutes the group was augmented by the stout woman in charge of secretarial services and by the single statistician with the mission. After some transparent excuses for the interruption had been offered, the conversation became severely general.

Now, anyone who has ever worked in any office anywhere, will realize that smoking, drinking coffee or tea, and exchanging gossip is a prominent and time-consuming part of the working day; only under the most exceptional circumstances does this activity lap over into off-duty hours. In this case, the exceptional circumstance was Mikhail Maseryan. There was a pervasive feeling that now was not the time to gain a reputation for clock-watching. Should Comrade Maseryan chance to call long after closing time, how satisfactory to be able to answer the phone in firm, workaday accents.

In addition the Russian Consulate, normally as faction-ridden, competitive, and at odds as any office in the world, was united by the descent of the man from Moscow to the point of needing the company of fellow-sufferers.

Every member of the consulate staff was a highly trained specialist of some sort; even stout Tamara Andreeva had been chief secretary at the disarmament talks in Warsaw for a period of time. This accumulation of brains, experience, and knowledgeability could not fail to grasp the obvious. Suspicion might fall on the United Nations delegation, on the embassy in Washington, even on ships' captains, but it fell most naturally on the staff of the New York consulate.

"Not that I am convinced that any Soviet citizen was implicated," said Durnovo when the preliminaries were over and the subject finally broached.

Anton Vassilich (records and regrettably pert) made a sardonic bow. "With all respect, Sergei Pavlich, it is not what you are convinced of but what Maseryan is convinced of . . ."

This speech alone demonstrated the changing climate in the consulate. Sergei Durnovo was usually far too conscious of his superior rank, of his growing reputation as a man making his mark, to tolerate familiarity from an underling. Today, however, he was somewhat awkwardly encouraging a comrade-in-arms atmosphere.

There was a shiver of silence broken by Tamara Andreeva.

"Well, I for one do not believe that Mikhail Mikhailich is convinced that someone here was responsible. No, not at all. He was sent for the sake of appearance—because it was the correct thing to do. It was decided it would look odd not to cooperate. But, you will see, it was some American who did this. Violence, murder—these are American habits, not Russian."

There was a murmur of assent.

"You do not agree, Feodor Ilyich?" Katerina asked anxiously. .

Voronin shrugged slightly. "I do not know. I simply do not know. I hope you are right—but those Soviet documents? All that detailed knowledge of our procedures— no, I do not know what to think!"

"That is not the attitude for us to take! We know that we are all innocent!" Durnovo was annoyed. This was no way for a comrade-in-arms to talk! "It is not for us to adopt a pessimistic attitude . . ."

But he could not meet Voronin's eyes.

The situation at the consulate was difficult; it would have been even more constrained if the participants could have overheard the conversation in a little known, but highly esteemed establishment on Mott Street. Tactful inquiry had disclosed that Maseryan was not letting the Sino-Soviet rift interefere with his enjoyment of Chinese cuisine.

Through the abalone soup Maseryan and Lyons had fenced warily, taking each other's measure. Over the Peking duck, Lyons, with the air of a man throwing caution to the winds, had relayed to Maseryan all his hard-earned information about Denger, Quentin, and Stringfellow and followed up with an elaboration of his "new life" theory.

Maseryan had listened carefully, responding to the information with a series of grunts and to the theory with rapt silence.

"It is interesting, what you say," he announced at last. "The new life, I can see that. Not clearly, you understand, but more clearly than I can see a Soviet citizen planning to steal a million dollars and continue his old life."

Inspector Lyons then went up several notches in Thatcher's estimation by abandoning the immediate problem and entertaining them over the steamed bass with a lively description of Baranoff's antics at the Denger funeral. Nothing in his manner suggested that he expected, or even hoped for, a *quid pro quo* from his Russian counterpart.

". . . that clown actually had a flag over the casket that he insisted on presenting to the sister-in-law. The poor woman was so embarrassed she didn't know where to look."

Maseryan was intrigued. "It is not customary to drape flags over your deceased chauffeurs?"

"Only chauffeurs being handled by Abe Baranoff," said Lyons, laughing.

His tactics paid off. By the time they were sitting over their melon, Maseryan had made up his mind.

"I know very well you are frustrated by not having access to the records of Soviet personnel who might be concerned in this crime." He examined Lyons shrewdly. "You are welcome to the background information I have. But, truthfully, I do not see that it will be of much help."

He was as good as his word.

Durnovo, they learned, was a rising man. Younger than he looked (he was only forty-five), he had capped a promising early career with a series of professional successes during the last ten years. Until he came to New York, he seemed to have a knack for being in the right place at the right time. It was no secret that he was destined for early advancement to a distinguished niche in the Ministry of Foreign Affairs—provided, of course, that he survived the current debacle.

"An enterprising man," Thatcher remarked.

"In more ways than one," said Maseryan sourly. "Ten years ago he married. His father-in-law is very superior in the Ministry. You see, I am frank with you."

Thatcher, mindful of Bradford Withers' nephew wreaking havoc in the Sloan's Paris office, refrained from witticism. Instead he suggested they pass on to Durnovo's assistant.

Feodor Voronin was forty-seven. He had been something of a war hero in his youth and entered the Ministry after a distinguished academic career. He had seconded important missions on every continent except Africa.

"This one married early," Maseryan said with approval. "His wife died three years ago. They had one daughter."

"And Katerina Ivanovna?"

She had graduated from the University of Moscow with the highest grades in English, French, and German ever achieved. Her career at the Interpreter's Institute in Geneva had been equally notable. She had come to New York after short tours of duty in London and Geneva.

Maseryan concluded her biography with one further fact.

"She is, of course, a very attractive young woman."

"I haven't met her," said Lyons with genuine regret. "And you're right. None of this sounds as if it's going to do us any good. But I've got something for you besides background material. We've finally dug up a solid fact, and I think it will interest you, Mr. Thatcher."

"Yes?"

"Baranoff finally gave us a list of the papers Denger was taking to the Registry of Deeds for him. Christ, I thought he was going to plead the Fifth Amendment! That lawyer of his made him cooperate."

"Well?" Thatcher could not keep all impatience from his voice.

"The papers were filed the day of the robbery, all right. But they use a time stamp at the Registry, and the papers are marked 4:30 P.M."

Maseryan leaned forward, his eyes bright with interest.

"But surely that is much too long. The Registry is not far. It—"

"Denger should have been there before two-thirty, if

he went directly from Quentin to the Registry," Thatcher cut in.

"Then," continued Maseryan, "he had over two hours in which to dispose of your check. In two hours he could have gone to a great many places."

Thatcher frowned in thought. "Of course, there might be some explanation unconnected with the theft. He could have been drinking, he could have been placing bets, he could have been buying socks for all we know. But it doesn't sound reasonable. He told us himself that he would be free for the day when he finished Baranoff's errands. You'd think that if he wanted time for himself, he'd rush through his work to have the rest of the afternoon off."

"That makes sense," Lyons agreed. "And there's one other point that makes the whole thing screwier than ever. One of the women at the Registry thinks Denger was there twice that afternoon, the first time shortly after lunch. She says she couldn't swear it was him—just caught sight of him in the doorway—but she's pretty sure. That would square with what he told us. That he turned the check over in the entrance shortly after leaving Quentin. We didn't ask him what he did with the rest of his afternoon, so we don't have his testimony on that."

"Denger's testimony," Thatcher observed realistically, "is getting more and more suspect, isn't it?"

Even as he spoke he remembered how Denger had looked, peering up at them, the visored cap pushed back, unable to conceal his spite, his smugness . . . his amusement. Was that the cause of his amusement? That they had failed to probe his activities after handing over the check?

Meanwhile Lyons was still musing: ". . . those two hours could be damned important. That must be when Denger cottoned on to something. Nobody could have known he was going to deliver the check. He found out something, but he didn't know what he had until we showed up at Halloran's. Then, what does he do?" Lyons glared around the table. "He rushes to the phone to call Luke Stringfellow."

"And becomes curious about the Russian Consulate," Maseryan reminded him severely.

"And wonders when Baranoff is coming back," Thatcher added, in duty bound.

"All right." Lyons shook his head as if there were flies buzzing around it. "I've got my boys going through everything we've got on Stringfellow. And I'm tackling him again in the morning. The same thing goes for Baranoff. As far as the consulate goes, I don't see what we can do. Hell, he didn't even know it *was* the consulate. Just asked what that brownstone on Seventy-third Street was. Anyway, that's not my department. But I still think— Yes, what is it?"

A waiter had come to announce that Centre Street was on the phone. Maseryan took advantage of Lyon's absence to pursue his own concern.

"Tell me, what he said just now, is it accurate? That Denger was asking about a brownstone on Seventy-third Street without knowing what it was?"

Thatcher frowned. "Yes, that's right."

"But don't you see? If he did not know what the building was, he could only be interested because it was associated with some person. And if he knew what the building looked like, then it would be because he had seen someone entering or leaving it. As you know, there is no insignia or sign identifying the building."

"That's true. But where does it take us? Every single person involved in this case has a perfectly good reason for visiting your consulate. And they have all been doing so, quite regularly. Except . . . but no, that's ridiculous," Thatcher had suddenly been reminded that there was one person who should not have been entering the consulate on the afternoon of the robbery.

Maseryan had become tense. "What is so ridiculous, my friend?"

"I was thinking that Denger would have been very interested to see Baranoff enter any building in New York that afternoon. But I can't believe that Baranoff wasn't on that boat. It's so easy to check."

"It is certainly easy to check that someone using Baranoff's name was aboard. Baranoff himself could have flown over later in the day."

Thatcher shook his head. "No," he said stubbornly, "I refuse to believe that any man slipping in and out of the country clandestinely would encumber himself with a hundred and twenty-two otters."

Maseryan was prepared to debate the point, but he broke off his argument as he saw Inspector Lyons striding across the room with sudden urgency. Imperiously the detective summoned for the check. He did not sit down when he reached the table.

"Having the boys go through Stringfellow's file again paid off," he announced tightly. "A car is picking me up in a couple of minutes. I'm going out to Huntington right away. If you want to come along, I'll explain as we drive."

Luke Stringfellow was alone in the big house in Huntington. They could hear the mechanical chattering of a television set in the distance as the door swung open. Their host was not pleased to see them.

"Everybody's out. I thought I'd get a little peace . . ."

Red-rimmed eyes finished his accusation for him.

"No use offering you a drink, I suppose," he said defensively, grasping his half-filled highball glass.

Maseryan interrupted an awed inspection of Alice Stringfellow's robust notions of elegance (currently including three oversize geometric paintings and a huge, weathered Buddha ensconced on an ivy-twined pedestal) and replied:

"Excellent! It has been a dry day. And with all this talk . . ."

Luke Stringfellow smiled, a little contemptuously, and moved to open a Venetian-mirror door. Behind it was a small well-stocked bar, with vodka for Maseryan and Scotch for Thatcher. Even Inspector Lyons yielded, if beer can be described as yielding.

"Now, what's this all about?" demanded Stringfellow, sounding less truculent.

Lyons carefully put down his glass and described the latest discoveries about Gus Denger's movements on the day of the robbery. As he spoke, Stringfellow listened without expression. Thatcher, watching him over his glass, knew that he had been tensed for something quite different.

"So, why come to me?" Stringfellow said when Lyons finished.

"I want to go over this call Denger made to you."

Stringfellow slammed a big hand on the table with enough force to move the heavy cigarette lighter. "Look, why don't you try changing the record? I've told you Denger never got through to me. I know he called because you say so—and Tessie says so. *Why* he was calling me, I don't know! I *do* know that I don't know a damned thing about the robbery! Somebody used Stringfellow paper—but it wasn't me! Hell, for a while it looked as if we were going to get stung for $985,000 instead of . . ."

"Instead of the Sloan," Thatcher supplied when his outburst came to an abrupt end.

Stringfellow grinned at him. "Sorry, Thatcher. But you can afford it better than we can."

"Especially now that you're investing in that industrial park in Trenton," said Thatcher. Whatever his intention was—and in retrospect he was not altogether sure he knew—he had touched a nerve.

"That's right," said Stringfellow almost savagely. "Here, I'll top that up for you."

Maseryan agreed to this suggestion with enthusiasm; his performance as early-vintage MGM Russian was impeccable. Lyons gave him a calculating look as Stringfellow busied himself at the bar. Maseryan rolled his eyes slightly.

From the bar, Stringfellow spoke with a weariness that struck Thatcher as quite genuine. "I don't have any idea —at all—why this Denger should be calling me . . ." Suddenly he broke off and his head went up. "I think I hear my wife. Excuse me a minute . . ."

Without waiting for a reply, he hurried from the room. There certainly had been sounds from the hallway but, to Thatcher, Stringfellow suggested a man suddenly struck by an idea. An unwelcome idea, at that.

The three men sat in silence while Luke Stringfellow alerted Alice to the usurpation of her living room. Her reception of the news was quite audible:

"Luke, you've got to tell me what's going on. You were drinking all afternoon, you wouldn't go to the Shaw's, and . . ."

The voice died away as if Stringfellow were drawing his wife farther from the living room. But the indistinct rumbles went on for some minutes before he returned, more red-faced than ever.

"Alice is upset," he said, trying to play the protective husband. "She's frightened at having police in the house. You might have gotten me in the office in the morning."

Lyons put his empty glass down deliberately. There was nothing easygoing about him when he next spoke.

"If you'd come clean, Stringfellow, we wouldn't be barging into your house."

"Look, Inspector, I don't have to take that kind of talk from you," the wheat broker blustered. "I've been willing to try and help you guys out—"

"If you want to be helpful, Mr. Stringfellow, tell us

about your military service," said Lyons with dangerous calm.

Stringfellow went white.

"The service?"

"More particularly, your service in Korea. You could tell us what outfit you were with."

"Now look, I can explain all that."

"Can you?" Lyons let the silence grow for a moment. "You're going to explain to me how you and Gus Denger served together for over eight months without your noticing him?"

"My God, I can't be expected to remember every man out there. I was a captain and he was a sergeant."

"Remembered his rank, have you? And the fact that he was in your artillery unit at Pusan."

Stringfellow mopped his brow.

"I know it looks funny." He looked around the unbelieving circle. "Goddammit! I did forget! That was a long time ago, and there wasn't anything special about Denger."

"And his being in the headlines for a week didn't remind you?" Lyons pressed remorselessly.

"All right, all right! I did remember after it was in the papers about his being murdered. But not before! It wasn't until I saw that he'd been in Korea with my outfit that I remembered. You didn't even tell me he was Gus Denger when you first asked me about him. You called him Augustus or something."

"He remembered you, all right. That's why he was calling you."

"I can't help that. I didn't have anything to do with him for over fifteen years!"

And from this position, Stringfellow could not be moved. Lyons kept at it, alternating accusation with cajolery, threatening a massive investigation into Denger's movements, but Stringfellow's answers were all the same. He had not recalled Denger until he read the accounts of his murder in the newspapers. Then he hoped to keep the connection a secret from the police.

And since Luke Stringfellow, by turn belligerent and self-exculpatory, stood accused of no crime, the three investigators eventually found themselves back in their car.

Lyons was far from displeased.

"We've got him rattled, that's for sure."

"Tell me, I am unfamiliar with your army," said Maseryan. "Is it possible that he did not remember Denger?"

"It's possible," Thatcher was trying to be fair-minded. "Denger was not particularly notable and would have been less so as a young man in the army. His captain would not have seen much of him. And it is a long time ago. What's more, some men forget their military experiences very easily. It's a different life altogether."

"One thing's certain," Lyons announced grimly. "Whatever Stringfellow forgot, Denger didn't forget him. It stands to reason. Stringfellow is a kind you remember, and he's stayed the same. Burly, bull-necked, red-headed. Then there's the name. You don't meet two Luke Stringfellows. We've found out something. When Denger handed over that check, he knew it wasn't to Luke Stringfellow."

"Yes, I think that's obvious." Thatcher pondered a moment. "One point might help. Do we have any idea whether Denger asked for Luke, or for Mr. Stringfellow, when he called Stringfellow's office? That should tell us if there had been any recent intimacy."

"I don't know. But we'll find out right now. We can stop at Tessie Marcus' place in the Village."

Maseryan nodded approvingly. Swooping down unexpectedly on people late in the evening accorded perfectly with his ideas of police investigation.

But not with Thatcher's.

"It's after ten, Inspector," he protested.

"She'll be expecting us. We'll warn her over the phone." Lyons grinned. "But we'll phone from the corner. You can't be fussy in this business, Mr. Thatcher."

In spite of the call, made from a booth on West Eighth Street, Tessie Marcus looked stunned, almost frightened, when she opened her door to them. She also looked unexpectedly human. A turkish towel wrapped around her hair, the ironing board they could see set up in the living room, attested to a domestic evening into which a vice-president of the Sloan Guaranty Trust, an Inspector of the New York City Police Department, and a visiting Russian investigator were now intruding.

"I always wash my hair on Thursday night," she said unguardedly. "What do you . . . I guess you'd better come in . . ."

It was a small room. Awkwardly they watched her unplug the iron and remove it to the kitchenette that led off the living room. The ironing board pointed an accusing finger at them. Tessie Marcus disappeared into the darkness beyond the kitchen for a few minutes, then reappeared in a white blouse and full black skirt instead of the maroon wool robe. Her coarse black hair was combed and wet; she had put on lipstick. Her unstockinged feet were still in flat, shapeless slippers.

His own Miss Corsa went home to Queens to a large, food-loving, multi-generationed family, Thatcher was suddenly happy to remember. But how many of New York's Tessie Marcuses lived their real lives in their Stringfellow & Sons and came home to drab apartments, to washing their hair very Thursday night?

To a solitude so profound that visitors rattled, and finally, cracked the hard protective shell.

"It's crowded," said Miss Marcus after directing them to the sofa and the easy chair and bringing a hard-backed kitchen chair out for herself. "My mother died last year, so when I moved in here I brought some things from the old place . . ." She looked around, seeing the overstuffed furniture, the polished old-fashioned end table, the betasseled lampshade for the first time. "I suppose I should have thrown this junk out and started from scratch . . . but I didn't get around to it . . ."

There are some people who enjoy stripping the pretenses of others away, exposing the naked flesh. John Putnam Thatcher was not of that kidney and neither, he was pleased to see, were Lyons and Maseryan. Lyons' voice sounded surprisingly gentle:

"My mother went four years ago," he said, "and I've still got St. Francis staring down at me every time I have a beer. And I haven't been to confession for forty years . . ."

The Slavic approach was more direct.

"Miss Marcus," said Maseryan with sincerity, "is it discourteous to ask if you would make coffee? I do not know in America but . . ."

Tessie Marcus became Miss Marcus as she busied herself in the tiny kitchen alcove. By the time excellent coffee was steaming in the four flower-decorated cups, she was herself—as much as she could be away from Stringfellow & Son.

"Now, why are you here at this hour?" she asked. In her own home, she sounded amost vulnerable. Maseryan sipped his coffee with appreciative noises and examined a large file of records near the turntable and loudspeaker at his elbow. Lyons looked unhappy.

John Putnam Thatcher made a note to demand more money—much more money—from the Sloan if his official duties were to include much more of this sort of thing. He cleared his throat. "Miss Marcus, we are sorry to burst in on you like this . . ."

"But this is a real home," said Maseryan with the approval Huntington had failed to elicit. "You have Qistrakh, I see . . ."

Tessie Marcus was torn. In a room this size it was hard not to respond to Maseryan's overpowering personality.

"Music always meant a lot to me," she said to Thatcher, making it sound like a shameful confession.

He forced himself to persist, ". . . but it was about that call from Denger."

As far as wet hair and slippers allowed, Miss Marcus became all business. Gus Denger had called the office of Stringfellow & Son. He asked to talk to Luke Stringfellow.

"Luke? Not Mr. Stringfellow?" said Lyons trying not to lead the witness. The Russian was still engrossed in the records.

Tessie Marcus frowned in thought. "I just don't remember. I think he said Luke Stringfellow—but I can't be sure. We all call him Luke . . ." She let the sentence trail off.

"He didn't say anything else?" Lyons asked.

"Not a thing."

"Sure, Tessie?"

Thatcher was appalled by this familiarity, but Inspector Lyons had apparently recognized a kindred native New Yorker and, more important, Tessie had too.

"Oh God," she said with a half smile that transformed her heavy features into a kind of bittersweet beauty. "Sure, Inspector. 'Is Luke Stringfellow there?' 'No, he isn't.' 'Click.' That was it."

Inspector Lyons pressed her on this point several times but to no avail. Then, without warning, he told her about the Korean connection between Stringfellow and Denger.

"Oh, Christ! So that's what it was!" She looked at the three intent faces awaiting her reaction. She took a deep breath that was almost a sigh. "I knew there was something. Luke's been behaving like a maniac the past week. But you don't know him." She threw out a hand that pleaded for understanding. "It probably happened just the way he said. He didn't remember anything until he saw the papers. He loses his head, you know. When things go wrong, he gets scared and then makes them ten times worse."

They dropped the subject. Thatcher, at least, was reminded that Alice Stringfellow had not felt it necessary to enter her living room and explain to them that her husband panicked in times of crisis. In this threesome, that was Tessie Marcus' job.

Inspector Lyons accepted this. Maseryan seemed to as well; he also apparently felt that Miss Marcus could be of use.

"What excellent coffee. Well, yes, another cup. Four lumps of sugar, if you don't mind. Oh, the trouble with those four lumps! When I was a young man, enemies said they showed I had bourgeois tendencies. Now Miss Marcus, you are an intelligent woman. Will you help me?"

Tessie Marcus grew wary, and Thatcher did not blame her.

"You said that you cared for music."

She looked as though she regretted the admission.

"No, you must tell me. Here in New York. Imagine a woman—a young woman. She works hard, but she does not make much money—not as much as capitalists like my friend Mr. Thatcher, here, or his friend Mr. Victor Quentin . . ."

"You mean she's a secretary," said Tessie Marcus tartly.

"Yes, say a secretary. Now here, I see that drink costs much money. To go to the theater in New York—that is for the rich . . ."

"You can say that again," said Tessie.

Maseryan was momentarily puzzled, but continued. "Can a secretary afford to go to concerts? Is not this music too expensive, like the theater?"

Tessie Marcus could not resist the opportunity to impart information. "Have another cup . . . and I've got some plum brandy. No? Well, yes, your secretary could afford concerts. You see . . ."

Only after an exhaustive description of Town Hall concerts, of subscription series at City College, of standing room at the Met, did they escape. At least, Miss Marcus seemed more like herself.

"And she could go to the Y," she called down the ill-lit hallway after them.

On the sidewalk, they all relaxed.

"I tell you I'm glad that I haven't got any sisters," said Lyons. "That is, sisters who don't have six kids."

"Ah," said Maseryan, ambiguously. "Ah, you Americans. In Russia, *that* one"—he jerked his head in the direction of the apartment they had just left—"that one, with that intelligence, she would be a doctor. In fact, that is one of the trifling drawbacks of our society. There are too many women doctors. It can be very embarrassing . . ."

"Observe," said Maseryan, as they were dropping him at the consulate, "observe a part of American life that is not generally seen. All this going to concerts! Think of it!"

He disappeared within. Lyons and Thatcher looked at each other.

"I suppose he meant something by that," said Lyons.

"He meant something," Thatcher agreed. "But what?"

15

The Bread of Adversity

THE NEXT DAY STARTED inauspiciously. Thatcher had barely, and tardily, reached his desk when Miss Corsa came in with a message; Mr. Lancer would like to see him.

"And," she added, noting that her employer was beginning a survey of the morning papers, "Mr. Quentin is waiting outside."

As she spoke, Quentin himself materialized at her elbow. He looked anxious.

"Can I have a few minutes, John?"

Much as he would have liked to, Thatcher could not refuse this plea.

"Come in, Vic," he began as Miss Corsa, apparently disgusted, contributed the last word.

"Mr. Lancer," she announced inexorably, "is coming down in fifteen minutes."

She then withdrew, ostentatiously washing her hands of the whole situation, including the menace implicit in Lancer's Coming Down. This left Quentin apologizing and

Thatcher wondering what was exacerbating Miss Corsa; true, he had promised her time for correspondence and she was clearly not going to get it. But was this the moment for Miss Corsa to turn on him?

"No, Vic. That's fine. You heard Miss Corsa. Let's see what we can do before George gets here . . ."

Courtesy and kindness alone produced that invitation. Quentin was oblivious to the lack of enthusiasm. He was obsessed by his own difficulties.

"John, I'd like your advice . . ."

Instinctively Thatcher stiffened. The words, ominous at best, here had a doomsday ring. It was too early in the morning for a confession. He was casting about for a non-committal response when Quentin hurried on:

"I'm sorry to barge in this way—I know you're busy—but, my God! that Russian has been taking up hours . . ."

Thatcher relaxed as the quiet, bloodless voice droned on with nothing more alarming than extraordinary demands on time and staff, interruptions to work schedules; at the same time, it told Thatcher clearly—if without words—that Mikhail Maseryan had shaken Victor Quentin badly.

Without really listening, he heard about Quentin's recital, which still lacked shape and form.

Maseryan, of course, was a man of considerable force of character, and the arm of a powerful agency, whatever its initials were. But why had this disturbed Victor Quentin? Particularly after what Quentin had already survived?

Perhaps there was an innocent explanation; Quentin was simply not up to Maseryan's weight.

Or perhaps the explanation was less innocent.

With what he liked to think was lightning decision (actually, a longshot player's hunch), Thatcher interrupted:

"I know you're being pushed down in Commercial Deposits, Vic. I'll see what I can do about getting you some help. But at least"—he carefully kept from looking at Quentin—"at least you're not in as bad shape as Stringfellow & Son."

Quentin took out a cigarette, although Thatcher seemed to recall that he smoked only after meals. "That's true enough, John. I went over the other day. And I did sense a real change. They used to be—well, almost too easygoing, if you know what I mean. Now, they're pretty tense . . ."

Awkwardly, he relit the cigarette that had gone out.

"Are there . . . has anything new come up? At String-fellow, I mean?"

Without editorial asides, Thatcher described Luke Stringfellow's military history, and the questions this raised. Quentin sat motionless as Thatcher concluded with the discoveries that Lyons had made about Denger's two trips to the Registry.

"That's interesting," Quentin finally said. Thatcher suddenly realized how often those words are spoke without truth; Quentin was not interested, he was fascinated.

"Yes," Quentin said almost to himself. "That makes it bad for Luke . . . I see that . . . Not that I think he could . . ." He broke off.

Quentin was still plunged in thought when George C. Lancer appeared.

"Busy, John? Oh, Vic . . ."

During the highly stylized ritual that got Quentin out of Thatcher's office and Lancer firmly settled, Thatcher let his thoughts wander. First it occurred to him (as Lancer, speaking a shade too loudly, sped Quentin on his way with injunctions not to worry) that Lancer's brushing past Miss Corsa could produce no softening of that redoubtable young woman's current disapproval.

His second thought was less frivolous; he had given Victor Quentin grounds for hope. But what the devil had he given him to cause so much tortuous thinking?

"Poor fish!" said Lancer with his customary ease. "Looks like hell! I don't suppose . . . no!"

"No," said Thatcher firmly. "Now, George, what is it . . . ?"

In the interests of variety alone, he hoped that he was not about to learn of another large theft from the Sloan.

George C. Lancer, statesman-banker and utility business-man-intellectual, had the grace to look slightly embarrassed.

"Potato chips."

Thatcher maintained his equanimity. "I know you're going to expand that, George."

George did. Several years earlier, a Soviet premier had toured the United States. Commuter traffic, expressways, even Hollywood left him cold. Disneyland had been closed to him. The only two aspects of American life that had made a hit were Hosmer Chuddley's farm at Parched Stream, Iowa, and potato chips.

"Very interesting," said Thatcher ironically. He was beginning to feel that the inmates were running the asylum.

"Now, John," said Lancer, "just bear with me."

The net effect of the premier's enthusiasm for potato chips was a desire to introduce this comestible to the Russian cuisine. As a result, delegation after delegation of Soviet specialists had been forced to round off tours of U.S. farms, universities or laboratories with pilgrimages to the nearest available potato chip factory.

"Fine," said Thatcher. They had their troubles, and he had his.

"Now, I don't know if you keep up with potato chips," said Lancer with due caution. He knew full well that, while he was composing replies to George Kennan, John Putnam Thatcher was keeping up with American industry —including small local potato chip producers. "You may have noticed that they have just formed an American Institute of Potato Chip Producers . . ."

"I missed that," Thatcher admitted.

Lancer continued. Three important happenings were converging; the trade association was launching itself on the waiting world with the usual hoopla; an enterprising potato chip producer was unveiling a new, automated facility (with significantly increased capacity) in Bridgeport, Connecticut; and a Soviet delegation, sent expressly and solely to study the potato chip, was arriving.

"Today," said Lancer heavily.

Thatcher temporized. He saw, all too well, where this was leading. "Tell me, why this enthusiasm for potato chips? After all, they've had several premiers since . . ."

With his usual expertise in these matters, Lancer could cite findings from Harvard's Russian Research Center, where eminent kremlinologists had analyzed Russian agricultural programs, Politburo personalities, the narrative poems of youthful rebels, and come up with a conclusion: Russia had a lot of potatoes.

"Well, George, this is all fascinating," said Thatcher, letting his eyes stray meaningfully to the thick folder that was currently exercising Miss Corsa. "It will no doubt be a great day for potato chips. I don't quite see . . ."

Lancer hitched himself forward and interrupted. In view of the precarious state of current U.S.-Russian trade relations, it had been decided—"at the very highest level,

John"—that potato chips, and visiting Slavs, merited red carpet treatment.

"Fine," said Thatcher.

Furthermore, since the Sloan was so intimately connected with the darker side of U.S.-U.S.S.R. trade, it was felt that the bank should send a high-ranking representative.

"To show the flag, as it were. I'd like to go," Lancer assured him, "but I've got to testify this afternoon . . ."

Three hours later, despite silent but burning reproaches from Miss Corsa, John Putnam Thatcher sat not at his desk but in the stifling luxury of an improbable limousine, part of the cavalcade of sixteen such behemoths being escorted up the Merritt Parkway by snappily uniformed motorcycle police. Brilliant cold sunlight bathed a frozen landscape as they sped through. Inbound traffic, comfortably multihued and winter-grimed, stared curiously at all this black splendor snaking its way north. They were wondering, Thatcher knew, what politician had died.

Thatcher repressed a sigh and inclined his head to the stately enunciations of the chief dietician of the American Institute of Potato Chip Producers. She was a formidable female who was describing the many ways to cook with potato chips. There were two other occupants of this car; the agricultural attaché of the United States Embassy in Moscow (who had been winkled out of home leave in Laconia, New Hampshire) projected bad temper; the senior agronomist of the Murmansk Institute of Horticulture was actively confused.

". . . crumble potato chips, add mushroom soup, then bake in a 300° oven!" Miss Rorely concluded triumphantly.

"Mushroom soup?"

The Russian was probably regretting Joseph Stalin, whose shortcomings, whatever they were, had not included efforts to supersede borscht.

Thatcher himself was regretting—for perhaps the first time in his years at the Sloan—the absence of Bradford Withers. According to postcards, Withers was inspecting Angkor-Wat, but Thatcher doubted it. In any event, his chief's innocent enjoyment of ceremony would have removed potato chips from Thatcher's overcrowded agenda.

Chippsies, Inc., was a photogenic one-story building carefully centered in a genteel grove. Americans in the official party descended from the transport to look around with open pride. Russians nodded approvingly.

"Er . . . these cars," Thatcher overheard the under-secretary confide to the notable he was escorting, "all those cars belong to our workers."

The Russian was stolid.

"Your undersecretary," said a sour voice in Thatcher's ear, "he, too, reads too much propaganda. We know about American workers—and their cars."

Thatcher turned to find Mikhail Maseryan falling into step beside him as they neared Chippsies' neo-colonial entrance.

"You don't know about potato chips, do you?" Thatcher retorted. "Otherwise we wouldn't be here."

"There is truth in that," Maseryan conceded, looking elsewhere.

His game was just alighting from the last limousine, Thatcher saw by glancing over his shoulder. He had overlooked Sergei Durnovo, Katerina Ivanovna, and Feodor Voronin at the assembling ceremonies in New York.

"Yes," Maseryan said placidly following his gaze. "I watch my friends from the consulate go about their daily chores. And you would never guess how much they travel . . ."

Thatcher had no opportunity to reflect on this. Almost immediately he was plunged into the wonders of modern potato chip manufacture. With moderate interest he obeyed the guide and watched a complex piece of machinery scrub, wash, rinse, then slice two tons of Maine's best.

Nodding sagely, the Russians crowded closer to study the apparatus with concentration. They sustained this attention at dipping vats, at ovens, at conveyor belts moving mountains of chips toward a demonic bagging machine.

"Now, here in our Broken Chip Department . . ."

The party moved past a watchtower where white-coated technicians twirled knobs with the eagel-eyed dexterity of test pilots.

After too long, it was over. "Now, to our Chippsies Research Kitchens!"

It was as the technology of potato chips was being unveiled—"Now, at 400 degrees fahrenheit, the chip remains crisp, with absorbative vegetable oil capability"—that Thatcher felt the tap on his elbow.

The sleek young woman looked worried. "They said you were Mr. Thatcher."

Thatcher wrenched his attention from waffle-cutting techniques and admitted it.

"Good. You're wanted on the phone."

If her name card could be believed, the young woman's name was Nona and she was Chippsies' Potato Girl of the Week.

Thatcher sighed and backed out of the kitchen to follow Nona to the phone.

For a reason he was unwilling to explore, Thatcher knew who must be calling.

"It's me, John. Vic Quentin."

"Yes, Vic," he replied with extreme caution.

"I think we've found something important."

There was no excitement in the voice, nor any exultation. With his customary quiet-spoken competence, Victor Quentin outlined a standard operating procedure; the thoroughgoing search of the Sloan files had unearthed an application from Barling Realty Corporation to transfer certain titles and credits in Trenton, New Jersey, to one Luke Stringfellow.

Thatcher had a vivid picture of Quentin's recent reaction to news of a possible Stringfellow-Denger connection.

"We already know that Luke Stringfellow is planning to buy into real estate in New Jersey," he began, matching Quentin's calm.

"But *Barling,*" said Quentin with understated professional emphasis. "John, Barling is one of Abe Baranoff's real estate operations!"

He succeeded in startling John Putnam Thatcher. So much so that, not until several days later did Thatcher find himself asking the question that should have leaped to his mind—potato chips or no:

"Vic, just *when* did you discover this?"

While Thatcher was on the phone, the official party had proceeded into the Chippsie Pub, where several pretty girls offered them their choice of remarkable meals consisting of chippsburgers, chippslaw, chipps foo yung, tuna chip salad, and like fare. This kept Katerina Ivanovna fully occupied; moving from table to table she interpreted and tried to explain to her bewildered compatriots precisely what their hosts were saying. The difficulty did not rest in finding Russian equivalents for the English words but in convincing the assorted Russians that she was not making the whole thing up.

"Now that cannot be right. Chipped steak? You must have made a mistake . . ."

"I assure you, Ivan Ivanich, that is precisely correct. Americans take steaks, dip them in crushed potato chips, then broil them!"

The Red Army had given Ivan Ivanich the opportunity to travel abroad some years earlier. Reaching back into memory, he came up with an appropriate comment.

"Wunderbar!"

"Yes, isn't it?" said Miles H. Orville, of the American Institute of Potato Chip Producers. "And, miss, do tell him to try this chocolate-chip cookie!"

At a small table, Sergei Durnovo looked at Feodor Voronin with amusement and resignation. Like all officials stationed abroad, he had learned to conceal his intense boredom (and annoyance) when visiting parties of dignitaries passed through town, demanding aid, comfort, and amusement while disrupting normal operations, then returned home to point out that the Russian Consulate in New York was staffed with wastrels and worse.

"They could not have chosen a more awkward time to come," he remarked to his assistant.

Voronin, watching Katerina Ivanovna with sympathy, was unwilling to join Durnovo, whom he now distrusted, in indiscretions. "These are busy times," he said.

Durnovo recognized the rebuff and did not like it. Voronin was his assistant, but he was far from being a comfort. Still, despite the basic discord between the two men, they shared a common awareness of the awkwardness, even the dangers, of their current position—as well as a suffocating awareness of Mikhail Maseryan's bright eyes watching, always watching.

As they sat in silence, they saw Thatcher return to the room, catch Maseryan's eye, and make a brief summoning gesture. Maseryan rose from a nearby table and went out into the hall.

"What are they doing, do you suppose?" Durnovo asked with unguarded venom.

Voronin absentmindedly ate some virgin potato chips. Like Durnovo, he was so deflected by curiosity that he forgot their profound lack of sympathy.

"I do not know," he replied. "Mikhail Mikhailich spent all morning with me, asking question after question."

"Not all morning," said Durnovo in the tone that Voronin had come to loathe—suggesting as it did Durnovo's sense of official and personal superiority (as well as Moscow contacts). Voronin saw he was being unjust when Durnovo continued, "He spent a goodly portion of the morning with me. With, as you say, question after question."

Voronin, the older if the junior man, was also the more reflective. "Since it is apparent that anyone in our consulate could have doctored the fraudulent invoices, I do not see how these questions contribute anything."

Durnovo made a gesture of distaste. For a moment they sat isolated from the bustle, talk, and laughter around them.

"And the banker," Durnovo added unwillingly. "What he is doing I cannot see."

Voronin took a sip of his beer. "I know that both of them are spending much time with the police. No doubt they are cooperating . . ."

Durnovo's slashing gesture spilled beer over the table. Only after a waitress had rushed over to mop up, smile kindly, and depart, did he reply, "Cooperation! I tell you, Feodor Ilyich, I do not like the way things look. All these questions! All these telephone calls! It is clear to me that they have decided to find a criminal! And who knows who may be cast for the part . . . ?"

Voronin looked at him with real surprise. The agitation in Durnovo's voice was a far cry from his usual armored nonchalance. And naked emotion made it difficult, indeed impolitic, for Voronin to comment. Before the silence could become embarrassing, they were interrupted.

"Whew!" said Katerina Ivanovna, dropping into the chair beside Voronin. "This is exhausting. Never will Yuri Blekhov believe what I am saying . . ."

Despite his anxiety, Voronin smiled at her. The irrepressible smile, the sparkling eyes, always reminded him of his much beloved daughter. His heart warmed to Katerina Ivanovna—and, sometimes lately, ached for her youth and vulnerability. But Voronin was not the man to reveal such feelings.

"You are a very fine interpreter," he said in his precise way.

"But I know nothing about cooking," she replied. "Now, about good restaurants . . ."

She broke off guiltily, shot a look at Sergei Durnovo. He had not been listening.

"Now they are coming back," he muttered, almost to himself.

Katerina Ivanovna followed his gaze. "Who? Oh, them." She was elaborately indifferent. Voronin suddenly felt very old and afraid.

Thatcher and Maseryan had resumed their places in the Chippsie Pub only because of the difficulties of transport in America; the one efficient way to return from Bridgeport to New York City at this hour of the day was via official cavalcade.

"And besides," said Thatcher as he dialed. "It may be difficult to track Baranoff down. Miss Corsa? Good. Will you see if you can line up Abe Baranoff for me? I'd like to talk to him tonight, if that's possible. Yes, it looks as if we'll be here for quite a while . . ."

(There were to be official ceremonies during which American Potato Chip Producers presented the chip-starved peoples of the U.S.S.R. with two potato slicers of advanced model and design. Thatcher knew this could not be accomplished without considerable oratory.)

He gave Miss Corsa the number and turned to find Maseryan sunk in thought.

"You have told the police?" the Russian asked.

"I told Quentin to call Lyons," said Thatcher.

"I would like to talk to both of them now," said Maseryan with emphasis.

If Maseryan talked to Quentin again, thought Thatcher, the Sloan might as well write off Commercial Deposits.

"Neither Stringfellow nor Baranoff is likely to run away," he said as they strolled into the Chippsie Pub, unconscious of Sergei Durnovo's almost feverish gaze.

"We will see," said Maseryan. "We will see."

By the strange logic governing current events, John Putnam Thatcher should not have been surprised that the discovery of a link between Luke Stringfellow and Abe Baranoff propelled him from the frontiers of modern potato chip manufacture (in Bridgeport) to the basketball courts of City College of New York. Maseryan, he had expected to accompany him. But Dmitri Vlozhnov, analytical chemist from the Smolensk Institute of Food Research, was something else again.

As Thatcher had foreseen, Miss Corsa located Abe Baranoff and called Thatcher back only minutes before the presentation ceremonies ended and a general exodus toward the cars had begun. It was, therefore, seven o'clock before they returned to the United Nations Plaza. There, Thatcher had already decided, the simplest thing to do was bolt.

Upon prearranged signal, he and Maseryan turned on their heels, marched briskly, and snaffled the first available taxi without looking back.

This was when Dmitri Vlozhnov manifested himself. As the taxi accelerated, they suddenly saw that they were not alone.

"Look here!"

Russian expletives!

The newcomer presented a face last noticed over a chippsburger. Thatcher relaxed. Maseryan thundered imperious questions. The cabby sped toward Twenty-third Street.

Vlozhnov was a small, nut-brown man with thick glasses and a merry manner. He recovered his breath during Maseryan's furious tirade, and replied at length. Maseryan translated. Vlozhnov had been so weighted with instructions to follow his guides that when he saw two members of the party set off to the street, he had fallen into comprehensible error; wrongly assuming that this was the official route, he had hurtled after them. Here he was. With open faith, he surveyed them.

Maseryan's reply did not shake his trust.

"If we take him back to the United Nations," Thatcher said after consulting his watch, "we may miss Baranoff. Miss Corsa said that he had an appointment later this evening."

Rounding on Vlozhnov, Maseryan spoke savagely. Vlozhnov chuckled and replied.

"Bah!" said Maseryan. "I told this idiot they will think he has defected. Do you know what he says? They will know better. He says that after potato chip soup, no one would defect . . ."

Fortunately at this moment, the driver pulled up to the gymnasium of City College. Miss Corsa had reported that Abe Baranoff expected to be here and Thatcher trusted Miss Corsa. He did wish she had more curiosity. It had not occurred to her to find out why Abe Baranoff should be using basketball courts.

The explanation became speedily apparent. Baranoff was not in sight under hanging baskets. What met their eyes was the Leningrad Symphony, members of Baranoff's retinue, fourteen weedy students moving wooden chairs, and several sharp-featured dark-haired women brandishing instrument cases.

"Ah!" It was a cry of pleasure from Vlozhnov as a violin scale wafted toward them. His nose wriggled slightly, he quickened his pace.

"Another music lover! As if I did not have enough!" said Maseryan, putting out a restraining hand. "Where is Baranoff?"

Thatcher had just located the ubiquitous George. He was standing, nay drooping, amid a healthy group of floppy-trousered men.

"Where is Baranoff?" Thatcher yodeled. He was forced to repeat the question at higher volume when Vlozhnov hailed his compatriots in a jovial slavic outburst. George was pained.

Maseryan shook his charge slightly, but this did not abash him. Inconsequentially Thatcher decided that, for an analytic chemist, Vlozhnov was remarkably perky. As such, he compared favorably to George.

George minced forward and in refined accents vouchsafed the information that Mr. Baranoff could be found in the small office off the far end of the courts.

There Baranoff was, hunched over a battered desk, bellowing into the telephone. The plain room was lit with a single naked bulb; the rightful owner of the room—who was an official of the CCNY credit union—as well as his secretary, stood looking on with resentment.

"So, Weinstein, be sure to check with this Kiley . . ."

After more shouting, Baranoff hung up, waved a manicured hand at his visitors, and addressed the secretary.

"Now, be a good girl and remember to call my downtown office. Tell them to send a car for me in about an hour . . . and if you will type the rehearsal schedule . . . well, Baranoff will see to it that you get something nice tomorrow."

He patted her cheek and rose to join Thatcher. The secretary, a thin intelligent young woman who had attended Hunter, glared after him, but Baranoff swept out of the office he had highhandedly preempted, exuding pleasure upon seeing Thatcher again.

"So, you do come to Baranoff again, to talk. Ah, Maseryan, is it? Yes, I have heard that name. Dr. Vlozhnov? Enchanted. Here, we can talk in here . . ."

He led the way into somebody else's office. Soon they

were settled at the desk. Baranoff, Thatcher observed, had quite unselfconsciously chosen to seat himself behind it.

"This morning, the Leningrad Symphony arrived," Baranoff said. "Since Lincoln Center is busy, we telephoned here. They must practice. Ah, such artists . . ."

Dmitri Vlozhnov uttered an ecstatic comment. Baranoff turned to look at him absently. "Better to talk English . . ."

"Have you forgotten your Russian?" Maseryan asked softly.

Baranoff was put out. "No. I have not forgotten my Russian! But with Mr. Thatcher here, it would be discourteous . . . ah, George!"

His call halted the minion who swept into the office, looked around with patent contempt, and presented Baranoff with a paper before leaving.

"George! Close the door!"

The door cut off the distant thunder of drums, the throat clearing of cymbals, shouted commands and pleas. The silence in the bare little office was sudden, complete, and almost ominous.

Dmitri Vlozhnov, unaffected by the atmosphere, began a scientifically thorough study of the portraits lining the walls, although it was hard to see what luminaries of bygone City College basketball greatness could mean to him.

Baranoff thrust a telegram into a pocket and confronted his visitors.

Trying to free himself from an oppressive sense of unreality, Thatcher said, "Mr. Baranoff, are you Barling Realty?"

The flamboyant showman facing him narrowed keen businessman's eyes.

"Do I need Weinstein?" he asked in a low voice.

Thatcher was back in a world he knew very well. "No, you do not need your lawyer when you talk to us. I have no doubt that the police will be speaking to you later—as a matter of form, the Sloan has informed them. I'll leave you to decide if you'll want legal counsel then."

Baranoff raised heavy eyebrows, shot an unfriendly look at Maseryan, who was waiting to pounce, and said:

"All right, Mr. Thatcher. I am Barling Realty—yes . . ."

Before Maseryan could intervene, Thatcher described the problem in bald terms. "Barling Realty just sold five acres in Trenton, New Jersey," he said. "To Luke Stringfellow."

Baranoff's mobile face was a study in conflicting emotions. Did fear or surprise predominate? Thatcher could not be sure, but he soon saw that whatever emotions Baranoff felt, his brain was working at its customary high speed.

"When I talk to the police," he said with a half smile, "I will have Weinstein."

He was as quick as Maseryan and Thatcher to see what this suggested; collusion of some sort, collusion that had first used Gus Denger, then contrived at his murder. Baranoff was, for once, choosing his words with care.

"I have many interests. I buy and sell. Not all these sales do I personally know about. After all, each year I spend many months in Europe, on the coast. And when I am away, my business does not stop . . ."

Maseryan stared at him. "What? Do you claim that you did not know that you sold this land to Stringfellow?"

It did not take a communist to feel suspicious of a man who admitted selling something worth nearly a million dollars, and professed ignorance of the details, including the buyer's name.

Baranoff looked angry. "My friend, I do not claim—I tell you! Of course I knew that land was sold—and I knew the price. I did not know who bought it—because I was in Iran, at the time. That is what my lawyers are for . . ."

"An odd way of doing business," Maseryan reflected aloud. "I come all this way to find a capitalist from Omsk —and what do I find? A very odd way of doing business."

Abe Baranoff swelled with rage. "We are not in Omsk now!"

Maseryan was acid. "And that is lucky for you!"

As their voices rose, Dmitri Vlozhnov turned to stare at the protagonists with disapproval; then he returned to CCNY's notable fives. Thatcher felt obliged to interrupt the exchange, which showed signs of growing even more acrimonious; for some reason, Omsk had sparked ancient enmities.

He said mildly, "I agree that the police are going to be hard to convince."

Baranoff broke off his glaring duel with Maseryan and shrugged. "That, Mr. Thatcher, is what I pay Weinstein and the others for!"

Baranoff leaned back at these words. A glint of cold uncompromising light struck a gold thread in his richly embroidered waistcoat as he did so. These were the wrong surroundings for him, Thatcher thought suddenly. Abe Baranoff was not at his best in shabby functional offices.

He kept his eyes on Thatcher, but there was no doubt that he was addressing Mikhail Maseryan.

"I hire many lawyers, Mr. Thatcher, in order that I do not have to convince the police of anything. Weinstein and the others will do it for me. And no doubt this—did you say the name was Stringfellow?—no doubt he will agree with me. And his lawyers, also."

Maseryan leaned forward with a ferocious smile. "Then tell me this, my friend Baranoff, why do you talk so seriously to this woman who owns the garage? Why are you so interested in this Denger—if he was only a chauffeur. Denger—who knew Stringfellow? Are you sure you did not tell him to do something . . . ?"

"How do you know that I have been to Halloran's Garage?" he demanded.

Maseryan rubbed the side of his nose with a thick forefinger. "Is it then a secret?"

Abe Baranoff fell into stylized outrage. "Then you are following me? Well, do so, Comrade Commissar! We are not in Omsk now!"

His voice again mounted and gathered strength. Thatcher withdrew into his own thoughts. Could the U.S.S.R. have placed an agent in Halloran's Garage? A short week ago he would have snorted at the idea, but now . . . When he returned to earth, Abe Baranoff had moved from fury to awful irony. "And remember, Comrade Commissar, I am a rich man. A very rich man. I buy and sell—and talk to many people, about many things. And I do important business in my car. Sometimes I say things there that not everybody should know." He broke off, directed a knowing look at Thatcher. "As Weinstein reminds me. Naturally, when I learned that this Denger was a crook, I was worried . . ."

Thatcher could believe this too. Not all the details of every business transaction—even those of less swashbuckling businessmen than Abe Baranoff—would benefit from indiscriminate publicity.

"So there is your truth!" This explosive sentiment signaled the return of Abe Baranoff, entrepreneur of the arts. "Wonder if you will—that is all I can tell you!"

It also signaled—unmistakably—Baranoff's intention to terminate this conference. For a brief moment Maseryan looked at him, almost contesting the dismissal. But, at a sign from Thatcher, he shrugged and rose.

Baranoff let a small breath of anxiety escape. Then he rose and magnificently flung open the door to admit the great cascades of Tchaikovsky's *Fifth* that were echoing through the high-roofed auditorium.

"But we cannot sit here—talking about such things! Not when these great artists are bringing magic into our lives! Even you, Comrade Commissar, must be stirred. Ah, listen to the crescendo . . ."

Still declaiming, he led the way to the corridor.

As they followed, it was apparent that only Dmitri Vlozhnov was completely satisfied.

16

Harrowing Details

JOHN PUTNAM THATCHER had been too modest in his appraisal of the forces flushed to the surface by the current difficulties. He had neglected one group that was all but taking over the act—namely, the People.

Long ago the citizenry of a nation minded its own business. It farmed its land, raised its family, fended off the elements, and limited its relations with any governing body to the payment of ridiculously small taxes and occasional participation in some brief martial endeavor. Affairs of state were left to those paid for the job, and bad cess to them.

But, we were told, this was no way for a democratic electorate to act. Democracy depends on you! Know the issues! . . . inform yourself! . . . keep abreast of the personalities! . . . reach your own conclusions!

Any government in its right mind would have thought twice, had it known what was coming. But governments —or the men who compose them—are the same everywhere. Until reality intrudes, they always imagine that participation is synonymous with support. They see a keen-eyed, clean-cut, diligent populace reviewing the aspirations of its leaders and shouting enthusiastic approval.

And sure enough, that's the way it began. American voters started by trooping obediently to the polls. Magazines sprang up to slake the sudden thirst for information about the country, the world, the personalities, the issues. Television came, and it was no longer possible to be totally ignorant. Then support occasionally faded into criticism. Even worse, critics sometimes seized the initiative.

The Soviet Union, undeterred by this appalling precedent, started lecturing its own nationals on social responsibility. Predictably, the same pattern unrolled. First, they cooperated, then demurred, then went on the rampage.

Suddenly every great power found small groups not only giving it advice, but turning ugly if that advice were not immediately followed. Young men burned draft cards in Central Park. The rich declared war on poverty. Poets in Moscow told Russia what was wrong with it.

In this heady atmosphere, no matter how prudent the official actions of the United States and the Soviet Union, it was only to be expected that various individuals and groups would insist—loudly, clearly, and in as inconvenient a manner as possible—on some eerie policy of their own. And all too often they discovered the power to implement that policy without recourse to any higher agency.

An obscure bus driver for Intourist somewhere in outermost Siberia was the first individual to take power firmly by the horns. Abandoning his cargo of thirty-six American tourists and their Intourist guide in the middle of nowhere, he departed with his bus after being inflamed by a tacky, uninformed article about the longshoremen's strike in New York.

"If they don't carry Soviet wheat, I don't carry American tourists," he announced. From this position the tearful pleading of the Intourist guide was unable to budge him. The party was totally isolated for a day before the gallant efforts of the guide ultimately brought them to a town from which news of their dilemma flashed west.

Unfortunately, that evening it reached Kharkov where an American opera company on tour was preparing to give a performance of *Boris Goudonov*. Futile alike were the demands of the company's director, the impassioned reasoning of the local leader in cultural exchanges, and the call for solidarity among artists delivered by the principal of the Kharkov Musical Academy. Instead of performing *Boris,* the company marched on stage en masse and launched into a deafening rendition of "The Star-Spangled

Banner." The Kharkov critic assigned to the event, a man who did his duty with the heavens falling, conscientiously reviewed their performance. Never had he heard anything like it. But then, he added, never had he heard it performed by the world's leading basso supported by two hundred trained operatic voices. There had been a subtlety of phrasing, a command of nuance, too often lacking in familiar pieces, that gave the intelligent listener pause for thought.

Among those who paused to think were the members of a Soviet track team in Cleveland, Ohio. Mutinously downing their fibreglass poles and spiked shoes, they first threatened a whole medley of Russian music, starting with the *Internationale.* Cooler heads, however, advised against competition with trained musicians. "Leave that to the Leningrad Symphony," counseled the world's champion broad jumper. He himself was tone deaf. "For us, the two-minute silence!"

So Cleveland track fanciers were subjected to the moving spectacle of the Soviet team, standing grimly at attention, as seconds passed in the lofty stadium. Broadcasters, trying to emulate their brothers in Kharkov (if with less material) did what they could. "Well, sports fans, this really is something! On the left of the Russian line-up is Konnie Levsky, who broke the outdoor record in Tokyo in 1964. And now a message from Gillette . . ."

Each incident inspired some fresh partisan reprisal. The great vortex, spiraling wider and wider, caused wild-eyed government agencies to cast about blindly, seeking the intervention of responsible, sober non-belligerents. Notables in every field were pressed into the service of urging their more inflammable fellow-citizens to maintain absolute calm. But no sooner was one hole plugged than another would start spouting, as patriots, determined to show their bureaucrats what the national will demanded, kept springing into ill-advised action.

"The amazing thing is that so many of them are on the other country's soil," said Mikhail Maseryan, as he called to break an appointment so that he could go soothe, gag—and, if necessary, kidnap—some Russian astronauts pugnaciously on their way to an international space program.

"If this is what happens with restricted travel, it makes you think twice about opening up the borders," Thatcher agreed tartly. Maseryan had no trouble assigning a cause to his irascibility. "And you, whom do you have to calm?" he asked.

"Hosmer Chuddley," replied Thatcher. He rejected the thought of further comment. Nothing that came readily to the tip of his tongue was going to bolster the image of the United States or promote international harmony.

When they met for a belated lunch at Luchow's, Maseryan reverted to the topic.

"I do not quite understand. I thought Chuddley had already made his protest."

"Oh, you saw that article in the *Times?*"

"I do not know what makes you think we have to resort to the papers where Chuddley is concerned," Maseryan said wearily. The astronauts had been determined young men. "He keeps descending on our Trade Delegation, telling them what is wrong with our agriculture program."

"I doubt if you'll be seeing much of him now," Thatcher said. "He has other fish to fry."

"Does he ever!" exclaimed Inspector Lyons, who was with them. "He wants the Commissioner to crack down on some meeting in Washington Square."

Maseryan was puzzled. "But there are no Russians meeting in Washington Square."

"He's protesting the other American protesters," said Lyons in a confused attempt to clarify. Almost all attempts to explain Hosmer Chuddley became confused, sooner or later.

"He likes to be in a minority of one," said Thatcher. "He thinks the rest are just claim jumpers."

Actually what had bothered Chuddley was the quality of his unexpected supporters.

"What have they ever done?" he had demanded of Thatcher. "Why should people listen to them?"

Chuddley, like many a millionaire before him, regarded the acquisition of great personal wealth as a prerequisite to the expression of views on public matters. The only prerequisite.

Anxious to get the man out of his office, Thatcher had cunningly argued that the new protesters must have been swayed by the eminent good sense of Chuddley's highly publicized statements.

He had no intention of telling Maseryan any of this. We all occasionally feel the necessity of sweeping something under the rug in the presence of foreigners. But his intention to introduce a change in topic was forestalled by the police inspector. Lyons was not only shifting the conversation, he was doing so to some point.

"I see Dave Yates is eating here too," he said, indicating a table across the room. "That's a good-looking girl with him. His fiancée, I suppose."

Thatcher and Maseryan looked across the room. The dark, vivacious features were familiar. There was a long silence. Finally Maseryan spoke:

"That is not Mr. Yates's fiancée, whoever she may be. That is Katerina Ivanovna Ogareva, an employee of the Soviet Consulate. As Mr. Thatcher knows—and as I suspect you do, too."

Lyons was mildness itself. "I'm not acquainted with either of the young women. But it seems to me that I did hear something about this."

Ever since the discovery that it was the attractive Russian interpreter to whom Yates was sending presents, Thatcher had expected some development. If Yates bought his presents in Russian stores and the two lunched together openly in places like Luchow's, it was inevitable. But he had hoped that the *eclaircissement* would not have to be made by Americans to Russians. Apparently this was not going to be necessary.

"You must think we are idiots," grumbled Maseryan. "I have known of this for some time. After all, I have access to Katerina Ivanovna's dossier. She probably does not realize herself why she was transferred so suddenly from Geneva."

"Happened before, has it?" inquired Lyons, lapsing into his easygoing interrogation methods.

Maseryan's face suddenly saddened, as if with some knowledge old to the human race. "There are girls like that, you know. We have a proverb in Russian about them. About how the wind will blow them a man wherever they are."

"We do too, as a matter of fact," said Lyons, suddenly erudite. "Only with us it's a poem."

"That is very interesting. So you are familiar with the problem."

Thatcher made a gesture of impatience. "I expect the Bantus have found it necessary to have a tribal legend on the subject."

"But this could be important," Lyons persisted. "A combination between Yates and this girl would give us just about everything we need."

"Yes, but what do we know?" objected Maseryan. "These two, they have a romantic attachment. It is not a state of affairs that recommends itself to me, no. But it does not make them murderers and thieves. Oh, it is possible, that I admit. So far, Katerina Ivanovna has been lucky. This time, she may have been unfortunate."

"You mean?"

"I mean that she is an attractive young woman with a taste for adventure in these romances of hers. So far she has attracted men who wanted from her the normal, obvious things. But if she attracted one of the other kind, someone who saw in her a very useful accomplice—and Katerina Ivanovna has a top rating as interpreter-translator—someone who could engage her affections, then I do not know what would happen. I would have thought that basically she was too firm-minded, but who can tell with women?"

"We don't have to tell about women in general," said Lyons bluntly. "But isn't it about time that we found out about Miss Ogareva in particular?"

Maseryan frowned. "This is a matter of some delicacy. Part of my mission is to protect our nationals from suspicion by the American police. We would not consent to an interrogation of Katerina Ivanovna by anyone other than a Soviet official. That duty I intend to undertake myself. However, having taken this position, it becomes awkward for the Soviet to urge the American police onto an American citizen. You see what I am driving at? We are not going to get anywhere unless Katerina Ivanovna and your Mr. Yates are both questioned. But I do not think that I can ask you to undertake the second task if I will not surrender to you the first."

"Look," said Lyons with heavy patience, "this has been the problem all along. You people—both of you—want this mess cleared up. You want our help in doing it. But you want to call all the shots. Okay, I'm not objecting right now. I know we've all got problems. But don't think if this turns out to be a joint deal by Yates and his girl friend, that the New York City Police Department is going to sit back and let everybody else carry the ball. Like I said, for now it's all right. It doesn't have to be me that talks to Yates."

Across the room, David Yates rose and instinctively they all turned their faces downward. Yates drew the lady's chair, tossed a bill on the table and began threading his way out behind Katerina Ivanovna. She laughingly said something over her shoulder; with a grin, he reached forward and put a proprietary hand on her elbow.

Katerina Ivanovna was dressed so simply that it could have—and did—pass for elegance in the company of David Yates. They were both obviously bursting with youth, health, and high spirits.

Thatcher heard somebody—he thought it was Maseryan —sigh.

When normal conversation could be resumed, Thatcher was not surprised to have Maseryan and Lyons look meaningfully at him. He had seen this new aspect of their strange international cooperation coming for some time. But his thoughts were elsewhere.

"Yes, yes," he said briefly, "I'll talk to Yates. Although there's very little I can do, if he refuses to discuss the matter with me. But there's something else you said that interests me. You said that he was engaged. Somehow I assumed he was married. Not that he looked married, I grant you."

"No," replied Lyons, "he never has been. We've got some information on him, if you want it." He flourished a small notebook. "Let's see. He's twenty-nine, came to Willard & Climpson a year after he left Yale. Spent the year traveling abroad. His family owns the firm, or a big chunk of it anyway. Has a nice income, both from the firm and a trust fund. About thirty-five thousand a year. He has an apartment on the East Side—one of those expensive, bachelor-service affairs—and a cottage on Fire Island. Got engaged about six months ago to a girl from an old New York family with money of her own. Debutante, charity balls, a society figure. The wedding certainly hasn't been rushed through. There doesn't seem to be any reason for them to wait around. That could be important." He looked at Thatcher. "You remember we were talking about the New Life theory the other day?"

Thatcher shook his head. "I don't agree. It's not surprising the wedding's been delayed if Yates has started this affair with Miss Ogareva. On the contrary, the engagement has made me think David Yates may be totally unimportant in our concerns."

Even so, with Katerina Ivanovna fresh in his mind's eye, he felt rather sorry for that unknown debutante from an old New York family—money of her own, or not.

17

Comin' Through the Rye

ALTHOUGH THATCHER THOUGHT David Yates unimportant, he was nonetheless anxious that the young man prove this to be the case. But his opening move ran into an obstacle he had not anticipated.

"I would like to speak with you, Mr. Yates, about something that's come up," he said into the phone later that afternoon. "If you have time, I could come over to your office right now."

Yates did not hesitate. "Of course, I'd like to help you out, but I'm all tied up right now. Maybe we could get together some time later in the week."

Thatcher frowned slightly. This was the first actor in their drama unprepared to lay everything aside for the pressures of the investigation. To be fair, however, Yates was also the first person encountered who might legitimately consider himself a bystander. Thatcher decided to be more specific.

"I'm sorry to insist," he replied, "but later in the week would be too late. I understand that Miss Ogareva is being questioned now."

There was a lengthy pause. When he resumed speech, Yates sounded harassed. And, as he was speaking to someone else, this was not surprising. "It's all right, Dottie," he said in an audible aside. "This won't hold us up. I'll be with you in a minute, dear. It's just about the wheat shipments." Then he spoke again to the phone:

"Look, Mr. Thatcher, I am busy right now, and will be for the next couple of hours. Could you drop by my apartment about seven-thirty or eight this evening?"

Thatcher agreed at once. But he was far from satisfied when he hung up. It was unfortunate, of course, that Dottie—presumably Yates's fianceé—should have been in his office at the moment of the call.

But why did the young wheat broker want time? Was it simply to shed his fiancée? Or was he going to prime her to corroborate his denial of serious involvement with Katerina Ogareva. He could always admit to a lunch or two on the grounds of business courtesy.

When, later that evening, Thatcher debarked from his taxi in the upper sixties and gave his name to the doorman, he was still uneasy. A discussion of Yates's Russian romance conducted in the presence of Dorothy would not necessarily embarrass Thatcher. He was old enough to make sure that the embarrassment fell elsewhere. But it would cloud the nature of Yates's reactions. And one thing this case could do without was transparent evasion for no purpose other than the demonstration of fidelity.

But Yates was alone when he arrived on the sixteenth floor. Alone and mildly apologetic.

"Hello, Thatcher. Sorry to cut you off the phone that way, but my fiancée was with me. And you can understand, I didn't want to discuss Katerina in front of her."

He took his guest's coat and hat and urged Thatcher to a seat near the glass doors overlooking a terrace and the city lights beyond. From the closet, he spoke over his shoulder:

"I had to squire Dottie to a cocktail party at her parents'. But I managed to leave early."

"I hope I haven't upset your evening," said Thatcher with insincere civility.

"No, you haven't. You also haven't explained why the hell I should talk to you about Katerina. What business is it of yours? You're not even my banker."

Yates was perfectly pleasant, even amused, as he seated himself, but there was a challenging tilt to his eyebrows. Just for a moment the suppressed laughter in his voice, the dancing eye, and the rumpled dark hair made him look very much like Katerina Ogareva. Thatcher could easily understand how they came to be attracted to each other.

"You're telling me that your affairs are none of my business, and indeed they are not. But this theft from the Sloan *is* my business."

Yates merely looked puzzled. "Sure it is, but what's that got to do with my love life?"

"It has been suggested that you and Miss Ogareva, together, would have had no trouble in acquiring the expertise needed for these forgeries. The authorities"—and there, he thought to himself, was a nice ambiguous word to cover the strange alliance he represented—"have had trouble figuring out who could have known both the Russian end and the wheat broker end. Then they stumbled across this partnership of yours. Inevitably the question arose—"

Yates broke in impatiently: "Why in the world should Katie and I run around robbing the Sloan?"

The question was reasonable. Inspector Lyons' answer was not. Nevertheless Thatcher dutifully advanced the detective's hypothesis.

"If your attachment became deeper than you originally contemplated, you might have wanted to run away with each other. A million dollars would come in handy for a new life somewhere."

The laughter was no longer suppressed. Yates roared. "But why?" he sputtered between spasms. Calming down. he continued: "I grant you, we might have decided to get married. But where do you get the running away business? I mean, what's wrong with just getting married and living happily ever after in New York?"

"There is this matter of your other engagement," Thatcher remarked.

"Engagements are broken every day," Yates reminded him. "I don't say there wouldn't be a little embarrassment. But what's that in the face of a grand passion? As a matter of fact, Katie and I haven't considered marriage and, speaking personally, I don't intend to."

Thatcher could only nod. It was the first thought that had occurred to him upon hearing Inspector Lyons' encapsulated biography. He could have pictured a married Yates fleeing with his Katerina. A wife entrenched behind the barricade of domesticity and maternity could make divorce so difficult that a man might well cut and run. But no mere fiancée could be such an impediment.

Conscientiously he continued to play the role of prosecuting attorney. After all, he was here as Inspector Lyons' proxy.

"That would be true if Katerina were American, but she is a Russian."

"So?" challenged Yates. "That wouldn't make any difference, and you know it. What would the Soviet government do? Even if they objected, it would be more in sorrow than in anger. And the U.S. government? They wouldn't refuse to let Katerina become a resident. In fact, the way things are going right now, both governments would probably celebrate the thing as a joyous omen. And it wouldn't make any difference to me. I'm not running for election, I'm not a top-security scientist. Nobody would be interested."

Emotions are fine for the young; eminent bankers are interested in something else.

"There's still the question of a million dollars."

"But I don't need money. And, if I did, Dorothy has plenty waiting around the corner. Anyway, what's a million? Say fifty or fifty-five thousand a year. I'm already in that league, and I'll be doing better in another ten years' time."

At this point Thatcher dismissed David Yates from further consideration. The mind that automatically thinks of a million dollars as a capital sum for prudent investment is not the mind that robs banks and streaks for South American beaches.

Yates, satisfied that he had disposed of any suspicions, moved toward his liquor cabinet. "You'll have a drink, won't you?"

Thatcher absently agreed to a Scotch and water. "It's a shame," he murmured, half to himself. "Collusion between a Russian and an American would solve so many problems."

Yates paid no attention. When he did speak, it was to continue his answer to Thatcher's original accusation.

"The thing is, I'm happy. I even like being a wheat broker. I've done a lot of thinking about my life recently, and I realize how lucky I am. Most of my classmates went into management training programs of some kind. Now they're assistant to an assistant to the assistant division manager. Of course, I know I couldn't have stepped into my spot if my family didn't have connections. But now I've got the spot, I sure as hell am not leaving it. There aren't many operations left where you can be involved in million-dollar deals and still have a small outfit. Willard & Climpson is one of them. There isn't so much goddammed red tape and paper work. Most important of all, we're not cogs. Everybody's still a human being."

Thatcher grunted. What Yates said was true insofar as it concerned himself. But remembering Tessie Marcus' life, as opposed to Miss Corsa's, he doubted if the clerical help at Willard & Climpson enjoyed the high degree of rounded individuality permitted to Yates.

Yates was continuing: "No, if somebody's planning to

skip to Brazil, you want to look for someone with problems. Me, I don't have any problems."

That final declaration would have roused anyone.

"None?" Thatcher inquired genially.

Yates flushed. "You're thinking about my engagement. Look, I don't want you to get the wrong idea about Dorothy. Six months ago I was closer to her than any other person in the world. And, it may seem a funny thing to say, but I think I still am. She's a girl in a million. But the day the ring went on her finger and that damned notice was sent to the papers, I tell you I felt as if someone had dug a deep, cold grave for me."

"Quite a few men feel that way just before they're married," Thatcher said automatically. Usually he had to produce this sentence on the steps of the church.

"It's not the ones who feel it before getting married who worry me. It's all the ones who seem to feel that way afterward," Yates retorted. He rubbed a hand over his hair. "I don't know. Sometimes I think the guys who get into harness when they're twenty-one have got the right idea. Then they never know what they're missing."

"The realization is merely postponed," said Thatcher dryly. "The thought does finally emerge."

But he could not give full rein to his irritation. Much as he disliked being made party to elaborate analyses of marital—or premartial—discontents, he had brought this on himself.

"I suppose so," Yates said, lapsing into gloom. Then, with a sudden burst of frankness: "You know, you tried to make something about Katie and me wanting to get married and running into trouble because she's Russian. I tell you, half the reason I fell for Katerina is that we can pretend it's the Iron Curtain that's keeping us apart. We don't have to think about marriage. Sure, Katie's a damned attractive girl, but the final attraction for me has probably been that I can list her as unattainable. And I wouldn't be surprised if the same thing holds true for her."

Thatcher smiled in spite of himself. He wondered how many hours of self-analysis had been required for young Yates to realize that Katerina Ivanovna was impelled by the same motives as he was. "You think she's just giving way to her sense of adventure?" he asked, recalling Maseryan's phrase.

Yates nodded. "Sure. I doubt if she's ever given a serious thought to me. She's having a good time and she will, for another year or two. We're a lot alike, you know. But when she does settle down, it will be with a good, solid Russian, believe me. Because she's basically just as contented as I am. And I'll bet it won't be a Russian in the foreign service. That was all right for sowing her wild oats. But when she puts the toys on the shelf for good, it will be with an engineer or a doctor in some suburb of Moscow. Just the way it will be Dorothy and Westport for me. We both need a sobering influence. And as for your robbery," he concluded with a rueful grin, "if you want to know, it's been a damned nuisance for Katerina and me. Everything was fine before. Nobody paid much attention to what Katerina was doing off hours. Nowadays they're watching everybody at the consulate like a hawk."

"Aren't you worried about Katerina? I gather you're fond of her."

"Certainly I'm fond of her," Yates said hotly, "but there wasn't anything to be worried about. It never occurred to me that anybody would think of us in terms of the robbery. It's only that with all this surveillance, somebody may catch on to us."

"And that isn't anything to worry about?"

"Not according to Katerina. She says that when they find out, they just transfer you instantly. It happened to her before in Geneva." Yates paused. "They never found out in London."

Thatcher was amused. Katerina Ivanovna was more perceptive—and more enterprising—than Maseryan knew. It was as Yates had said. She was contented. She was young, attractive to men, competent at her work and seeing the world. But it was only a youthful deferral of adult responsibilities. When she did settle down, it would be far from the temptations that might concern a prospective husband in Moscow.

"You've convinced me at any rate, and I doubt if Miss Ogareva will have any more difficulty convincing the Russians," he said at last. "The combination, I confess, always seemed unlikely. But it fitted our requirements so neatly."

For the first time Yates became really interested in Thatcher's problem, rather than his own. "Why is this combination such a good thing? I thought everybody and his little brother knew about the wheat deal."

"In general, yes. But specific knowledge was needed to

carry through the forgeries. It involved both Russian and American documents, you know."

"I don't know anything," Yates declared. "The press just said forged shipping papers. And Luke—Stringfellow, that is—hasn't seemed to want to talk about it much."

Thatcher was glad to have his host's attention. Here was somebody inside the wheat world. Maybe Yates would have some suggestion. Thatcher had forgotten how few people knew all the details of the forgery.

"Perhaps you'd like to look at some of the documents involved. I'd be glad to have your opinion," he said, pleased that he had brought photostats along.

Yates agreed readily, pulling over a table and producing a pair of horn-rims for the inspection. Thatcher left him to his examination and looked around the room. There was none of the impersonality often found in luxury bachelor housing. The service kept the place clean, the furniture polished, the windows washed, but it had not tidied the apartment into sterility. Probably Yates's habits made that impossible.

There was a long cabinet-and-shelf-unit housing a hi-fi apparatus on which records in gay colored jackets were tumbled. The collection would have won the approval of Tessie Marcus and must have pleased the Russian in Katerina Ivanovna. Here were the concerts Katerina had mentioned. No wonder she had blushed! A lively Mexican rug brightened the wall opposite the terrace, and part of Yates's sports equipment had escaped from its assigned quarters. Ski boots and golf balls jostled together on top of a chest.

In a way, all this comfort was a shame. If Yates had not succeeded in making his bachelor quarters so cozy, he would be looking forward to marriage with more enthusiasm. If this building had found a way of providing home-cooked meals, Dorothy might have a long wait.

Yates had finished his inspection. "I don't see anything that socks you in the eye," he admitted. "Of course, I don't know much about the Russian stuff. But I can see how you might think a Russian was involved. The typewriter alone is enough to make you think so."

"The typewriter?" said Thatcher, suddenly alert. He had been awaiting Yates's judgment on the American documents, not expecting anything from the others. "What do you mean by that?"

"It's not easy to get a typewriter with Russian characters. Several times, when the Russians wanted to make changes in some bilingual agreement, they've had to send all the way uptown for the typing to be done."

It was so obvious. Yet no one had mentioned it. Maybe Lyons had not commented because of its obviousness. Maseryan was probably unaware of the difficulties.

Yates was taking back some of what he had said. "Of course, there are Russian typewriters around. NYU once let us use one. But they're hard to come by."

"Anything else?" asked Thatcher.

"I was wondering about the Stringfellow invoice. It's certainly a beautiful forgery. Even uses their abbreviations."

What a mine of information Yates was proving to be, thought Thatcher. Aloud he said: "I thought abbreviations were standardized."

"Well, they are and they aren't. Some things, there are one or two variants, and firms get into the habit of preferring one usage. Here, I've got some of our invoices. I'll show you."

In a few moments he had produced some Willard & Climpson invoices from the corner desk and was proceeding:

"See, we use f.o.b. in lower case. This invoice uses FOB in upper case, without the periods. That, I know, is the way Stringfellow & Son does it. I've noticed it before. And the same thing for 't.' and 's.t.' We abbreviate the word 'ton' and they abbreviate 'short ton,' but we're both using the 2,000-pound ton. Now about this, I don't know," he said, pointing to the destination. "We use periods in 'U.S.S.R.' Some firms omit the periods and write 'USSR.' I don't know what Luke's people do."

The question in Thatcher's mind was not whether Yates knew, but whether the forger knew. Patiently he kept the young man plodding through the invoice, stopping to question each period, each comma, each abbreviation, each formalized use of numbers. By the time the job was done, they had a list of eight points in which the forged invoice differed from Willard & Climpson's usage, three points being marked departures from trade custom.

Now Thatcher was in a hurry to be gone, to disrupt Victor Quentin's evening, to examine genuine Stringfellow invoices. For if the eight points were all duplicated in the Stringfellow file, then the odds that the forgery had emanated from the Stringfellow office became very, very good.

"I can't tell you how helpful you've been," he said, taking a hurried farewell. Yates seemed surprised at the genuine warmth of his guest's thanks.

"Anything I can do to help, you know——" he started, but Thatcher was already impatiently ringing for the elevator. His mind seethed with speculation. Why hadn't Luke Stringfellow pointed this out? Why hadn't the helpful Tessie Marcus? The woman who, according to Lyons, would answer truthfully but would never volunteer information against her employer.

Or was he being too harsh? Was it simply that all invoices looked that way to the workers at Stringfellow & Son? That no question had ever occurred to them?

Harsh or not, three hours later he was uttering a triumphant shout across the desk to a bedraggled, shirt-sleeved Victor Quentin. Open files were strewn over the office.

"Got them, by God!"

All eight points had checked out. Two of them had been used by Stringfellow & Son only once in the past five years.

18

Thrashing It Out

VICTOR · QUENTIN stared at him, and Thatcher beat down a flicker of impatience.

"My God, Victor, don't you see what this must mean? It has to have been a Stringfellow insider . . ."

Quentin shook his head. "No," he said. "The police will still think that anybody who did a lot of business with Stringfellow could have done it . . ."

Thatcher was incisive. "No, Vic," he said, "nobody could have picked up these details from a few invoices. We had to go through five years of files to find them. They just happen to be the way somebody works."

Quentin smiled sourly. "Try convincing Lyons of that," he said.

Thatcher thought for a moment. He had already suggested that Quentin take sick leave, instead of running Commercial Deposits during these trying days—but Quentin, gritting his teeth, had been determined to stick it out. Thatcher understood, and sympathized; the man's resolve to salvage his old life argued forcibly that he was the last person on earth to steal a million dollars for a new life. Still, the strain was showing.

Well, Commercial Deposit's customers would simply have to like it or lump it. Since Commercial Deposit's customers were borrowing money they would, Thatcher knew, lump it.

Wearily Quentin rose and resumed his jacket.

"By the way, John, did anything come from that String-fellow-Baranoff connection?"

When Thatcher shook his head, he shrugged. "All these damned coincidences! I give a check to Baranoff's chauffeur to give to Stringfellow! Stringfellow and Baranoff are doing business! And it's all coincidence—coincidence that's drawing a noose around my neck!"

"No," said Thatcher. "Both of them claim that it was a routine commercial transaction. Their lawyers back them up, naturally. And, for all we know, Vic, it could have been. At any rate, the police had to let Stringfellow go."

"Then I can expect the police first thing in the morning," said Victor Quentin as they were emerging into the darkened lobby to be greeted by the guards and let out into a deserted Wall Street.

Gallows humor, but it was better than none.

But morning did not bring the police for Victor Quentin; nor did it shake Thatcher's strong and growing certainty that only somebody at Stringfellow & Son could have duplicated the Stringfellow invoices with such meticulous fidelity.

This virtually narrowed suspicion to a single point—a single point, moreover, already interrogated and released by the police.

Could trickery explain the Stringfellow invoices?

Could somebody have been gulled into preparing the fraudulent *Odessa Queen* papers in all innocence? Could the Stringfellow insider even now be ignorant of having been a murderer's accomplice?

Deep in these tentative explorations, Thatcher strolled into his office. Miss Corsa, no respecter of executive daydreams, greeted him with a full docket of work. Mr. Trinkam, Mr. Gabler, and Mr. Bowman had all expressed urgent need to confer with their superior.

"Fine!" said Thatcher, who wanted time to think. "Send them all in . . ."

Miss Corsa protested. "I believe they wanted to see you separately."

Thatcher was stern. "Miss Corsa, since I am on twenty-four-hour call by the Department of State, the Russian Embassy, the New York Port Authority, and God knows who else, it is apparent that the only way we can get any business done in this bank is to use the efficiencies of mass production. I didn't watch those assembly lines in Detroit for nothing! It's all of 'em—or none."

He stalked into his office, leaving behind a palpable atmosphere of disapproval. This, in turn, injected a note into Miss Corsa's voice that was immediately identified by the secretaries of Messrs. Trinkam, Gabler, and Bowman. Thus, when they converged on Thatcher's office, they were prepared to tread warily. The most explicit channels of communication at such institutions as the Sloan Guaranty Trust do not rely upon mere words. Charlie Trinkam, tuning his ebullience low, reported quickly and succinctly on new and unwelcome developments in some Sloan-held securities.

"What do you know about it, Walter?" Thatcher demanded.

His big, comfortable chief of research was not the man to break under fire.

"Not a damned thing!" he replied forthrightly.

With the cameraderie born of common misfortune, Everett Gabler turned the discussion; he had spotted an accounting irregularity in the annual report of a New England electronics firm. He wanted to summon the lawyers. He, too, could stick to his guns.

"We'll have to think that over," said Thatcher shortly. "At the moment, let's put it on ice."

His subordinates, being no fools, neither pressed their issues nor tried to prolong this session.

". . . so, if you'll just sign that Angleworth estimate, John," said Trinkam, "I'll put Nicolls onto it."

"Send it up," said Thatcher.

His staff was departing, faces carefully composed to conceal relief, when Walter Bowman felt the call of disinterested duty which frequently afflicts the conscientious professional.

"Oh, John . . ."

Thatcher, already deep in a file Gabler had left, looked).

"I heard a rumor you might be interested in," Bowman id. "Down at the Travel Analysts Association, they're ying that Halloran's Garage is up for sale . . ."

"What?" Thatcher was jolted out of his bad temper.

Bowman was too experienced to reveal satisfaction.

"Ev here told me that that Halloran woman was involved the robbery. Just thought you might want to know."

Before Thatcher could demand particulars, Bowman rried on.

"I picked this up an hour or so ago. I've put Phil Neale to it. As soon as I get more info, I'll shoot it up to u . . ."

With this, Bowman lumbered off, feeling, quite rightly, at he had handled the Thatcher storm perhaps more droitly than his colleagues.

They were in the corridor outside Thatcher's office when ey saw a new Christian heading for the lion.

Charlie Trinkam summed up. "Poor bastard."

But, as he settled across from Thatcher's desk, Mik-ail Maseryan was met with a different kind of impatience. hatcher was eager to compare notes with him. An in-rnal metronome had started to race; Thatcher knew at solution of the murder was in sight, if not within asp.

Why the enigmatic Mrs. Halloran was pulling up stakes as not instantly apparent to him, but it added to Thatch-'s conviction that things were, in some way, breaking.

Now he studied his visitor. There was, he noted, a cer-in weariness about Maseryan.

"I came down," said Maseryan. "It seemed easier. At the onsulate our friend, Comrade Capitalist, is talking about ringing Russian horses to race at your Aqueduct—is that ght?—so there is no peace."

Thatcher interpreted this without difficulty. Abe Bara-off had taken possession of the Russian Consulate, his out-ders rushing in and out with important messages, or surping other people's secretaries. As Maseryan said, o peace.

". . . so, I thought it best to come to you," Maseryan ontinued. "I have talked to Katerina Ivanovna. I have gain looked at that forged seal. I have studied these consular forms again. And I have looked for a Russian typewriter . . ."

The grim cadence in Maseryan's voice puzzled Thatcher. However, he was not letting anybody else claim monopoly on dogwork.

"I interviewed David Yates last night," he said, frowning slightly.

"Yates?" said Maseryan. His eyes became bleaker than ever. "Ah . . . Yates."

This dredging up of a name from the ocean deeps of memory nettled Thatcher, since it was the real possibility of criminal, as opposed to amorous, alliance between Katerina Ivanovna Ogareva and David Yates that had sent Thatcher to Yates's apartment and those interesting insights into life and love among the young.

Maseryan, however, was retreating into Russian melancholia and spoke, almost to himself:

"It can be no other way. It was someone at the Soviet Consulate. Who else knows these formulations for certificates? And"—his voice dropped heavily—"who else can find a Russian typewriter?"

These ruminations testified that Russian dramatists were not exaggerating when they put speeches into the mouths of their soul-tormented heroes. Thatcher was interested to note that, despite his abundant misery, Maseryan had not failed to register the point made by David Yates—it is difficult to locate a Russian typewriter in New York City.

Thatcher smiled slightly, which set Maseryan off again.

"Does it please you to learn that the criminal is Russian? Oh, unworthy . . ."

"We bankers," Thatcher retorted, "are scrupulously non-ideological." There was no point in trying to out-Jeremiah Maseryan. "I take it your research has more or less duplicated mine."

With economy, he described his interview with young Yates. The details of the relationship between Yates and Katerina produced a head shaking.

"Precisely what she told me," said Maseryan. "She called it only a passing friendship. I fear little Ogareva is falling into very unfortunate patterns. It must be back to Moscow for her."

Thatcher relayed David Yates's opinion that Katerina Ivanovna was destined to end up in the Soviet equivalent of Westport.

"Ah, he is not such a fool, that young man," said Maryan. "I myself think that . . . but, no. These young people are incidental. The important part is what you have learned about the Stringfellow invoices."

Thatcher repeated his findings. There could be no doubt that the extreme accuracy of the duplication of the Stringfellow procedures pointed inescapably to a Stringfellow insider.

With an oath, Maseryan slammed a heavy hand on Thatcher's desk.

"How can it be? It was assuredly someone who knows the Soviet consul's forms. Only a Russian . . ."

"And I say it was someone from Stringfellow," Thatcher persisted. "Now look here. It was, after all, the possibility of a Russian-American conspiracy that set us off after Yates and this girl of yours. Although if David Yates had anything to do with it, I'll eat my hat . . ."

Thatcher was just hitting his stride when Miss Corsa cast routine to the wind and buzzed him. Fighting a feeling that he was a whale surrounded by minnows, Thatcher demanded enlightenment.

"It's Mr. Withers on the phone," Miss Corsa reported.

Not even the president of the Sloan Guaranty Trust was enough for Thatcher in his present mood.

"From Katmandu?" he demanded.

"From Rome," said Miss Corsa impassively. "He wants to talk to you about bringing back a new Alfa Romeo to be used as the bank's car . . ."

The frustrations of a frustrating morning came to a boil.

"Tell him I've left for Alaska!" Thatcher snarled. "Tell him he can bring in a dozen matched Rolls-Royces, for all I care! Tell him . . ."

Pointedly, for she too was having a trying day, Miss Corsa left the switch down so that Mr. Thatcher could hear his message relayed:

"Mr. Thatcher suggests that you contact Mr. Brady when you get to Paris about the customs forms . . ."

Abruptly he switched off. Automatically he began to describe Walter Bowman's hint about Rita Halloran, before suddenly snapping his fingers.

"That call!" he said.

Mikhail Maseryan was courtesy itself. "I am impressed. Alfa Romeos, Rolls Royces—like so many potatoes. It is capitalistic exploitation, no doubt—but I do not deny that it is impressive."

Again Thatcher smiled. "It may well be capitalistic exploitation—but it is also the solution to our murder!"

19

Reaping the Whirlwind

"WHAT DO YOU MEAN?" Maseryan demanded.

John Putnam Thatcher was not smiling now; instead he somberly paused to marshal the facts that damned two criminals. This mental review uncovered no loopholes, no further unknowns. His argument, when he began to speak, was as logical and complete as any report he submitted to the Investment Committee.

For a full five minutes Maseryan listened without interrupting, his eyes narrowed as Thatcher moved from link to link along the chain of robbery and murder.

"It was Miss Corsa's call just now that made me see it," said Thatcher in conclusion. The facts he had described were irrefutable, and depressing. "I don't know whether or not I should tell her that she showed me how the whole scheme was arranged."

"No," said Maseryan absently. "Perhaps it would not be conducive to high office morale."

They fell silent. In Thatcher's outer office, Miss Corsa was typing, blissfully unaware that she had just demonstrated exactly how to weave an intricate pattern of crime.

"You are right," said Maseryan with heavy finality. "You explain everything—first the robbery, then the murder. And they are the only ones who could have done it. But"—he made an angry gesture—"but now, our clever murderers will wait for a week, then disappear with a million dollars!"

"A week, or a month," Thatcher amended. "They're very careful and prudent, remember. But even if knowledge is power, I'm not sure where this leads us. There isn't any indictable evidence here—the murder took care of

hat. And I confess I don't look forward to the prospect
of waiting for weeks or months."

Maseryan smiled in an exceptionally ferocious manner.

"Waiting? No, I am not by nature a patient man. As I
have said, my friend, we are a good team. You have seen
now these crimes were committed—yes, I am convinced
hat you are right. Now I will play my part. I will make
he criminals condemn themselves. That we Russians know
now to do."

Thatcher's heart sank as Maseryan spoke. It was true
hat his own reconstruction of the crime was no more than
ingenious hypothesis, without the support of hard evidence. On the other hand, Russian methods concerning
self-incrimination, although undeniably effective in their
sphere, were inadmissible here. Or, so the Supreme Court
kept saying. He was casting around for a way to express
his when Maseryan forestalled—and relieved—him.

"We will bait a trap for them!"

Cautiously Thatcher projected skepticism.

Maseryan hitched himself forward. "Let me explain."

After hearing him out, Thatcher made the only comment suitable under the circumstances.

"Oh my God!"

In later days, he was to maintain that, had he been given
any choice, he would—at that moment and subsequently
—have opted to write off the Sloan's $985,000 to experi-
ence and leave the miscreants free to enjoy their ill-gotten
gains. Moreover, as he never failed to point out, as things
turned out, he would have been saving the Sloan money.

But the choice was not to be his. The prospect of de-
finitive action exhilarated Maseryan. He was bulldozing
ahead with zest.

"Theoretically it could work," Thatcher finally conceded.

"It *will* work," Maseryan assured him. "But to make it
work, we must bait the trap. There are arrangements to
be made . . ."

Unfortunately, these arrangements involved sovereign
nations and major financial policies; they further involved
four full days. And, indispensably, John Putnam Thatcher's
cooperation.

Maseryan had barely left his office before Thatcher set to
work. The whole Russian-American Trade Treaty had

triggered extravaganza after extravaganza already; what did one more matter?

His first telephone call was to George C. Lancer. Lancer listened to Thatcher's terse recital, squared his already square jaw, and said, "Good work, John. I'll get the Ambassador on the phone . . ."

This in turn was followed by further telephone calls, and inevitably conferences with: the director general of the International Monetary Fund; His Excellency, Manuel Ribiera y Ribiera, Minister of the Treasury of the Republic of Mexico; Otis Hammer (of the Wall Street exchange specialists Hammer & Hammer); three men from the U.S. Treasury; and platoons of underlings.

The result of this activity, and of certain powerful arguments advanced jointly by the governments of the United States of America and the Union of Soviet Socialist Republics, finally budged rigid Hispanic ideas of national dignity.

"But of course," said Señor Ribiera with the feline grace that had not deserted him even when Baker, from the Federal Reserve, broke down and wept. "But of course, if it is within the province of the Ministry of Finance of the Republic of Mexico to cooperate with our great friends, the United States of America and the Soviet Union—we are most happy to do so." But Señor Ribiera y Ribiera had, to put it bluntly, been leaned on. He wanted his pound of flesh. "Permit me to say, furthermore, how happy my country is to witness this eager cooperation between two great nations . . ."

He allowed himself to embroider this theme. Across the table assorted U.S. and Russian officials glared at him. Thatcher pointedly averted his eyes and studied the dour features of a portrait on the wall. He, at least, was willing to pay the price of listening to a lecture; he had got what he wanted.

This was a small notice in the financial press.

Tessie Marcus called it to Luke Stringfellow's attention the next morning. In her flat, matter-of-fact way she had spent a good part of the morning advancing small pieces of information like this toward him, trying to spark some interest, to revive the Luke Stringfellow she had known. The silent, brooding giant slumped in his chair, listlessly watching clouds through the window, disturbed and rather frightened her.

Without interest, Luke Stringfellow took the newspaper he handed him and obediently read, " 'The Ministry of Finance of the Republic of Mexico, having been advised of certain defects in series four of its 1979 50,000 peso bearer bonds (A8273 to TC 9483) hereby recalls such bonds. Holders may present them for redemption or exchange at any Mexican bank within the week. Thereafter such bonds may be redeemed only at the Ministry of Finance.' . . . yeah. So what, Tessie?"

She fought a temptation to shout at him to be a man, to hold up his head, to show some pride.

"Don't you see it's a trap, Luke?" she said harshly, and only an intimate would have realized that she was pleading with him. "Lyons tried to get you this morning. He said they've traced that Sloan money to Mexican bearer bonds! And now they're calling them in! That means that the thieves are going to have to cash them in Mexico within the week. Otherwise they'll be stuck for years and years."

He looked at her dully, and she broke off. "For Crissake, Luke!" she snarled. "This means that maybe they'll clear everything up! Don't you see what that means?"

Stringfellow swivelled to stare out the window again.

"If they catch them," he said. His voice sounded distant.

Tessie Marcus slammed a desk drawer viciously.

Katerina Ivanovna Ogareva, looking woebegone, listened while Durnovo and Voronin discussed the item.

"It is clear enough," said Durnovo with a revival of his superb condescension. "Mikhail Mikhailich tells me that this will cause the criminals to panic. But I tell you that —had I been asked, which I was not—I would have pointed out that this will not work."

He paused. Voronin exchanged a quick look with Katerina, then dutifully asked:

"Precisely why will it not work?"

Durnovo expanded. "Because the criminals have already cashed these bonds! Already they are far away . . ."

He developed this theme at length, before departing to his own office.

Voronin frowned. Then, although he regretted having to do so, he asked a personal question. "What is the matter, Katerina Ivanovna?" His voice was low, troubled.

For a moment her eyes were bright with unshed tears. 'I thought you must know. They have recalled me."

In his heart of hearts Voronin had known that this was inevitable. Nevertheless he looked at her with comprehension and worry. There was little comfort he could offer. Helplessly he said, "It could be worse."

Her voice grew hard as she stood up and prepared to leave. "Yes. It could be much worse."

Joe Kiley's telephone call came just after Rita Halloran finished a long talk with Phil about a dented Rolls Royce fender. It found her in a salty mood.

"No, I don't read the financial pages . . . well, what does that mean?"

Kiley was not put off by her tone.

"It means that they're closing in," he said with the authority of someone with good police contacts. Still choosing his words carefully, he continued, "I think it's a trap, Rita . . ."

Keeping one eye on the work she could inspect through the hatchway, she listened. "Yes, I'm still here . . . well, Joe, that's their problem. When are you going to have those papers done? I'm in a hurry."

Kiley was unhappy. "You're rushing this through awfully fast, Rita. Are you sure you want to sell?"

"It was your idea," she snapped. "Now that I've made up my mind, I don't want to hang around waiting longer than this week."

Kiley forced himself to ask another question.

"What are you going to do?"

"Travel," she said grimly.

There was a long pause.

"Well then," said her old friend and lawyer, "just remember, Rita, the world's a mighty small place these days!"

David Yates read the financial pages because he read the entire paper every morning, not as a prelude to work but as an integral part of it. Secretaries and accountants at Willard & Climpson were not allowed to indulge themselves this way, but read the morning paper at breakfast, on the subway, anywhere—so long as it was on their own time. Young Mr. Yates, however, was a partner, and the morning paper was part of a long-established ritual.

His pleasant features gave no hint that his thoughts were racing furiously even as he read an editorial about Albany, even as he read the obituaries of New Jersey dentists, even as he read about Mexican bearer bonds. But David Yates, who was not given to introspection, was thinking, as indeed he had been thinking since John Thatcher's descent on his apartment. Finally he put down the paper, drummed his fingers on the desk in a final moment of indecisiveness. Then he reached for the phone:

"Dottie? . . . oh, I'm sorry, I thought you'd be up . . . yes. Listen, Dottie, I've been thinking . . . yes . . . we ought to set a date . . . soon. Yes, Dottie, I know that it's eleven o'clock in the morning . . ."

"Weinstein! Did you see the *Journal?*"

Weinstein moved the receiver several inches from his ear and acknowledged that he had.

"I've got to see you right away! Do you understand?"

Weinstein did.

"That's going to flutter a lot of dovecotes," said Walter Bowman when he inspected the notice in the morning papers.

Thatcher, who had put in virtually eighteen unbroken hours of negotiation to achieve that notice, evinced no sympathy for those members of society who require numbered accounts for bearer bonds for their assets.

"Those dovecotes, Walter, can take good care of themselves."

"I agree," said Bowman. "You don't catch me crying for the Mafia. Or for tax evaders either, for that matter. And just how in the hell did you get Mexico to go along?"

This was a question that was going to be asked in many quarters when the full story came out, Thatcher reflected. The answer, however, must not leave the confines of the Sloan. Happily, Señor Ribiera y Ribiera was not likely to make any statements on the subject.

"The United States is helping out with a desalinization project off Yucatan. The U.S.S.R. is building a dam . . ."

"And the Sloan?" asked Bowman, incorrigibly parochial.

Thatcher was resigned. "I expect that we're investing in low-income housing near Acapulco . . ."

Bowman did some mental arithmetic. "Adds up to eighteen or twenty million—to get back $985,000," he commented.

"This proposition," said Thatcher with genuine weariness, "has become strictly noncommercial."

It was easier to say what the proposition was not than what it was. Enormous efforts were being made, but

Thatcher was not sure to what end. His own travails, however acute, were comprehensible; unwillingly, he had started out to retrieve the Sloan's money. The low-income housing in Acapulco simply testified that once again he had underestimated high-mindedness, public responsibility, and a number of other attributes of which he had become heartily sick. Why the Russians were building a dam he would never understand.

"So," Bowman summed up, "the criminals can trade the bonds in Mexico for the next couple of days pretty freely. After that, there'll be a lot of questions when they try to get their money. Right?"

"Right," said Thatcher.

"Well, I understand that much," said Bowman. "But how do you think you're going to catch them before they break and run?"

"That," said Thatcher, "is Maseryan's problem. He and Lyons have been thick as thieves this last two days. Presumably they're hatching an elaborate system to trap these poor fools. But exactly what it is I don't know."

At this very moment, Miss Corsa buzzed.

Flags fluttered in a cold wind. A dull gray sky sneered at the efforts of men and nations to make galas in the Northern Hemisphere before summer came. The men and nations persisted and, currently, gleaming limousines bearing high U.S. and Russian officials were proclaiming an event. This time, however, there were no potato chips in the offing. The site was Kennedy International Airport, and photographers were immortalizing yet another historic step in the Russian-American rapprochement by snapping shots of important men and women ducking into the great terminal.

There were even pickets; these hurried-up arrangements had caught Hungarians, Ukrainians, and the American Legion short; not so the enraged citizenry of Jamaica, Long Island, up in arms about jet noise.

"Let the Reds Keep Their Jets Home!" screamed a sign borne by Mrs. Barbara Benbine, present, indignant, and the mother of two cold infants.

For the occasion of this latest gathering of luminaries was the expected arrival, at any minute, of the mighty Ilyushin-62. Aboard would be Vladimir Lusklov, deputy premier of the U.S.S.R., plus thirty-two leaders of high-achievement Stakhanovite stations.

This august party was being welcomed to the new world by the Vice President, the U.S. Secretary of Agriculture, the President of the American Farm Bureau Association, and the president of the Farmers Union.

(Which proved, Thatcher reminded himself as he moved out of the path of a large congressional party from wheat-producing states, that Maseryan had considerable power and authority indeed; what explained the presence of the Vice President, he refused to contemplate.)

On hand with political, commercial, fraternal, and professional greetings was a very large cast. There at the desk, handsome in a mink stole and cream wool liberally bedecked with diamond clips, was Alice Stringfellow. Beside her, Luke Stringfellow smiled at a representative of the Food and Agriculture Organization. Dark shadows under his eyes attested to his recent ordeal. But he was still out of jail, and perhaps that was enough for Luke Stringfellow at the moment.

As Thatcher looked on (and made no move to near this part of the throng), David Yates pushed through a group of Indian economists to join the Stringfellows. He was glancing impatiently at his wrist watch. The Ilyushin was ten minutes late; Maseryan, nowhere in evidence, had probably arranged that as well. Already a certain impatience was stirring the huge crowd that was milling around the airport's angular waiting room; cigarettes were being smoked, then stubbed out too quickly. Small groups were forming and reforming in a minuet of polite restlessness.

For two criminals, the minutes must be dragging.

Yates, however, looked suitably grave and untroubled. The picture, in fact, of the solid young businessman.

Was his mind exclusively on the business of selling wheat to Russia, Thatcher wondered?

Over intervening heads he could see the Russian delegation stationed in ranks near the corridor, ready to greet their distinguished compatriots. They showed the slightly embarrassed, forced geniality that characterizes welcoming parties. Behind the head of the United Nations delegation, Thatcher thought he saw Durnovo. Far behind him, in the midst of a less orderly group of lower officials, he noticed Feodor Voronin stepping aside to allow an airline official to pass.

There was no sign of Katerina Ivanovna Ogareva.

Thatcher sighed. Wherever she was, he hoped she could still smile.

"Flight twenty-six, American Airlines Astrojet to San Francisco, is ready for departure . . ." The disembodied voice intoned, barely audible over the steadily rising din. din.

Thatcher shifted slightly as the Mayor of New York strode into the terminal accompanied by four uniformed policemen. The other policemen present, Thatcher knew, were decorously disguised as farm economists.

"Great day for the city of New York . . ."

"Great day for Soviet-American friendship . . ."

"United Airlines Flight two oh one, non-stop to St. Paul . . ."

In the mounting uproar, Abe Baranoff had managed to corner a reporter and was busy telling him something. The crush, however, hampered his style; he could brandish neither arms nor cane.

The Ilyushin was now eighteen minutes late, and even the vast confines of Kennedy International Airport began to take on that tattered look that a large mass of impatient people impart—smoke hazing the air, crumpled cigarette packages littering modernistic furniture. Some of the waiting throng even abandoned their postures of spurious eagerness and rested briefly. With increasing desperation, official told official that it was a great day.

Finally the hum of private conversations was stilled, the thousand fidgetings and stirrings were frozen. Triumphantly the loudspeaker spoke:

"The Ilyushin-62, non-stop from Moscow, has just landed on runway six and will be unloading . . ."

Thatcher watched the quick return of party manners as Russians, Americans, wheat dealers, policemen straightened ties, smiled brightly, and began slowly seeping toward action stations. From somewhere, two little girls with baskets of flowers were produced and ruthlessly shoved ahead of the Russian delegation, the Mayor and three directors of the Kansas Cooperative Council.

This was John Putnam Thatcher's signal. If those long hours of debate with Señor Ribiera y Ribiera had any meaning, now was when he would find out. He turned and began to walk down the nearby corridor that snaked away from the main terminal. Each step that bore him away from the subdued roar of the official party rang louder and louder as he hurried on. With only its normal quota of bona fide travelers, the corridor managed to impart an illusion of emptiness.

But unless Mikhail Maseryan and Inspector Lyons had made grievous blunders, Thatcher was but minutes behind another member of the official welcoming party— a member who had slipped away earlier.

He turned a handsomely paneled corner and glanced at his watch. It was all a matter of seconds now. The Ilyushin-62 had set down precisely on schedule; not, to be sure, the schedule of the airline or Kennedy International Airport, but a schedule, all right, that was tight as a drum. Elaborate calculations had produced a kind of certainty, in some minds at least; the Ilyushin-62 was coming in just as a Panagra Turboprop took off for Mexico.

But at the desk a man was hurriedly stuffing tickets into a pocket, the tension of his stance identifying him as late, hurrying to catch his plane.

As Thatcher stood at the door watching, Mikhail Maseryan appeared on cue from the office near the counter and moved swiftly to block the way to the loading gate. The tardy passenger snatched up his bag and swiveled to take the last steps toward freedom.

He saw Maseryan—and was turned to stone.

Despite the blank, familiar ticketing clerks, the gay travel posters, the sudden eruption of two small children with blue flight bags from a neary bank of leather sofas, the scene was chillingly stripped of the commonplace.

"Hurry up! They've called . . . Oh God!"

It was a cry Thatcher would never forget. Tessie Marcus was half running as she appeared under the sign pointing to Gate 7. For a moment she stood rooted in horror, until Inspector Lyons appeared behind her. As he put a hand on her elbow, she gave a compulsive shudder and broke into agonized sobbing.

Mikhail Maseryan had not looked up at her cry. Nor did his face have the involuntary pity that Thatcher could see in Lyons'. Maseryan looked darkly implacable as he slowly approached his motionless quarry.

Feodor Voronin's face remained carefully, painfully blank.

20

In Clover

ONCE AGAIN Kennedy Airport was en fête. The Soviet dignitaries who had arrived only the week before were now returning home in a blaze of glory. Their short stay had seen the recovery of the Sloan funds, new hopes for the Big Thaw, and the completion of yet another trade treaty promising further grain shipments in exchange for platinum and bauxite. Sweet harmony was everywhere. American operatic companies, Soviet track teams, Intourist bus drivers, and New York longshoremen had all returned to duty amidst pledges of undying fraternal affection.

The Ilyushin-62 was waiting to fly the distinguished visitors back to the Soviet Union. Its silver flanks glistened in the brilliant sunshine under a clear blue sky. Fountains tossed feathery spume in the breeze, brass bands stood ready to launch triumphal refrains, and throngs of spectators lined the roadways. The whole world seemed to have joined hands in a giant *entente cordiale*. Nothing marred the occasion. True, the Ukrainians were still dissenting but, as their nationalist purism prohibited the expression of their views in any language other than Old Ukrainian, they could not hope to find an appreciable audience.

While joy and amity reigned supreme on the field itself, John Putnam Thatcher was lurking with his companions in the shadows by the Air France loading gates. He had been lurking steadily now for seven days. His successful excision of a malign international growth had produced hysterical gratitude from Washington and Moscow which, to Thatcher's mind, bordered the pathological. The Soviet government wanted to give him the Order of Lenin. The State Department wanted to arrange a solemn presentation ceremony in the Rotunda of the Capitol.

And Abe Baranoff had offered to handle him.

Even worse, George Lancer, apparently brainwashed by his recent experiences into viewing the Sloan Guaranty

Trust as an extension of the World Court, had been receptive to this appalling proposal. ("Naturally I don't want to twist your arm, John, but think what it would do for our image!")

Long ago Thatcher had learned that you can't twist the arm of a man who isn't there. Accordingly, he had decided to remain on the move until the departure of the Soviet deputy premier effectively removed all threat of dramatic galas with himself in a leading role.

But deliverance was at hand. Another hour and the peril would be over. He had broken out of his solitary haunts to pay farewell respects to Mikhail Maseryan. It was Maseryan who had arranged this rendezvous. Now four men stood in the shadowy corner. Thatcher was supported by Victor Quentin and Everett Gabler.

It was a new Victor Quentin. The apprehension of the culprits and the return of the missing $985,000 had trimmed twenty years from his face. Relief was already giving way to curiosity.

"Tessie Marcus! Of all people!" he exclaimed. "I've worked with that woman for over ten years, and I could have sworn she didn't have a thought outside her job at Stringfellow's."

"It would have been healthier if she had," Thatcher replied. "That was one of the troubles."

Everett Gabler, whose life was filled very satisfactorily by Rails and Industrials, was unprepared to let the conversation stray into undesirable generalities. "But what made you suspect her?"

"Looking back, I find it incredible that we didn't spot it sooner. But I suppose you could say that light began to break when Maseryan, here, proved conclusively that the criminal had to be a Russian, and I proved it had to be someone at Stringfellow."

Quentin blinked. He was a slow, thoughtful man. Flights of fancy were not up his alley. "I don't see how you could do that."

"The forgeries were too good."

The old bitterness momentarily reappeared on Quentin's face. "They certainly were. They fooled me completely."

"If you will forgive me," Maseryan interrupted, "that should not have been too difficult. You had never seen Russian documents like these. Nobody in New York had. Much less accurate forgeries would have sufficed. Only the absence of the Consul's signature and seal betrayed them. How then was the thief able to produce certificates prepared exactly as the consulate would do them? When there were no previous papers to copy from? The answer was obvious. They were forged by someone familiar with this type of documentation, from his work with a Soviet trade delegation in another country. Hence a member of the Soviet staff."

Quentin nodded slowly. To Everett Gabler the whole thing was clear as day. This was what came of shifting people around the world willy-nilly. You didn't find the Sloan acting that way.

Thatcher took up the story. "But none of the Soviet officials was an old hand in New York. They were all comparative newcomers, brought over within the last year or two. And the criminal had to be someone from the New York wheat world, who knew exactly how you worked, Victor. The critical period in the entire crime was the interval during which you were examining the shipping papers and releasing the check. You had been conditioned for over a week to act exactly the way you did. On top of that, the same observations could be made about the Stringfellow papers that were made about the Russian ones. Where there was nothing to copy from, still the forger went ahead and produced an invoice exactly the way Stringfellow's office would have done it. Inevitably, we were forced to think in terms of collaboration between a Russian and an American."

"But how could you narrow things down any further? Theoretically, any combination of two people would have been possible." Gabler's normal testiness had been mellowed by the Sloan's recovery of the loot. Personal outrage no longer underlined his every reference to the robbery.

Thatcher shook his head.

"Theoretically, perhaps. But actually, no. Try to imagine an American wheat broker and a Soviet official first suggesting a million-dollar theft to each other. Think of Yates and Durnovo, for instance. It simply doesn't stand up. Total strangers don't make that kind of suggestion to each other. There has to be some sort of intimacy first, some grounds for thinking the proposal will be acceptable."

"And life being what it is, the intimacy would be between a man and a woman." Maseryan was nodding like a

andarin sage. "We have had some experience with
e intimacies of Soviet personnel abroad, and that is al-
ys how trouble starts. A man and a woman."

Gabler snorted. "Not just with Soviet personnel!"

"We had no trouble getting that far," continued Thatch-
"That's why we were so attracted by the possibilities
the situation between Yates and Miss Ogareva. But
en that didn't stand up, we were at a loss. We've all
en so indoctrinated with the myth of young love, that
e didn't think in terms of a woman of thirty-eight
d a man of forty-seven. If I had paid more attention to
e realities of life, I would have been thinking along
e right track as soon as I talked with Yates."

"But you redeemed yourself nobly, my friend," said
aseryan generously. "Your insight was positively bril-
nt."

"What insight?" Quentin demanded. "That's what I want
know. What made you zero in?"

Thatcher leaned against the building to collect his
oughts. "All along I was bothered by the luck our crim-
als had. Stringfellow's calls alerting the Sloan, String-
llow's absence in Jersey on the critical day, Stringfel-
w's contemplated land purchase being brought to our
tention so that a delivery at the Registry of Deeds was
aonable. That's what I meant about conditioning you,
ctor."

Quentin was no longer unnerved by references to his
nocent but vital role in the fraud. He was moved to
ter an objection.

"But we proved that an outsider could have found out
out these things."

"Finding out wasn't enough. This robbery was planned
onths in advance. The criminal's problem wasn't finding
t himself. It was making sure these things happened—
d that you, at the Sloan, knew about them. The timing of
ringfellow's movements and the timing of the *Odessa
ueen* were interlocked. It looked almost as if the crim-
als had to be moving Luke Stringfellow around, arrang-
g his calls and his trips. All that was explained if
ringfellow were the guilty man. Indeed, the suspicion
s reinforced by the exceptionally tense atmosphere at
ringfellow & Son after the theft, when they hadn't lost a
nt. It didn't seem possible that it could be anyone else.
nd then I asked Miss Corsa to make a call for me."

Gabler's mellowness had its limits.

"Well?" he demanded impatiently. "That's what she
there for. To make your calls."

"Exactly. But I told her to say one thing and sh
quite properly, said another. To be honest, I told her
tell Withers that I'd left for Alaska, and she translate
that into some acceptable message. If anybody had aske
me four days later, I would have immediately agreed th
I told her to give *her* message to Withers. And Withe
would have said that he got that message from me. W
both think of Miss Corsa as my alter ego. But it starte
my thoughts along a certain path. Who makes calls fo
me? Who arranges my appointments? Who can make a
solutely sure that at a certain moment I will be at th
aquarium meeting Abe Baranoff? Who, in short, can pu
me around the board like a chess piece?"

He received an unexpected reply.

"It is a great mistake, my friend, to allow yourself to l
managed by a woman," said Maseryan broodingly. "Yo
should assert your authority."

Thatcher snorted politely. It was all very well for M
seryan to talk big, here safe in Kennedy Airport. In h
only face-to-face encounter with Miss Corsa, the Russia
had been mild as milk. Thatcher was ready to swear th
somewhere in the Kremlin, or wherever Maseryan mai
tained his office, there was a soft-voiced, strong-minde
young woman named Ludmilla who saw to it that Comra
Maseryan toed the line.

"Never mind that," he said diplomatically. "All th
made me think of Tessie Marcus in a new light. We a
agreed that it was unfortunate the last call to Quentin b
fore the forgery gave him the impression that the *Odes
Queen* papers would be delivered any minute, instead
any day. Stringfellow adopted the language of the call u
hesitantly. But actually the call had been made by Tessi
She could twist it to leave any impression she wante
And she could easily arrange her superior's movements
suit herself. Finally, the atmosphere at Stringfellow & S
could result from her tension, rather than Luke Strin
fellow's. Anybody who doubts that simply has to visit n
office when Miss Corsa is displeased."

Quentin still had difficulty with the outlines of the pl
"I see all that. But how in the world did you move on,
her liaison with Voronin?"

"That was the easiest of all," said Thatcher sadl
"That's why I should have listened to Yates. He told n

at happy people do not rob and murder to start a new
fe. And he was right, of course. But a simple examina-
on of the records eliminated quite a few people. Compare
oronin and Durnovo, for instance. Durnovo is the clas-
c example of a man on his way up. Every year has seen
a improvement in his position. Before the robbery, he
ad clear sailing for a brilliant future. Voronin was ex-
ctly the reverse—brilliant beginnings petering out into
ediocrity. A war hero, a top student, then downhill. That
ight have meant nothing by itself, but his personal life
ad become equally unsatisfactory. First he lost his wife,
en his daughter got married and left him alone to
ove to a strange city. Tessie Marcus' mother had died two
ears ago, leaving her to solitude. They were both prob-
ly very unhappy. They had been working with each
her on these wheat shipments for over a year. What
ore natural than that two lonely people should come to-
ether?"

"Have they spoken of this at all?" asked Maseryan. He
ad lost touch with the criminals after their arrest. Voro-
n's diplomatic immunity had been waived by the Soviet
nion; he was now imprisoned in New York, under a
arge of first-degree murder.

Thatcher's information was more recent, and he was
le to reply.

"Yes. Tessie Marcus has told Lyons all about it. She's
ot the least bit remorseful. She says she'd do it again if
e had the chance. She and Voronin met quite acci-
entally at a concert one evening almost a year ago. You
ere right about all that music being a link. They had
offee together afterward. Within a month, they were
ving together. Within two months, they had decided they
ouldn't live without each other. It's a great mistake to
ink it's the young who take their love affairs seriously.
eople like Miss Ogareva and Yates still have the illusion
inexhaustible time and opportunity. And it's not such
a illusion. Yates can find himself a new attachment any
ay. Katerina Ivanovna knows very well that she has
ly to lift a finger to bring a man to her side. It's the
iddle-aged, the lonely, the failures, who bring the edge
desperation to their relationships. As far as Voronin and
ssie Marcus were concerned, this was their one, their
ly chance to seize happiness."

Everett Gabler was markedly unsympathetic. "That may
plain why they persisted in an improper relationship,"

he said stiffly. "It does not explain why they found i necessary to rob the Sloan of a million dollars."

"Ah, you are not acquainted with Feodor Voronin's rec ord," Maseryan interjected. "He was what you might call a perpetual assistant, constantly being moved from country to country, whenever there was need for extra personnel."

Thatcher had a vivid collection of the first time he had seen Voronin on the *Odessa Queen,* sitting modestly with drawn from Captain Kurnatovsky's convivial circle; then later at the consulate hovering deferentially at Durnovo's elbow. After twenty years of being the deferential assistant a man begins to be weary.

He tried to explain this to Everett, although he knew that Everett was beyond understanding.

"Look at the situation they faced. It was very differen from the Yates-Ogareva tangle. Voronin would soon be transferred away from New York. And he couldn't even defect successfully. He had spent his entire professiona career as a junior Soviet administrator and was virtually unemployable in any other capacity. He didn't know any thing that would make him a catch to American intelli gence. Quite the contrary. In the present climate of good relations between the two countries, even sanctuary would have been extended reluctantly. And Tessie? Was she will ing to go on dedicating her life to the affairs of String fellow & Son? No, of course not. They had both reached the point where they were ripe for the attractions of wha Inspector Lyons calls the new life in Brazil. And between them, they had an ideal opportunity to achieve it."

Quentin was still preoccupied with the aspects of th robbery which had impinged on him personally. "And Denger? How did he come into it?"

"He wasn't supposed to come in at all. When Voronin was casting about for a way to deliver the forgeries anonymously, he remembered how Baranoff would set tle down at the consulate, ordering the nearest secretary to call Halloran's and deliver instructions to Denger. Re member, Voronin never dreamed it would be Denger a the Registry of Deeds. He thought it would be a bank mes senger from the Sloan. By a terrible fluke, Denger knew Stringfellow . . . knew him well enough to realize a sec ond after he made delivery that an imposter was con cerned. So he followed Voronin back to the consulate without any idea of what was involved. That's how he spen the time between his first call at the Registry and his sec ond. As soon as the police became active, he realized his information must be worth money to somebody. Tessie says it was the biggest shock of her life when she picked up the phone and Denger announced himself as an old Army buddy of Stringfellow's. He told her he'd followed Stringfellow's stand-in back to Seventy-third Street."

"We shouldn't have overlooked that," Gabler said reproachfully. "That call was the only one in which Denger actually spoke with a suspect. It must have been the motivation for the murder, and the person involved was Miss Marcus."

"Yes. She acted very promptly too. Got Denger's number and promised to call back. Then there was a hurried consultation with Voronin, and they set Denger up for the murder. They were in hourly danger that the papers would report the Sloan robbery. After that, they couldn't count on Denger's staying away from the police. There was bound to be a sizable reward from the Sloan."

Maseryan shook his head at violence by a Soviet citizen. "It was Voronin who did the actual shooting, after making an appointment at the consulate with Denger. He was very familiar with the terrain. He was back inside, by a rear door, almost before the alarm had been given."

Thatcher drew Quentin's attention to a point he might have overlooked. "That's why Voronin left us so abruptly at the *Odessa Queen*. He was uptown an hour before we were, waiting to keep his appointment."

"And Mrs. Halloran didn't suspect Denger of being up to something?" Gabler asked dubiously.

"Oh, she suspected all right. She was desperately afraid that the entire robbery had been engineered from her garage. And she thought there might be other things going on that she didn't know about. That's why she was eager to sell. And the closer we seemed to be coming to a solution, the more eager she was to be free and clear before the revelations were made."

Gabler, with his usual concentration on the fine print of commerce, had an inquiry.

"But exactly why did Abe Baranoff buy Halloran's Garage?"

John Putnam Thatcher rarely found it possible to score off Gabler in this context.

"Because, Everett, Baranoff is always ready to buy— in a buyer's market."

To add to Gabler's pique, Mikhail Maseryan chose to illustrate this truth by quoting from Marxist scripture.

"Accumulate, accumulate . . ." he said with disapprobation.

Before Maseryan could continue into a denunciation of Baranoff's habit of buying garages with the right hand and selling real estate with the left, Victor Quentin dragged the conversation back to the straight and narrow.

"I understand Abe Baranoff," he said, incurring a frigid glare from Everett Gabler, "but Luke Stringfellow beats me. Why was he so upset? I know you say it was Tessie who made the difference in that office, but Luke was on edge too."

Thatcher cleared his throat. "Well, Vic, I wasn't going to bring this up right now, but perhaps it's just as well. If I were you, I'd be careful of the business Luke Stringfellow brings to Commercial Deposits these days."

Quentin gaped at him.

"Yes," Thatcher agreed. "It's hard to believe, after all this, but it seems that Luke's up to his ears in trouble, over that Jersey real estate operation. It's a highly dubious deal, I gather. And the rumor is that Luke Stringfellow is acting as strawman. Not exactly illegal, but flirting with it, you might say."

"Tsk, tsk," said Maseryan.

Quentin flushed. "Stringfellow? After all this? John, believe me, I'm going to watch him like . . . like . . ."

Since words failed him, Thatcher came through. "Like a hawk. Yes, I would. At any rate, that's why he's been so worried about bank and police attention. It's reasonable . . ."

Both Victor Quentin and Everett Gabler embodied an outraged Sloan Guaranty Trust, but Quentin still retained enough human frailty to experience personal emotion.

"This whole thing, the robbery and the murder, has been unbelievable," he said.

"*Now* it is unbelievable," Maseryan told him sternly. "But it should have been foreseen. Our friend Sergei Durnovo will have to answer for this. His future may not be as bright as he—and his father-in-law—expected. This went on for months, under his nose. Voronin should never have been exposed to such . . . such temptations. As soon as his daughter left, he should have been transferred back to Moscow. Two years of home duty, and he would have been contentedly remarried!"

"No one could possibly have expected such irregular conduct." Everett Gabler did not anticipate human shortcomings. He demanded the ideal. When he didn't get it, he was incensed.

"To expect is one thing. To defend yourself is another," retorted the Russian.

With some amusement, Thatcher intervened. "As you have, I understand, with Katerina Ivanovna."

"What has he done with Katerina Ivanovna?" demanded Victor Quentin, who had pleasurable, if hazy, memories of the *Odessa Queen* party they had shared.

Mikhail Maseryan met the question with dignity. "She has been appointed my secretary, in Moscow," he said blandly. "That way I can assure myself—that she does not get into further trouble."

Confronted by undisguised incredulity, he hastened to change the subject. "But you are wondering why I have brought you out here for this meeting. I wanted to introduce you to Voronin's replacement. He has just arrived on the flight from Paris. Ah, there he is."

They turned to watch a baggage-laden group being ushered over by Maseryan's driver.

"And I suppose that this time you have protected yourself against any possibility of unhappiness or loneliness?" Thatcher asked skeptically.

"He may be unhappy," said Maseryan, "but I guarantee that he will not be lonely."

The handsome blond couple in the lead were introduced as Akim and Anna Maltsev.

"And you must introduce us to the others," urged Maseryan.

Proudly Akim Maltsev stepped aside to reveal the tail of the procession and began the enumeration:

"And this is our little Vanya, our little Sasha, little Volodya, little Natasha, little Olya, little Doonya, little Grisha . . ."